A DANGEROUS KISS

His fingers trailed up to the spot where her garnet eardrops brushed against her neck, then along the line of her jaw until he drew the outline of her lips. He looked into her eyes, as if that would help him see through her mask before leaning forward until his lips hovered over hers. Her lips, so lustrous, so full; the scent of her, so heady; the feel of her, so tantalizing. He gave way to temptation and kissed her.

It was his slow tenderness that trapped Cecilia. If he had pulled or mauled her as other young bucks had tried to do, she might have had the strength to push him away, to bring them both back to their senses with a caustic set-down. But his gentle coaxing lulled her into believing that she was almost unaffected until he pulled back slightly—perhaps to take air, perhaps to end the kiss—and some uncontrollable urge pushed her forward to take his lips with hers this time.

Cecilia abandoned all clear thought as her instincts overcame her reason. She reached for Ormiston, pulled him closer, and in doing so, broke his self-control. His hunger for her was matched by hers for him as their kiss deepened. . . .

Books by Madeleine Conway

SEDUCING SYBILLA

THE RELUCTANT HUSBAND

Published by Kensington Publishing Corporation

The Reluctant Husband

Madeleine Conway

ZEBRA BOOKS
KENSINGTON PUBLISHING CORP.
http://www.kensingtonbooks.com

ZEBRA BOOKS are published by

Kensington Publishing Corp.
850 Third Avenue
New York, NY 10022

All Kensington titles, imprints and distributed lines are available at special quantity discounts for bulk purchases for sales promotion, premiums, fund-raising, educational or institutional use.

Special book excerpts or customized printings can also be created to fit specific needs. For details, write or phone the office of the Kensington Special Sales Manager: Kensington Publishing Corp., 850 Third Avenue, New York, NY 10022. Attn. Special Sales Department. Phone: 1-800-221-2647.

Zebra and the Z logo Reg. U.S. Pat. & TM Off.

First Printing: February 2004
10 9 8 7 6 5 4 3 2 1

Printed in the United States of America

One

The gaming room was brightly lit with the latest gas lamps, revealing its high ceilings, gilded and frosted with intricate plasterwork, its walls richly hung with tapestries and landscapes of Dutch ports and sylvan idylls. Busts of notable Roman statesmen and Greek philosophers sat solemnly on side tables topped with Italian marble, impassive as the English nobles exchanged their vowels. There were more than two-score gamblers, gathered around in threes and fours to watch or wager on the action. Footmen paced the floor, removing empty glasses, refilling others, serving platters of cold ham, beef, and cheddar cheese. The room remained quiet apart from the crackle of the fire and the soft clink of coins against the baize tabletops. In a corner near the long sash windows sat two men deep in their cards.

"Piqued, repiqued, and capoted." The larger of the two, his coat turned inside out for luck, threw down his losing hand.

"Another partie, Dacre?" His slim-faced companion tallied up his winnings with long fingers free of rings.

"I might if I had anything left to wager. I think it more prudent to withdraw, though I never was fond of prudence." The marquis reached across the table to survey the hand his opponent had held.

Mr. Marchmont spread out the winning cards and quipped, "A puritanical trait, it's true, never something one could hold against you, my friend."

"Depends of which Prudence we speak." Dacre leaned back and stretched. "Now, Lady Wetherby is a Prudence one might happily hold."

"Roué."

"Ah, my dear Marchmont, I cannot deny it."

"So do we play again?"

"So long as it is not for money. More claret, while we ponder on a suitable stake?"

"Aye, fill my glass." Marchmont shuffled the cards lazily, running them through his elegant fingers with expertise born of long years of play, while his companion poured more wine.

"Piquet is your only vice. And your fondness for your plaguey offspring." Dacre swallowed the contents of his glass in one draught.

"Is paternal love a vice, Dacre?"

The marquis smiled wryly, his brown eyes apologetic. "It is when your child spurns it. Well, we shall see whether Ormiston's distaste for me is mended by his absence."

"When does he leave for Europe?" Marchmont had ceased shuffling and was watching his friend carefully.

Dacre poured himself another glass of wine. "In five or six weeks. The London house will be all the pleasanter without his brooding presence. But I worry that he will find some means of defying me during his travels. It will not be drink or gaming, I know, since he makes his view of my indulgences all too clear. He will probably settle on finding some highly unsuitable young woman to foist on us all as the next marchioness. Some Galatea to whom he will wish to play Pygmalion."

"Get him betrothed before he leaves," suggested Marchmont. "Make sure you have your lawyers seal it and no other match can stand."

"Who'll accept him? He's a boy."

"Who won't? He's heir to a marquisate."

"Shame none of your brood is old enough for him," mused Dacre.

"Just as well, perhaps." Marchmont tried to turn the subject to the more immediate issue of a suitable stake. "What about that hunter you bought last season? I'll take him off your hands if I win the next rubber."

"What about that eldest girl of yours. Cecilia?"

"Still in the schoolroom and will stay there for another two years before Letitia takes her on and brings her out. The hunter?"

"Fourteen is not so young."

"Fourteen is too young to enter your disreputable family. Indeed, whatever her age, I am not sure I would wish Cecilia to form a connection with the Dacres." Silence fell over their table. Marchmont glanced up from shuffling the cards, afraid he might have overstepped the bounds of friendship with his baiting. Though he had certainly said much worse to the marquis in the past.

"For that, I will not play for my hunter. For that, the only wager I will accept is the hand of your daughter for my son."

"You are drunker than usual if you believe that I will wager away my Ceci's future."

"If I am so drunk, you should have no difficulty in winning the match."

"I will not play."

"Will not or dare not?"

Marchmont sighed wearily. "You will not provoke me that way."

"You have insulted my family." Dacre struggled to maintain his composure as Marchmont's eyebrows shot up in astonishment. "You owe me some reparation. I know." The marquis's brow creased as he unravelled the complexities of what he was about to propose. "The stake for the next partie is that if I win, you must play the following partie with Cecilia as the stake. And if I win the second and she is contracted to become my son's bride, you may knock five thousand from her dowry."

"Lord, I see how it is. I shall have no rest until you have played this partie." Marchmont gave way in the certainty that even if the marquis managed to win the next set of six games, he was in no condition to triumph in two consecutive sets. But the first cut went against him, so he had to deal and watch Dacre as Elder score high with a long suit of spades, which he used to take every trick earning the capot and thus, forty points. Even when Dacre was dealing, Marchmont's hand was weak, and the exchange did nothing to enhance his score. He scarcely scraped seven tricks to earn him a measly ten points, and by the end of the fourth hand, he could see that he would be rubiconed, failing even to reach his hundred points at the end of the partie. So now, he must play for Ceci's hand. He could not weasel out of the wager at this late stage.

Concerned for his daughter's fate, Marchmont made foolish errors, failing to exchange sufficient cards, allowing Dacre to take more tricks than necessary, and then, cataclysmically, declaring carte blanche in an effort to gain points, and thereby allowing Dacre a glance at his hand, which was not a point earner. It was with a nauseated, incredulous horror that he totted up his final score, and discovered that though he had this time at least crossed the Rubicon, Dacre's final tally was more than a whisker over his own. He closed his eyes. When he opened them, the room was still as it had been before, Dacre now looking on him in concern.

"I will not press the debt. It would not be honorable." The marquis collected up the cards and tore up his score-sheet. "There's an end on this nonsense."

"But you have won. I was the fool to have taken on the challenge."

"I cannot cause you grief, nor your child. It is between the two of us—no one else knows of the debt."

"No, Dacre. You have taught me a signal lesson and I must fulfill my due."

"At least present it to Ceci as a possibility, not a necessity. If she cries off, we shall forget the business."

"She will do whatever I ask. She is dutiful." Marchmont swallowed. "When do you wish the marriage to take place?"

"If that is the way of it, the sooner the better. Let them be married before he leaves. Then they have at least a breathing space and if he comes back and they find they don't suit, we shall seek an annulment."

"I shall bring Cecilia back to town with me three days hence. Perhaps you will be so good as to ensure that the marriage may be performed as soon as we return. A special license from that cousin of yours, the bishop. Now, if you will excuse me, Dacre, I must arrange my return to Sawards on the instant."

Birdsong in Saint James's greeted Marchmont as he left his club and the depth of night had lifted. He walked back to the rooms he kept in Albany and summoned his carriage. If the roads were clear, he might be in time to sit down with his family at half-past two. And then he must speak with Cecilia. Would she remember Ormiston, who had visited around the time she was nine? Five years ago now. He seemed to remember tears and teasing and mutinous frowns on being told that however obnoxious a guest might be, his presence must be endured with grace. No comfort there.

He spent the journey down fretting over his predicament with his daughter. He was relieved that he had not used his curricle, for if he had been driving himself, he would have crammed his horses and surely caused some grievous injury if not to himself, to some other more innocent traveller. Additionally, as he rattled along the road, he remembered his failure to carry out all the commissions for books from Hatchards and haberdashery and succulent favours from Fortnum and Mason on behalf of his children and their long-suffering governess, Mademoiselle Lavauden. So he arrived home in a defensive temper, fuming and dusty and dry in the throat, even the climb to the house on the brow of a hill overlooking the Weald failing to raise his spirits as it normally did. Matters were not helped by the sight of Reggie and

Amelia cavorting about the stableyard as the carriage pulled in, and consequently able to bombard him with queries about his unexpected return to the country. Of Lavauden and his eldest daughter, there was no sign.

With Amelia clinging to his midriff like a lace-laden monkey and Reggie clasping his hand with a grimy paw, Marchmont made his way indoors and up to his rooms, where he admitted to his offspring that he had not completed any of the shopping he had intended. They bounced away, guilt-inducingly philosophical about his lack of bounty.

"Perhaps you will remember next time. Any road, half of the books were plaguey schoolbooks for Mademoiselle, and it is all to the good that you have had no time to buy those." Reggie hauled his sister over to the windowseat. "Did you see anyone grand, Father? Did you see the Duke of Wellington again?"

"No. I went to my club and I met with my man of business and that is all. There was no cause to see anyone grand."

"Did you see any fine ladies, Papa? A princess or the queen?"

"No more than I saw the Duke of Wellington, Amelia. Be sure that I should tell you immediately if I had seen anyone worthy of your notice. Now, you scamps, go find Miss Lavauden and Ceci and bid them help you wash and brush before we eat. You reek of the stables, the pair of you."

Marchmont picked at his food, which did not go unnoticed. After he declined syllabub and almond biscuits, his favorite sweet, both his staff and his family feared for the aftermath. Gruffly, he demanded that Cecilia join him in his study.

"What have you done, Ceci?" demanded Reginald. She bit her lip and shook her head. Four-year-old Amelia came and hugged her sister's legs. Ceci disentangled the child, dropped a kiss on her dark curls, and handed her over to Reggie's care.

"I wish I knew. Take Amelia up to Mademoiselle, Reggie. I must not keep Papa waiting."

The study was a rather dark room, and Ceci found she

could not see her father's face clearly in the gloom of the afternoon.

"Cecilia. Sit down."

"Yes, Father."

"You remember we discussed the notion that in a year or two you would go to your Aunt Letitia to prepare yourself before making your curtsey to the queen."

"Yes, Papa."

"I had hoped that you would then enjoy a Season or two before meeting some suitable gentleman. But it is not to be so neatly ordered." Marchmont cleared his throat. Cecilia waited apprehensively for what would follow. "Yes, well, that is what I hoped for, but circumstances have altered, and I must tell you that if you will have it, Dacre wishes you to be married to Viscount Ormiston in London next week."

Cecilia gaped. "If I will have it? What has come about that you agreed to broach this with me, Papa?"

Falteringly, Marchmont explained. Cecilia sat still as he stammered and blushed his way through an account of the previous night's—and morning's—events. Eventually, he stumbled to the close of his account. Cecilia remained still. Finally, she looked up and spoke.

"It seems, Papa, I must take Ormiston. We cannot back away from a debt of honor."

"Cecilia, you do not have to marry him. And even if you do, it is not irrevocable." Marchmont hurriedly explained, stumbling at the indelicacy of what he must discuss with his girl. "The marriage will not be consummated now, and indeed, if he returns from Europe three or four years hence and you find you do not suit, we shall dissolve the union, be in no doubt of that. I have Dacre's word on this. He only wishes Ormiston to be married to prevent the boy from any rash act while he is out of England."

"It seems a foolish way to control Ormiston, to be sure. However, that is not my concern. It would not look well if I refused him, would it?" Cecilia frowned and stood. "While you say Lord Dacre will not hold us to the agreement, I feel we should meet our obligations."

"Ceci, dearest girl, are you sure?"

"You have said that I am not tied by it. Not forever. If I had to live with him and be a true wife to him, I do not think I could do it, even for our family honor. But you seem to suggest that if we do not consummate the marriage, it may be dissolved."

"It can be annulled." Marchmont held her close and kissed her forehead. "It is a muddle, but we shall come about, never doubt it. Now, off you go and start your packing. We must leave for London the day after tomorrow."

"Papa, what shall we tell people?"

"We will claim a long-standing, private betrothal, made when you were in your cradles. It is now formalized. Do you think that will wash?"

"With the world, perhaps. I will see what Mademoiselle says. If she is prepared to accept it, the rest of our friends will. But there is one thing, Papa."

"What, child?"

"Please, do not play at piquet again."

At this request, Marchmont was filled with remorse. He looked once again into the wondrous eyes of his child, so like her mother's, and spoke. "Dearest Cecilia, my gaming days are done."

As Cecilia climbed the stairs back to the nursery, it was as though a thick mist had fallen, obscuring her future entirely. Fairy stories and novels ended in marriage and the promise of living happily ever after, but the union of happy lovers was surely meant to follow the adventures, not precede them. It had always been her intention to have many adventures. She had imagined herself boarding ship for Africa or distant Cathay, taking to camels in sandy Araby, dancing with dervishes, sledging in the deep snows of the Russian winter. Marriage had never figured large in her imagination. She turned as she reached the top of the stairs and gazed at the painted ceiling and walls, alive with nymphs and winds and gods and soldiers. She sat on the top step, remembering Ormiston's visit. He had seemed to frown perpetually, his being given over either to scorn or sulks, his nose and chin pimpled, his mien glowering. But there was no other course open; the marriage must proceed.

Reggie and Amelia emerged from the nursery door. Amelia sat beside her sister and took her hand.

"Are you in terrible trouble, Ceci?" she whispered.

"I'm not in trouble at all, my darling. None of us are. It is just that Papa has told me I am to be married, so you see that is no great tragedy at all."

"Married!" Reginald paled a little. "Does that mean that you shall leave us and live somewhere far away? I had rather he had found out all about the cricket ball and the greenhouse than you should go away."

"There is no need to confess to any such misdemeanour. There is no need for any commotion at all, my dears, for I shall simply go to London with Papa and return by the week's end. You will not remember the man who is to be my husband, but he came and visited us quite five years ago. Papa and his father, Lord Dacre, must have settled it then, but forgot, and now they want it all carried out quick as may be before Ormiston—that is the son of Lord Dacre—goes away for a good long while to Europe."

"You will not go with him to Europe?" Reginald continued to sound a little nervous.

"I should like nothing better than to go to Europe and see such things as we have read of in the library, but it is felt that I am too young just yet, and the next time Lord Ormiston goes away, I may accompany him. But that won't be for years and years yet, and by then, you shall both be quite grown up and going on your own travels."

The task of appearing matter-of-fact before her brother and sister gave Cecilia courage for her next interrogation with Mademoiselle. But while the Frenchwoman cultivated in herself and her female charges an appearance of calm compliance, she was shrewd and intensely practical.

"I think your papa would have had something to say to me regarding the matter of this long-standing betrothal, *ma puce*."

"I would have thought so, too, but he told me he had quite forgotten it, as had his friend, Dacre. It was only Ormiston's imminent departure for Europe that brought it to mind again."

"For me, it seems heathen that you should be married to a boy you scarcely know. It is a custom that was outmoded when I was a girl in France. Still, if you do not object, who am I to protest? At least you will not be removed from the family just yet. It is just as I have always said, my child. Men govern our lives, and we have no recourse against their judgements and decisions. It is barbarous."

"You have been reading *A Vindication of the Rights of Women* again."

"You, my child, would do well to make it an object of study instead of those foolish novels you love so. But now we must inspect your wardrobe. It is an age since you had any new clothes, but there must be something suitable for you to be married in. Ring for Sukey, and we will set about the packing."

Sukey, only a few years older than Cecilia, had joined the nursery to help Nurse with Reggie and Amelia, but following negotiations between the governess and Nurse Featherstone, the girl had been in training for six months as Miss Cecilia's maid, under the tutelage of Mademoiselle Lavauden, who once had had her own lady's maid. The practical Frenchwoman did not repine for her lost glories. Left a penniless orphan by the Revolution over twenty years ago, she had come to England to the house of a cousin who had married an English clergyman, much against the will of her family. While it was clear that Cousin Claire would willingly keep Mademoiselle Lavauden with her in the vicarage, an awareness of the burden of feeding an additional mouth made the young Frenchwoman eager to find her own way in the world. Armed with references from the vicar, she was fortunate to find governessing situations in families who were sufficiently sophisticated to feel that to converse fluently in at least one tongue other than English was a necessity. French, despite the rampaging and ravages of that villain Buonaparte, remained the language of choice.

It was now nearly ten years since Lavauden had been with the Marchmonts at Sawards. Taken on by the mistress of the house, she was immediately conscious that her path had fallen into pleasant ways, where the tone was set by Mrs. Marchmont, who had been a vivacious and intelligent woman with a love of learning positively nourished by her husband. In addition to Miss Lavauden, the Marchmonts employed a librarian, Mr. Hartley, who was also able to tutor in mathematics and classics. Miss Lavauden remembered still the celebrations which attended the births of Master Reginald and Miss Amelia, and even more vividly, the wasting sickness which had taken Mrs. Marchmont following Miss Amelia's birth.

Of the three Marchmont children, Cecilia was the only one who remembered her mother with any clarity, a circumstance which brought her close to her father, and also led her frequently to resort to Mademoiselle when trying to persuade her younger siblings toward what Mama would or would not have liked. Mrs. Marchmont's death secured Lavauden's place in the family circle, and while Mademoiselle would have been the first to disclaim the notion, she had in fact stood in for Mrs. Marchmont admirably. Hence her pique at this sudden betrothal. Pique, and a certain disquiet. She, like Cecilia, decided to make the best of the situation, and led her charge to the cupboards and drawers where her clothes were stored.

Cecilia had always been a robust young lady, but none of her intimates had really absorbed the effects of a recent spurt in growth, both upward and outward. She had numerous everyday dresses in muslin and poplin, but nothing that would do for a wedding.

"Does it matter?" she queried. Mademoiselle and Sukey harrumphed and rolled their eyes at each other. Time was too short to allow for anything other than a letting-out of a dull green gown which had been intended for Sunday best, but which was rarely used even then due to its unprepossessing color. It had been described as sage in the shop, but when made up, had come out sludgier and browner than expected. Lavauden draped her own prize Norwich shawl about Ceci's ample shoulders and chest and pinned it securely with an amethyst pin, and summoned up her most plausible tone to tell Ceci that she looked very well indeed, and did Sukey feel confident that she would be able to repeat the effect when the time came?

There followed a lengthy discussion about bonnets and it was decided that Ceci, a creditable needlewoman, might be left to trim her own Leghorn straw with an ostrich feather, and perhaps Sukey would fetch a posy of fresh white roses for the wedding day. Sukey and Mademoiselle did what they could with three other gowns, all rather the worse for wear. The bustle and banter kept Cecilia's mind from the terrors of the next few days. Before she knew it, bath and story-time for the younger ones was upon them, and then bed. She slept more soundly than she had expected.

Two

Ormiston arrived in London, carefully suppressing his excitement at the prospect of Europe. Of course, he had a bear-leader, but at least he had been allowed to choose an artist to share his passage around the Continent. Peter Buchan had made something of a name for himself as a watercolorist, but had insufficient funds to allow him to travel freely. The Scot had not leapt at the opportunity to accompany Dacre's heir on his Grand Tour, but when he had seen the viscount's own drawing and painting, he was reassured that the young man was no philistine. They might even get some good work done.

Dacre's secretary, Powell, a cousin of the family with few expectations and great ambition, had fixed on half-past eleven on the morning after Ormiston's arrival in town as a suitable time for an interview between father and son.

Dacre had not been minded to give his son a prosy jawing such as Polonius had passed on to Laertes. Apart from his disinclination to stand moral arbiter, he was well aware that Ormiston would roll his eyes and heave deep, poetical sighs and hurl himself from the room with a histrionic flourish modeled on that expelled literary lion who, in addition to bringing his own sister into disrepute, had caused Caro Lamb to let go of what little sense she had ever had.

The youth drooped into the room in slender disarray. Lord knew, the last thing Dacre wanted was a pattern card for a son, but he found Ormiston's willful shabbiness a repellent affectation. The scuffed boots, the half-buttoned waistcoat, the shirt points so limp, the shirt sleeves emerging shapelessly from coat sleeves, the slack necktie, the pomaded hair tumbling artfully in careless locks, all served to irritate the earl.

Ormiston's appearance was intended to convey that dress was a mundane adjunct to one whose mind was preoccupied with higher matters. Dacre could not help comparing his son to his secretary. Powell was always neat and unobtrusive and gentlemanly. It was a shame that Powell was not accompanying Ormiston, thereby giving him time to infuse the boy's precious artistic ideals with a little brisk good sense. Perhaps the artist fellow would prove to be practical-minded rather than high flown. Dacre had not yet met Buchan, but Powell had passed on a good report.

"You summoned me, my lord."

Dacre bade the boy sit. He had not intended to command his heir to attend him, but so Ormiston perceived it. Heavens, how tiresome was the quadrille he must dance about the boy's sensibilities.

"You have my draft. You know you may rely on me if you are in difficulties and you know that I wish you only the best for this journey. I do not look to see you back in London for at least two years, but you are at liberty to extend your travels if there is any object of study that demands more time."

"Thank you, sir." Ormiston did not sound grateful.

Dacre hurried on. "However, there is one piece of business we must complete before your departure, according to your mother's fondest wish."

"Sir?"

"Your mother wished to see you married to the daughter of her dearest friend."

"On my return from Europe, I would be happy to meet the young lady. If we suit, perhaps a betrothal would be possible." Ormiston sounded positively accommodating.

"That is very good of you, but there is a difficulty. You must marry Miss Marchmont before you leave for Europe."

"Why, sir?" The boy's tone was skeptical.

Dacre began to bluster. "It is a matter of honor, a matter of some delicacy, but suffice to say, if I do not have your agreement to this marriage, there will be no tour of Europe."

"Sir, this is preposterous! High-handed! It is Turkish behavior."

"Say no more. If you refuse, as I say, you bring the family name into disrepute. You may think on it. Marchmont will be here this afternoon to sign the settlements. I understand that he is accompanied by Miss Marchmont. If you choose, you may see her then. I have secured a special license for your marriage. If you comply, the ceremony will take place tomorrow morning at St. George's and I shall have a coach ready to take you to Dover immediately after. If you fail to comply, the coach will return you home."

Dacre was well aware that this approach would only deepen his son's resistance. With his next words, he sought to mollify.

"Consider this. If you marry her now, you will not see her further for several years. On your return from Europe, you may once again meet, and if you find that you do not suit, I will fund whatever is necessary to dissolve the marriage."

"How has this person been persuaded into such a match? Surely we cannot proceed without her agreement also?"

"She appears to have a more highly cultivated sense of duty toward both her father and her family name than you."

"Has she also been offered an annulment?"

"That, I think, is a matter for the young lady and her father."

"And you say you will not permit me to leave for France if I refuse?"

"Not only that. I will keep you without further funds. You may retire to Hatherley and produce daubs to your heart's content."

Ormiston stood and paced the room. He wanted to lash out, to kick, to hurl ornaments out of the window. But he would not. He turned and paced back. He would go to Europe. That was the vital thing, his real goal. Fury would be a waste. He was being manipulated into doing as his father wanted, but Europe was what *he* wanted, and after all, this match could be dispensed with on his return from the Continent. *If* he returned.

"Very well, sir. I shall do my duty."

This capitulation astounded Dacre. "Marchmont will be here at tea-time, with the lawyers."

"I shall join you then." Ormiston bowed and left the room, heading out immediately. There would be someone at Angelo's willing to spar or fence or wrestle—certainly his fellows in the prank which had seen them all sent down from Oxford to rusticate indefinitely. He would lunch with his friends, and then, for once, he would drink, deeply, and then he would return to Dacre House in time to meet his bride.

As Ormiston paced toward Bond Street and other less salubrious haunts, he tried to picture his betrothed. He remembered going down to Sawards years before, but recollect Miss Marchmont he could not. There had been two young children, he seemed to recall. She was the elder of the two children. She could be no more than fourteen now. What his father proposed seemed to him barbaric. But of a piece with the man.

Everything about Dacre repulsed his son: his bulk, his heartiness, his gambling, his mistresses, his drunken shamblings and late nights, his philistinism, his gun-dogs and horses, his farmer's talk and manners. Ormiston regarded the marquis as a crude vulgarian and strove to present himself in as different a light as possible.

The viscount saw himself as a sophisticated creature of some refinement. Of course, there were lapses from that ideal. It was hard to refrain entirely from the usual pursuits of young men and last term there had been the unfortunate incident with the provost and the fountain, following an unusually riotous dinner.

At least Ormiston's university career was only temporarily curtailed rather than terminated, due in part to the marquis's influence, and also because Ormiston had had to drop away from the main body of malefactors so that he might redistribute the dinner he had eaten in a convenient urn. The aftermath of the episode was a sense of shame and a continuing tussle between the conscience of the young viscount, which required him to eschew all frivolities, and his common sense, which dictated that a gentleman ought to be able to hold his drink in all company.

The viscount found solace in painting, a talent he had inherited from his mother. The marquis, who had been fond of his bride and saddened by her death in childbirth, was glad to see some sign of her in her son. He fostered Ormiston's artistic ability with the engagement of good drawing-masters at Hatherley and later at Harrow. By his fifteenth year, the viscount was producing creditable depictions of the Hatherley park and its environs.

Wild ideas of spurning his father's machinations and making off into London to apprentice himself to some master were considered and then dismissed. He had no funds whatsoever and had the idea that men only took apprentices on with some financial inducement. Besides which, Ormiston's *amour-propre* could accept neither the prospect of taking orders nor the notion that he might end up in the homes of his former cronies painting their portraits. While he affected dedication to art, the truth was that the viscount's true deity was comfort.

So, he would go through with this match with as much grace as he could muster and the devil take the marquis, which, given the old man's reprobate habits and loose morals, might occur soon enough, although not soon enough to suit Ormiston. At least, so he had resolved by the time he needed to return to Dacre House to meet his betrothed.

Instead of finding friends at Angelo's fencing salon, Ormiston found only a fencing master at a loose end. The man was newly from Italy and gave Ormiston a thorough practice with some new maneuvers. When he heard that the young man was hoping to go to Venice, the fencing master gave him the names of two people from whom he might learn a little more and wished him well for his journey.

So it was that Ormiston found himself back at Dacre House well before the appointed hour of his meeting with the Marchmonts and the lawyers. He found his sketchbook, then ran down to the garden and sat by the fountain, the centerpiece of which was a statue of Hercules overcoming the Nemean Lion. He was soon absorbed by the complexities of shadow and light on the black marble, the problems of rendering accurately the snarl on the lion's features, echoed by Hercules's own pained brow and twisted mouth. When he was drawing, he noticed nothing else, so he was unaware that from the library, a girl was watching him.

Within, Cecilia and Marchmont had arrived promptly, followed soon after by lawyers representing both families. All were ushered into the library while the servants were sent in search of the viscount. The men were discussing the price of corn imports and duties, so she drifted away to the windows, conscious of the discomfort of her tight dress and the corset, which had required the wrestling of two maidservants to fasten, and the prickling of overstarched petticoats. Like a shaggy pony in the heat, she longed to find a convenient tree or column and ease the itch between her shoulder blades, roll in the mud, and free herself of all ribbons and ties that bound her.

Then, looking into the garden, she saw a young man intent on his drawing, glancing up at the statue he was trying to capture on the page, every particle of his being concentrating on the task at hand. He was slim, and he shared his father's dark coloring, with almost swarthy skin and a thick head of hair. But his features were altogether more refined than Dacre's pug-like nose, heavy brows, and jowly cheeks.

The young man's mouth appeared wide, given the narrowness of his face, and his nose was of an elegant length. He had a high brow and neat eyebrows. His eyes were squeezed tight in concentration and against the sun, which now shone into the garden directly behind the statue's head. His chin was definite, and his neck was long, his shoulders broad. His clothes were all black and somewhat dusty. His coat was shabby, his cravat untied and dangling, his shirt points wilted, his boots scuffed, and his unmentionables skintight, molded over muscled thighs. Later, she was unsure whether it was the constriction of her clothes or the sight of this Adonis that caused her breathlessness and a sudden flush to rise unbecomingly to her face. She turned back to the room.

"Is the young man in the garden Viscount Ormiston?"

Dacre came over and gave an affirmative, unimpressed grunt. Marchmont came to stand behind his daughter, his hands on her shoulders. Watching thus, they saw a servant approaching tentatively, then breaking the concentration of the young man. He scowled, but packed away his things and followed without delay.

Minutes later, Ormiston came into the library and sketched a cursory bow. He mumbled an apology, then looked at Cecilia, who at that moment saw uncertainty and then distaste flitting across the viscount's face. She could not be sure, for he swiftly took her hand and bowed once again as he kissed it. By the time he straightened, his features were schooled into bland impassivity.

"The papers are ready for signing, your lordship," said one of the lawyers, and the group gathered around the desk to put their names to the documents that safeguarded Cecilia's dowry and provided detailed particulars of the calls that might be made on Ormiston's purse by his future wife and, heaven forfend, his widow. After, Dacre called for refreshments, and they drank a toast to the happy couple. Ormiston stood beside Cecilia. As soon as the champagne was drunk, Marchmont made moves to leave.

"We need to rest and dear Cecilia must gather her strength for the morrow. You have fixed the ceremony for eleven, is that right, Dacre?"

The marquis confirmed the arrangements for the wedding itself and the Marchmonts took their leave. In the carriage, Cecilia sat back, mute and confounded. Marriage to such a man as Ormiston—such a boy—was the last thing she had wished for herself. Yet, now she had seen him, she knew there was nothing more she wanted than to be married to him. To be loved by him. She gave a small gasp of surprise.

"Cecilia, is all well?" her father asked.

She nodded.

"We need not proceed. Dacre will understand."

She shook her head. "I will marry him." Her tone suggested she was taking a vow as binding as the one she was to speak the following day.

That night, as she lay in her bed, Cecilia searched her own heart. Now that she had seen Ormiston, the case had altered. She had not expected the sight of him to affect her so, and she wondered at it. But she also understood that he had been unmoved by their meeting, and probably would remain so. She could not imagine what powers of persuasion Dacre had used to force the young man to comply with the arrangement, but she had recognized that Ormiston was being coerced into the match in a way she was not. A way that could only result in a detestation of the match and anyone participating in its completion.

Recently, Cecilia had taken to reading novels. Marchmont was a subscriber to *Mudie's* and they had enjoyed reading aloud to one another and to Mademoiselle Lavauden once the youngsters were in bed. Marchmont had even purchased a special lamp for the parlor which shed more light than candles. All three had fallen into stitches at the antics of innumerable foolish heroines who persisted in exploring strange castles in the depths of night and who consequently had to flee villains, thereby allowing them to fall into the arms of some eminently suitable suitor. They had spoken of love at first sight and hopeless passions, and Marchmont had even felt able to speak of his own late wife and the very different, deeper passion he had felt for her, and the sorrow her death had brought. Cecilia had since hoped that she might inspire a similar devotion.

Now, the encounter with Ormiston had awakened in Cecilia an awareness that passion might strike one even without love. For how could she love the viscount? She had met him twice, and on this occasion, had seen him for scarcely an hour. Tomorrow, she was to become his wife, but it was clear that he had no interest in becoming her husband. Yet some small part of her wished, however foolishly, for the miracle that he might respond to her as she had reacted to him.

She spent the night building fantasies, imagining that Ormiston would insist on her accompanying him to Europe, that he would leave for Europe and then summon her, that he would find her presence absolutely necessary to his well-being. But every airdream came tumbling down when she remembered his swiftly concealed reaction to her appearance.

When she woke, she was wan and listless, her eyes red-rimmed and lackluster. A maid brought a tray of food to her room, but for the first time that she could remember, breakfast held no interest. A little while later, the maid returned to wrestle Cecilia into her clothes. More time was spent on fussing at her hair, attempting to fix onto it a veil and flowers. Finally, she was ready to meet with her father. He drew her to him.

"You look a picture, my Ceci."

"I look a fright."

"Well, I have something here that I hope may give you heart." Her father handed her a box covered in black velveteen. She opened it and drew in her breath. There lay a diamond parure that she remembered last worn by her mother.

"On this day of all days, she would have wanted you to have it. And it is yours to keep thereafter, as your mother requested when she was failing."

"What about Amelia?"

"There are other jewels set aside for her. But this came to us through your mother and was hers to dispose of as she wished. She knew you would do it justice." So saying, Marchmont lifted the necklace from the case and placed it around his daughter's neck as she held the veil carefully out of the way. Next came the bracelet and then the earbobs.

"Are you ready, Ceci? Hereafter, I must address you as Lady Ormiston."

"I am ready for anything but that. I hope I shall always be your Ceci, Papa."

"Of course, my pet. Let us go."

So they went, each longing to tell the other it was not necessary to proceed with the charade before them, neither able to speak the words.

Being a marquis with a full purse to offer, Dacre had had no difficulty in arranging for his cousin the bishop to officiate at St. George's, Hanover Square. The journey from Piccadilly did not take long, and soon, Marchmont was handing his daughter out of the carriage and through the grand portico of the church where so many fashionable marriages took place.

The church was empty save for the backs of four gentlemen and the dim figure of the bishop kneeling at the altar. The bishop stood, turned, and nodded toward Marchmont, who escorted his daughter up the aisle. There was no music. She recognized, through the folds of veil, Dacre and the lawyer sitting behind Ormiston and a short, stout man. The viscount slipped out of the aisle as Cecilia came past, but did not look at her.

The ceremony itself was brief and both bride and groom were scarcely audible in their responses. Ormiston threw back the veil and closed his eyes as he leaned toward her and made a kissing sound in the general direction of her cheek. He pulled back immediately. Cecilia swallowed. The bishop escorted the party into the vestry where they signed the register, and she found out that the short man, who smiled at her encouragingly, was called Peter Buchan. The party returned into the nave and out of the church and, in two carriages, repaired to Dacre House, where a wedding breakfast awaited.

It struck Cecilia that she could have walked the distance that she had travelled, from Piccadilly to Hanover Square and from Hanover Square back to Berkeley Square in half the time it took to drive, due to the press of people and carriages on the streets. London was a lively place, but she found it too crowded and very dirty indeed. She was relieved that on the morrow, she would be returning to Sawards. Dacre House was imposing, but hardly comfortable. Cecilia was shown the way to a bedroom where she might repair the ravages done by her travels that day. She rinsed her hands and smoothed back the hair that was escaping from its confines before returning to the fray.

The door to the library was ajar, and she could not resist another look at the room where she had first seen Ormiston. She wished to imprint the memory of that moment quite clearly in her mind. The curtains were drawn against the sun, but she slipped behind one into the embrasure to look at the garden and its fountain, merrily playing as Hercules struggled with his foe. Just as she had settled, she heard footsteps entering the library.

"Show me the picture you spoke of, Mr. Buchan." It was Ormiston who spoke.

"It is here, sir."

Cecilia was about to make herself known, when Ormiston spoke once again.

"So what do you make of my bride, Mr. Buchan?"

"A very young lady, my lord. She has fine eyes." Buchan's Scots accent was soft and his voice mellifluous.

"Fine eyes!" exclaimed Ormiston. "I had not noticed, for they are so buried in fat."

"She will grow. The time when a girl is attaining womanhood is not always a kindly one. I would have said there is great promise there, and certainly, some intelligence."

"You see more than I. Perhaps it is the artist in you. All I see is a pudding-faced doll foisted on me for a whim of my father's."

"She may have been compelled as you have into the match. You need only treat her with kindness for a few hours. Surely that is not beyond you. And then we are in Europe and free." Buchan sounded mildly censorious and Ormiston reacted immediately.

"It is not beyond me, but I do not choose to treat her in any fashion at all. I find her repellent, and I feel that even were she to turn into an Aphrodite on the morrow, I should still find her so. In foisting this child on me, my father appears in his true guise: a man who pays no heed to anything but his own convenience."

"With whom are you most angry? Your bride or your father?"

"I cannot tell, I detest both so heartily. He for using such weapons against me, she for taking on this invidious role of his instrument."

"It is an invidious role. You must remember she is a child with as little say in all this as you. She cannot like her position any better, and as the elder, it would behoove you to make things as easy between you as you may."

But Ormiston did not choose to follow his bear-leader's advice. When Cecilia came stumbling into the dining room, he ignored her and continued to do so throughout an uncomfortable meal during which the bishop, somewhat deaf, and Marchmont, exceedingly troubled, made the lion's share of the conversation.

When it was all over and she was safely back in her rooms, Cecilia tore off the coronet of flowers, the veil, the ugly dress and confining corsets and threw herself on her bed to sob out her misery. Soon her sorrow was overtaken by fury, by a rage which Cecilia could scarcely recognize, for she had never felt such a storm of sensation before. She would have her revenge on the boy who had spurned her so. She would become Aphrodite and she would charm him and bind him to her and then she would turn him over with the contempt and distaste he had shown her. As the fury rampaged through her, it cooled and hardened into a determination to see Ormiston at her feet—not this year, not next, but when next she saw him, she would be everything that a man could want and once she had him at her feet, she would trample upon him and make of his desire and his passion something of dust and ashes.

Three

Paris, February 1822

Ormiston gazed idly about him as he sat dutifully accompanying Henri de Ferrières's mother on her morning ride from the mansion near the Palais Royal, through the Tuileries and across the river to the Jardin du Luxembourg. It was an exquisitely crisp February morning, and as he watched some of the more spirited mounts curvetting in the sharp, sunny air, he wished he was astride Corsair, the highly bred chestnut stallion Henri had insisted he consider his own while he stayed in Paris. Horses were always lively on bright mornings like this, and he would, by far, have preferred the challenge of a ride to this docile trot in the comtesse's brougham, sedately wrapped in furs.

Five years in Europe with Peter Buchan had wrought immense changes in Ormiston. He had quickly discarded his down-at-heel romantic pose and mode of dressing. Buchan had insisted on neatness from the start, but as they made their way through Germany, Ormiston had discovered the advantages of his dark good looks and had learned to dress with a quiet elegance that set them off. He eschewed the barbarities and discomfort of dandified style, and chose instead the comfort of well-cut, soft fabrics. The allowance from Dacre was handsome, and Ormiston took advantage of it to insist on the finest leather for his boots, the best silk for his shirts, and the softest cashmeres for his coats. While choosing subdued colors for his main tenure—breeches of softest chamois leather, charcoal and bottle greens for his coats—he had made it a hallmark of his personal style to add improbable touches of color: in the facings and trimmings of his attire, brilliant acid yellows against dark green, flashes of fuchsia with dark gray, vivid scarlet with navy blue.

Buchan's robust common sense had also improved Ormiston's temper. Five years of being allowed, as he saw it, to follow his own desires had removed the need to rebel.

The Scot had spelled out his own views on the most profitable use of their time in Europe on their way from London to Dover, when Ormiston was at his lowest after the heartless ceremony of his marriage.

"M'lord," Buchan had said, "I know that you feel much put-upon by this insistence of your father's, but we are now privileged to enjoy a wee breathing space before you take up your responsibilities, and I think we might take some time now to plan how we wish to go on."

"What does it matter?" snarled Ormiston. "We are exiles, and when I return I shall be imprisoned by that dough-faced dowd."

Gradually, Buchan's arguments aroused some response, and eventually they agreed that each day must include what Buchan was pleased to call "the Four E's": Exercise, Enjoyment, Education, and Expression. Exercise they interpreted as riding and fencing; Enjoyment as painting, reading, and listening to well-executed music; Education as anything which would add to the enjoyment of the aforementioned; and Expression as both amassing drawings and watercolors of the sights they saw as well as the keeping of a diary to record experiences. By the time they took ship, Ormiston had begun to anticipate his new career with some relish.

They had met Henri, Comte de Ferrières, in Vienna, at the end of what Ormiston now thought of as the "northern" part of his tour, and he had promised the young count that he would spend some time with him in Paris on his way home.

As is common with young people of similar inclinations,

the friendship between the two young noblemen was swiftly cemented. Both were thoroughly bored by life in Vienna, a Vienna which was still lamely trying to recover the sense of being the center of the universe that it had enjoyed during the heady days of the Congress in 1814 and 1815, but failing dismally, offering only starchy palace receptions and staid private balls.

Henri was enchanted with the way that Ormiston and Buchan divided their time between serious study of language, music, and, above all, painting and sculpture, combined with excursions to see all that was to be seen.

"You English are so practical!" he had exclaimed. "You organize a program of utter pleasure, then make rules about how it should be carried out so that you create an illusion of being usefully occupied when you are doing no more than following your own inclinations."

"But we are learning every day," Buchan interposed, somewhat indignantly.

"Of course. But whoever said that learning should not be utter pleasure?" was Henri's answer. "I admire your illusion of discipline, that is all, *tout simplement*. It is such a compliment to *les aieux*, our forefathers—I am sure they, your ancestors, rest happier in their graves knowing that you are spending their money in such a disciplined way."

"It's not so much the ancestors that poor Buchan here has to worry about," said Ormiston. "He must send reports to my father explaining where we go and why. He has to answer to much more potent Lares and Penates."

"Then he is your father's spy?" Henri's face was a picture of puzzlement as he tried to understand the precise relationship between his two companions. Ormiston, dark and sardonic, but supremely elegant; Buchan, a stout, but not inelegant, red-headed Scotchman, some ten years older than the two young men.

"My dear Henri," it was Ormiston's turn to protest, "Peter has been my tutor and my mentor for two years. He has rescued me from a gloomy past and has turned me from a sulking romantic into the toast of the Viennese salons. He has taught me everything I know about the techniques and the styles of drawing and painting. When my father first had this idea of getting rid of me for a while by means of a pilgrimage around these tedious cities, I was against it. I absolutely refused to go, until he agreed to my demand that, if I were to be accompanied, only a serious teacher of art was fit to accompany me. It is Peter who has determined what we should see, and why. But, of course, he must send reports home. A man who spends his every waking hour gambling must needs be reassured that his son and heir is behaving as befits his station."

Ormiston's contempt for his father was only too evident in this piece of sarcasm. Henri de Ferrières was shocked at the resentful expression darkening his friend's face.

"But you ought to know that we write the reports together," continued Ormiston, his features lightening with mirth.

"And they are very truthful," added the Scot.

"Yes, because I do not play."

The Frenchman looked concerned. "You do not enjoy yourself?"

"No, you chump! Of course I enjoy myself, do I not, Monsieur Buchan? But I do not play at cards, nor gamble in any way. This means that our expenses are very simple to account for. Poor Buchan," Ormiston laughed at the absurdity, "in Leipzig we laid out a fair amount of money to get ourselves established as belonging to the best circles, and my poor, demented father complained that we spent too little. In his view, the best circles are those who waste all their money at the tables. He is utterly convinced that my time travelling is a complete loss, since we fail to report any substantial sums dropped in the course of games of chance. He refuses to believe that we have met everybody that we should, even though we spent hours waiting for the appearance of the Duchesse de Dino and paid homage to Mme. de Stael at her absurd menage in Geneva."

Henri was fascinated with Ormiston. He was so confident and so aware that he occupied, or would come to occupy, what might be called "a place in the world." Yet he was natural, easy-natured and easy to be with, until any mention was made of games of chance. Then Ormiston's face would darken and he would grow silent, moodily shutting up his pens and inks before striding off, refusing any offers of companionship. At times the viscount would disappear on solitary, lengthy rides, returning having exhausted both his mount and himself.

The young Frenchman had only been on one of Ormiston's "rides" during a visit they had made to Mecklen. The young viscount had ordered the most spirited mount from the livery stables. He strode around the stableyard, rejecting mount after mount, until at last the poor ostler had been prevailed upon to produce "something resembling a real horse." The beast had been hardly broken and was as vicious as could be. Once he had been given his head in the forest he had headed for all the lowest branches with the sole aim of unseating Ormiston, who clung low to his neck and laughed at his friend following in such tame concern on a more docile mount. Henri never forgot Ormiston and his horse returning to the stables. Neither had given in to the other—both had enjoyed their ride!

Henri had been recalled to Paris in the early autumn to attend his dying father, prompting Ormiston and Buchan to leave Austria and make their way to Venice. There at last Ormiston was able to indulge his twin passions for architectural drawings modelled on Guardi and Canaletto and fencing with exponents of the Neapolitan style of Rosaroll Scorza and Pietro Grisetti. But soon the November fogs made Venice unpleasantly cold and damp so that, intent on returning for Carnival, they had travelled inland through Padua, Ferrara, and Bologna to Florence, which they made their winter headquarters.

It was during the Christmas festivities in Florence that Ormiston first encountered Giugliana di Podenza. Giugliana was twenty-seven, tall and lissome, with pale features resembling Botticelli's Venus and long auburn hair to match. Descended on her mother's side from the Medicis, she had been married to the Marchese di Podenza at the age of nineteen, and had been heartily relieved when the very rich and very stolid marquess died at the age of fifty-five, some five years after their marriage. She was reputed to have spent the intervening years journeying from house to house of her numerous relatives who, between them, seemed to hold positions of influence in every court in Italy, surrounded wherever she went by a galaxy of aspiring young admirers of whom she clearly thought little.

The entire fortune of the marchese had passed to Giugliana. She was constantly sought out by suitors both rich and poor; the rich seeking to add to their immense wealth, the poor desperately hoping for some way to repair their aristocratic, albeit battered, fortunes.

The Marchesa and Viscount Ormiston had met formally and fleetingly on a number of occasions, but it was at the opening of a newly restored gallery in the Uffizi when they first spoke with any intimacy. Ormiston had wandered away from the main party and was standing quite alone in another part of the building, staring at the Simone Martini Annunciation.

"You do not mix with the throng, Viscount?" The voice was resonant and deep. "Are you one of the few who come to the Uffizi to look at the pictures? You have found one of my own favorites. I love the reluctant Virgin Mary—she does not look at all pleased to hear the Archangel's news."

"The angel also appears to have little confidence in the welcome accorded his message," agreed Ormiston as he bowed formally to the marchesa, "but I was studying the fabric behind the angel. He may have alighted but it looks as though his gown is still whirling in the air . . . astonishing technique." He paused. "But as to your question, the Gallery is so much more pleasant when emptied of the usual hordes. I could not resist the temptation to steal away and revisit some of the treasures on my own."

"Then perhaps you will allow me to escort you back to the reception via some of my own old favorites. My grandmother used to bring me here as a child—she told me that her mother remembered it before her aunt settled the Medici inheritance on the people of Florence, just over eighty years ago. I like to imagine my great great grandmother chasing along the galleries with her sisters and cousins when she was a little girl. What a wonderful place to play on rainy days!"

They strolled back slowly, stopping here and there before paintings that one or the other wished to admire. Ormiston was astonished by the acuity of her comments on the paintings and the depth of her knowledge. On their previous encounters, she had always been surrounded by her little court, flirting here, bestowing favors there, and appearing, from a distance at least, merely to be a frivolous and flirtatious widow. But here she let her voice relax to its natural, rather deep tones and showed the serious side of her character. Ormiston was fascinated by the combination of learning and beauty, albeit daunted by her ability to give such a different impression of herself in public.

No sooner had they met, however, than she disappeared. The next day he called to leave his card, but subsequently learned she had left Florence; it was rumored she had gone to Venice to visit her father's elder brother, who was said to be suffering from the agues brought on by those same winter chills and damp that Ormiston had fled.

There were endless rumors about the young widow. Her family was notorious for its political intrigues throughout the length and breadth of Italy, and stretching way beyond into the Hapsburg court of Austria and the Bourbon courts of France and Spain.

Buchan advised his charge to forget her, since the local wisdom in Florence insisted that her parents were determined to marry her off to a great statesman in order to extend their family influence yet further. But Ormiston had not forgotten, and even now, in Paris two years later, his pulse quickened as he remembered a chance meeting with Giugliana in the Piazza San Marco during Carnival. Her deep, sibilant voice. "Signore Ormiston, in a moment you will remember me from Firenze, but you must rescue me instantly from the unwanted attentions of the portly gentleman in the scarlet domino."

They had become firm friends, as she insisted on showing him less-known churches and other corners of Venice where largely undiscovered art treasures could be found. Ormiston was infatuated with her, not least because wherever they went they were accompanied by Buchan and Giugliana's duenna-like spinster cousin. Eventually Giugliana discovered an empty Palladian villa of her uncle's, Buchan was heavily bribed to distract the gaunt spinster cousin, and Ormiston and Giugliana could, at last, meet alone.

It had been a glorious spring and early summer for Ormiston, improving his swordsmanship, mastering the ever-changing light of Venice in paintings and drawings, and spending every possible moment with Giugliana. Their affection for each other deepened as the months passed. When she moved to Lake Guarda, he had followed, discreetly. When the time came for her to attend on yet another relative at the Vatican, she helped organize his route to Rome, making sure he visited Pisa, Siena, and Assisi.

The three months they were parted decided Ormiston that he was in love. She had forbidden him to write, promising that she would make suitable arrangements in Rome for them to continue the intimacy they had shared in Venice. And so she had, taking apartments for him in a palazzo separated from her own only by a secluded back garden. He had kept a diary of his travels, copiously illustrated, which he presented to her on his arrival. His accounts of the places visited were interspersed with odes addressed to his beloved, and all his drawings included somewhere a slender female figure, identifiably dressed in one of Giugliana's splendid gowns or cloaks.

Giugliana was touched by the accuracy of his recall of the

details of her wardrobe and their reunion had been passionate but, eventually, the idyll had been drawn to a temporary close. Giugliana's mother insisted on her daughter's company for a visit to her maternal uncle, a person of some eminence at the Bourbon court in Naples, and Giugliana had told him that Ormiston's presence there would be welcome neither to her mother nor her uncle.

"My dearest Ormiston, we shall be resident at court, and only be allowed to meet formally. Although your notorious Lady Hamilton held undisputed sway, it is a very different thing for Italian courtiers and the Naples town and court are the most arrant gossips. Furthermore, my mother will be everywhere. You have not met her," Giugliana said and smiled sardonically. "She is most intrusive!"

Ormiston resolved that he would use the time of this forced parting to travel home and insist on the annulment promised by his father. Once he was free, he would pay suit to Giugliana. After writing the necessary letters home, and to Henri de Ferrières in Paris, he had sailed to Marseilles from Rome, and made his way to Paris for a month or two before making the final stage of the journey home.

Letters from Henri awaited him at Marseilles, with recommendations for the best route north and what to see on the way. Young de Ferrières would meet him at Macon to introduce him to the delights of several of Burgundy's finest vineyards before the family gathered at their chateau in Auxerre for Christmas. He also warned Ormiston that his mother and her friends were planning a masked ball for Carnival, now that the mourning period for his father was officially over.

"But I fear that her principal motive in all this is to make sure that I meet every eligible girl in Paris. You also must be on your guard—she has made many acquaintances among the English families here and assures me that you would be a catch for any French girl prepared to tolerate your climate and customs."

Ormiston had been grateful for the week of having Henri to

himself in Burgundy. Buchan, sensing his charge's need for male company of his own age, effaced himself in the evenings, claiming to have been made drowsy by the wines en route and at dinner. The two friends thus strolled out every evening to enjoy the cool December night air before retiring.

The Comte de Ferrières had stories to tell of Paris, where he was entered into his country's diplomatic service, and of the endless efforts made by Talleyrand to reassert the power and influence he had enjoyed in earlier days. Ormiston, of course, had many traveller's tales to unravel, but mainly wished to talk of Giugliana and his plans to marry her. But even now, he could not bring himself to mention his odious marriage and merely expressed concern that his father would manage to foil his plans.

"But are you sure she will have you? I understand her family is notoriously ambitious for her. There are rumors of trying to marry her to some Bourbon princeling in Naples."

"That is why I must secure my father's agreement before I speak," said Ormiston fiercely. "I must ensure that my inheritance is intact and safe from the depredations of my degenerate father. Now I am of age, he cannot deny me. But I am sure that Giugliana will remain faithful until I return."

"If I were you, I should not concern myself so much about the marchesa's feelings as with the plans of her scheming family. They have influence in every court in Italy. Your wealth may be immense, but so is hers. It is power they seek. Her mother is known to be proud of her Medici ancestry and, like Talleyrand, longs to recover the powers of old. Have you met her?"

"I was presented to her in Florence, of course, but Giugliana has managed to avoid coinciding with her since."

"For good reason, no doubt. I suspect your liaison would never have been allowed to flourish if she had been closer at hand."

"But we behaved with the utmost discretion!" protested Ormiston.

"Ah, *mon ami*, your mother died when you were young. You do not know at first hand the persistence of scheming and ambitious mothers."

Christmas in Auxerre had been a revelation to Ormiston. Although Henri was his parents' only child, the de Ferrières' traditional gatherings were numerous, with seemingly endless aunts and uncles and cousins. A party of young cousins had ridden out to meet them as they neared Joigny, and from their boisterous greetings to Henri he realized that informality and high spirits were to be the tone of their sojourn in the country. The dowager countess confirmed this at their first meeting. She was petite, fine-featured, and behind her warm welcome he sensed that her shrewd gray eyes were assessing him keenly.

"Welcome to Joigny," she said, "and thank you for your many kindnesses to Henri in Vienna. Why, on his return, he could talk of nothing else but your expeditions. We are very informal here, as you can see—we come to relax, far away from the concerns of Paris. We do not dress for dinner except, of course, for Christmas Eve, and for church when the townsfolk expect us to make something of a show. Otherwise, the men seem to spend most of the day outdoors, hunting and the like, while in the evenings we make our own entertainment."

They were a party of over thirty, six of Henri's uncles and aunts with their spouses and children. Buchan was in constant demand to sketch family groups and produce likenesses, or to give useful hints to those who wished to improve their drawing skills. Several hunting expeditions were organized and the evenings sped by in music-making and occasionally more noisy games of charades. Despite his position as nominal head of the family, Henri was a great favorite with all his cousins, who were also determined to make a pet of his English friend.

Ormiston wished he could have belonged to such a large, uninhibited family. And he was strengthened in his resolve to escape the lonely vastness of the home where he had spent his neglected childhood. From time to time, he caught Henri watching him anxiously, but determined he would control his moods and deny himself the urge to ride madly through the woods to expunge his rage and resentment as he had used to do in Austria. Once the odious business in England was cleared up he would be free to return to Giugliana. He was sure he could persuade her to disentangle herself from her family's schemes. They would raise a large family, and one day, perhaps, he would convince her that they should return to England and set about turning Hatherley into a home such as this, ringing with happy laughter and companionship.

But late at night, alone in his room, sitting over the embers of the fire, he wondered whether he would really ever be able to induce Giugliana to leave her beloved Italy, with its bright sunshine, and her sense of being descended from one of the greatest families of art collectors that Europe had ever known. After nearly three years in Italy, he had to admit how pleasant it was to be once again in a northern country, rising early to hunt over fields shrouded in mists. But perhaps she would consent to France . . . and he would fall asleep musing on possible futures for them both.

One morning he rode out alone with Buchan.

"I have been thinking, my lord."

"Yes, Peter."

"Would you be thinking of returning to Paris with the family, sir? I understand you are bound to be in Paris for the dowager's grand ball, but that is not till mid-February, six weeks away."

"Quite so. I understand there is a great deal to see in Paris, but after these days in the country, I am not sure I am ready to return so soon to city salons."

"Well m'lord, I have been reading up in the library, and it seems there are a good many places we could profitably visit before rejoining your friends in the capital."

"Buchan, you are a splendid fellow. What do you have in mind?"

Buchan revealed a well-worked-out itinerary that would encompass the ruined abbey at Vézelay, the great cathedral at Bourges, as well as the remains of the once-glorious chateaux of the Loire before reaching Paris via Tours and Chartres. That evening Ormiston drew Henri aside and asked his opinion.

"In all honesty, it would suit me admirably. My days in Paris are damnably taken up, and my mother and I were wondering how best we should be able to entertain you, as she will be fearfully occupied with this wretched ball. And your *succés* in Paris will be guaranteed if you can express opinions about some of the glories of French architecture, which many of our aspiring dancing partners have not so much as heard of, let alone visited. Now, how do you wish to travel?"

The next few days were taken up in planning Ormiston's excursion, since all the uncles and aunts had favorite sights, or recommendations for especially comfortable inns. In the end it was decided that the bulk of Ormiston's luggage would travel to Paris with the family and that he and Buchan would travel light on horseback, accompanied by Sylvestre, one of the family's most trusted groomsmen.

While the excursion itself had proved a fascinating diversion, the news that awaited Ormiston in Paris had cast him down. Waiting for him at the Hotel des Ferrières was a letter from Giugliana, a cool dispatch informing him of the forthcoming nuptials of the Marchesa di Podenza to il Principe Vergara, with no personal message at all. At first, the viscount had read and reread the note in disbelief, pacing his chamber and driving his Italian valet to distraction as the man attempted to prepare Ormiston for dinner. But as the evening wore on, he found himself astonished by how little he really seemed to mind about Giugliana's cynical defection. A little wounded by the formality of her letter, yes, but he did not feel so devastated as love lyrics and stage dramas would have him believe he ought to have felt. He slept well, and woke the next morning somewhat at a loose end, but otherwise in reasonably resigned humor.

Thus it was that Ormiston now found himself on his second

morning in Paris, accompanying his friend's mother on her morning ride. The dowager Comtesse de Ferrières was busy pointing out who lived where and who was who. Their progress was stately, as the countess had many friends to greet or salute. Ormiston was increasingly bewildered as the roll call of those due to attend the ball on the following day was enumerated. Vast as the de Ferrières mansion might be, he could not imagine it accommodating such a crush.

As he had been warned, the dowager countess was obviously of the opinion that he must make a show in Parisian society. He noticed she was stressing the eligibility of the daughters and giving him what were, no doubt, invaluable hints on their interests, their pedigrees, and their fortunes. No doubt she was scheming. He suspected that she might already have earmarked him for some unsuspecting ingénue. Why the deuce were people so intent on marrying him off without consulting his desires? First his father's insistence on that absurd marriage before he had left England. Now Henri's well-meaning but busybody mother. He could not resist the temptation to tease.

"And which of all these beautiful and accomplished *mesdemoiselles* have you earmarked for my poor, unsuspecting friend?"

"Dear Lord Ormiston, you cannot think me such a goose as to tell you! Henri thinks I am a scheming *vieille dame*, but although I may have my favorites, it would be foolish for me to make this clear to Henri. His father and I were blessed with great happiness. I just wish him to see the best, and to make *une choix sage*—how do you say, a wise choice."

"And what of me, Madame la Comtesse? Do you not have someone in mind?"

"I do not think I would presume. A little *oiseau* has whispered that your heart is unsuitably engaged in Italy. But no doubt your own people at home are awaiting your return in order to show you the exquisitely eligible beauties of London."

Ormiston was silenced. How the deuce did she know about Giugliana?

"No, you may be sure that Henri has not told me any confidence that you may have made him privileged to. But the Marchesa di Podenza's family is not unknown. Rumors have spread that she has spent much time in galleries and artistic churches with a romantic, aristocratic Englishman, and that her mother has insisted on her wintering in Naples, under her especial vigilance. The identity of the English aristocrat is a closely guarded secret, but your appearance is undeniably *romantique*, and suddenly you are here in Paris on your way to conclude family business at home?"

Ormiston summoned up all his courage to look the tiny, bird-like creature in the eye. She laughed, and put out her hand to reassure him.

"*Non, mon fils*. I was just guessing. My late husband's brother is at Naples, and he knows how I love gossip. The story of the marchesa's attachment is rife in Naples, but has not yet reached Paris. You are safe here. But, since you are the friend of my son, I should warn you that the so-romantic Englishman is unlikely ever to see Giugliana di Podenza again. Her mother is determined that her next husband will be a Bourbon, no matter how impotent and discredited."

Ormiston was mortified. That his delicate affair with Giugliana should be known to half the wagging tongues of the so-called diplomats, the spies of Europe! And now, no doubt, would follow the humiliating information that he had been passed over for a man with sixteen quarterings on his shield. But there had been something else that the dowager had said which had touched on another raw nerve—her casual assumption that all at home was well.

If only that were the case, he thought. He was suddenly thrown back into the gloom that had obsessed him in Vienna. For the first time in years he thought seriously about the frightful truth that awaited him in England. He had become sufficiently a man of the world to recognize that his dreams of happiness with Giugliana might be beyond him. But the sure knowledge that he had no people at home who cared even a jot for his well-being was a harsh reminder of the realities of his life.

The Comtesse de Ferrières was aghast at the effect her words had produced. Ormiston had sunk into the deepest reverie. She continued with her recital of who was who, but Henri's friend was lost, sunk into a bleak and threatening world of his own. Perhaps she had been wrong to mention the Italian? Surely not. It was her duty as a friend to warn him that the affair was becoming publicly known, that sooner or later he would be identified as the romantic Englishman, and that he would be a fool to nourish hopes in that quarter. It was with some relief that she sighted the daughter of her best friend, and instructed the coachman to drive toward her.

But Louise was riding accompanied by the most extraordinary creature and, involuntarily, she cried out.

"This girl is mad. Who can she be!"

Ormiston roused to her unexpectedly sharp tone and his eye followed her startled gaze. There were three girls riding together, properly accompanied by what seemed to be elder brothers and grooms. But one of them stood out by the quality of her mount, an exquisite, spirited gray, and by the color of her habit, a brilliant, jewel-like blue. *Almost pure cobalt*, reflected Ormiston.

The horse was obviously affected by the combination of sharp air and bright sunshine which had made so many of its stablemates so frisky that morning. Her horsemanship was superb as she controlled her mount, and he noticed that this was indeed a horse that the girl was riding, not a docile mare or gelding. Her companions were all riding lesser animals, but he watched this girl's hands as she soothed the beast, as if promising a gallop in future, if he would just be good for a moment longer. As he watched her restless stallion, held to hand while she exchanged the time of day with her friends, he found himself drawing the furs up closer around his neck. Decidedly, the wind was getting fresher.

As they passed the group, he heard Henri's mother expressing her indignation that she had no idea of the identity of who that girl "riding that powerful horse and dressed in such an exquisitely pure blue" might be.

"The girl in pale gray is the Duchess of Dino's niece, the one in green is Louise de la Trémouillère, but this mad girl riding that savage horse that is much too strong for her, *aucune idée.*"

He felt a tinge of regret. Giugliana did not ride. The nobility of horses never ceased to amaze him. Despite the trappings of saddles and girths and bits, the instinctive desire to race forward was always there. He looked back, admiring the girl's skill as she kept the horse calm, despite its obvious desire for more freedom.

There was a sudden gust of wind. Ormiston felt the cold and was about to draw the furs even more closely around him when, still looking back, he saw that one of the duller girls of the three, dressed in a turgid green and riding a pale chestnut gelding, had lost her hat. He could hardly believe what happened next.

The girl dressed in blue did not hesitate. Suddenly she and her horse were in motion; she leant down the immense distance from the beast's back, retrieved the hat, and presented it to her friend.

The Comtesse de Ferrières had not missed the performance, nor failed to note Ormiston's interest.

"*Sans doute*, you would like to know who she is. I shall find out. She rides like a child of the circus, but she is beautifully dressed. I shall call on dear Louise's mother this afternoon. She is sure to know, and then we must make sure that such an exquisitely beautiful creature is invited to the *bal masque.*"

But how, he wondered, was he to divine the beauty's identity if she attended the ball? For of course, there she would be disguised. Still, his interest was piqued, and his anxieties regarding his return to England at least temporarily allayed.

Four

Bursting into her room, Cecilia flung her gloves and crop onto the bed before teasing out the hatpins securing her top hat. Almost immediately, Marston came bustling in, gathering up the discarded items from Cecilia's morning ride, muttering and snorting to equal the disapproval expressed by Lady Ormiston's bay mare when roused too early for her morning gallop. Having straightened the bed and arranged Cecilia's accessories on a bureau, the maid came to her aid to unfasten the glorious blue habit. Two weary undermaids were filling the bath before the fire with buckets of steaming water scented with lavender essence.

"How was milady's ride this morning?"

"Exhilarating, Marston." Cecilia twirled her way out of her petticoats, grinning broadly. "Simply splendid."

"Is that what you call it? Behaving like a hoyden is what I call it, from what the groom says. You should know better, and you a viscountess and such."

"Well, we don't discuss that, do we, Marston? And if you have heard about the ride from the groom, what need to fatigue me with your tiresome questions?"

"None of your airs, madam. If Lady Ketley hears about your circus tricks, there'll be a piper to pay and it won't be me as is shelling out."

"How should Lady Ketley hear, unless you choose to tell, my dear Marston?" Cecilia slipped out of her chemise and tested the waters of her bath with her toes. The temperature was perfect. In French, she thanked the maids and sank into the water. The girls left Marston alone with Cecilia.

"There is a great deal I might choose to tell Lady Ketley if you continue with your cheek, Madam High and Mighty."

Cecilia turned to face Marston and, leaning her chin on her arms along the back of the bath, she widened her eyes.

"But you wouldn't distress Aunt Letty. And you wouldn't give me away, dear Marston. I beg your pardon. I never intended to cheek you, I promise."

"Think you can weasel round me with your big eyes and your soft ways? How long is it since we arrived in Paris? A week? Ten days. And you've smoked out all manner of low dives in a trice. A fencing salon for ladies. Coffeehouses for ladies. Clubs for ladies. Gambling dens for ladies. It's iniquitous what ladies get up to here." Marston helped Cecilia to soap and rinse her hair.

"It's wonderful." The girl lay back and relaxed as Marston massaged her scalp. "After all the restrictions and hedging about one in London, all the worries about how one will take and whether one will get vouchers for an insipid evening at Almack's, which I swear is the dreariest place imaginable. Especially if one isn't hanging out for a husband."

"Aye, but the less you hang out for a husband, the more you have the men swarming round you. Wasps at a jam pot." The older woman poured clean water over her charge's head, and Cecilia came up for air, spluttering and giggling.

"Isn't it a joke, dear Marston? And all due to you and Aunt Letty. I'd be the frumpiest woman in England even now if you hadn't taken me in hand." She stood and pulled a towel about her, stepping gracefully from the bath and sitting so that Marston could dry out the wet mass of curls dripping down her back. Combing out the tangles took time, but Marston was patient and gentle.

"Good bones and fine skin will out. Given time, your mademoiselle would have ensured that you were dressed as befits a young lady."

"Perhaps." Cecilia went into a reverie as Marston eased the comb through the knots and snarls in her dark hair. She thought back to the days following her return to Sawards after her marriage to Ormiston. Reggie and Amelia had come out to greet Marchmont's carriage, but once Cecilia had given them each a brief hug, she had retreated to her room. Despite the best efforts of Marchmont, Lavauden, and her brother and sister, Cecilia had come back from London subdued and remained withdrawn from her family. She would rush through her lessons and then disappear on long walks or rides, missing lunch and even dinner, scavenging odds and ends from the kitchen, nibbling at one of the carrots or apples she intended to feed to her horse. It was as though she could not bear company at all, and she refused entirely to mingle with her former friends in the neighborhood. When she did return to the house, she would lavish affection on her brother and sister, but she would no longer join in their games and mischief.

The weather that summer had been sultry. The air grew dense and sticky, clouds rolled across the horizon without breaking, and Cecilia continued to ride at breakneck speed through the forests and across the fields, determined to rid herself of the echo of Ormiston's harsh words. Finally, one afternoon as Cecilia rode along the ridge way above Sawards, the skies darkened to a surly charcoal, thunder rolled around the valley, sheets of lightning shook the hillsides, and the first great gouts of water fell on parched land. Ceci raised her face to the skies and let the water rinse away the hurt and shame she felt. She headed for home.

Although the head groom would not allow her out on a horse again that week, Ceci contrived to escape the confines of the house whenever a storm broke and to return soaked and shivering.

Physically run-down, heartsick, her lapse into a fever which deepened until she was no longer conscious was inevitable. She remembered little of that time: just a haze of aching limbs and cold compresses and then the robust voice of Aunt Letty, saying, "You've given us all a fright, my girl, but there's no need to milk it quite to death's door."

Marriage to a naval captain had removed Letitia Marchmont from her family sphere for many years, but now that young Ketley had achieved fame, fortune, and the rank of admiral, their peregrinations were less frequent and she was able to reacquaint herself with her brother's family at Sawards. She had reencountered the haunts of her youth to find the place in uproar, Marchmont and his two children in high agitation, the French governess close to exhaustion from watching over Cecilia's bedside, and her eldest niece afflicted with pneumonia. Slim, languid, and prone to sarcasm in regular life, in an emergency Letitia Ketley displayed energy, dependability, and stalwart good sense.

The Ketleys' union had not been blessed with offspring. While this had allowed Lady Ketley to accompany her husband on his voyages, it was a source of some disappointment. Seeing the need for feminine guidance at Sawards, Letty installed herself with enthusiasm, which was further galvanized when her brother reluctantly recounted the events that had led to Cecilia's precipitate marriage. Roundly declaring her brother to be a nitwit, as soon as Cecilia was convalescing, Letty set about winkling out of her niece her reactions to the viscount and the notion of being a married lady. One evening, she did not withdraw as usual with Miss Lavauden when Marchmont's port was brought in.

"Pour a glass for me, brother," demanded the admiral's lady. Marchmont complied, somewhat disapprovingly, as Letitia savored the wine. "It takes me back to Lisbon. I do not customarily drink port, but this is a particularly fine specimen."

"Your husband sent it to me. But it is not simply the port you wish to discuss."

"Of course not. How you could have been so totty-headed with Cecilia is my chief concern."

"Totty-headed? What do you mean?"

"What I say. I know that in Dacre's company you have always been prone to folly, but this is not some boys' scrape that can be cleared up with a few judiciously spent guineas and fulsome apologies. Annulments do not fall off trees. Nor can they be secured quietly and privately. Whatever possessed you?"

Marchmont dropped his head and cradled it in his hands, clearly distraught. "Lord, Letty, if I only knew that, I'd never have taken the wager in the first place. At the time, I felt invincible, but it has brought nothing but misery on me and mine."

"It's not simply that, Marchmont. It's Cecilia. You and Lavauden have done a fine job on her mind and her morals, but between you, you have neglected entirely the womanly arts."

"She can sew and draw and dance and all that business."

"My niece is singularly accomplished, but she has the skimpiest acquaintance with proper behavior. If she was to go out into Society now, she'd be pronounced a gauche hoyden. We know her to be charming, but dressed like a quiz and prone to say the first thing that comes into her head."

Marchmont preferred to ignore this attack on his child-rearing abilities. Instead, he tackled Letty's confident knowledge of marital law. "But what's this you say about annulments, Letty? What do you mean about it being so difficult to get one?"

"Ketley was in charge of some young fool of a lieutenant who had entered a marriage of convenience and sought to dissolve it. You will parade the family name through the courts if you proceed with an annulment, and you must prove not only nonconsummation but inability to consummate. Would you foist that reputation on either of these children?"

"What's to be done, Letty?"

"We must make the match permanent. It's a good marriage on both sides—hardly astonishing, given the friendship between you and Dacre. If only you'd the sense to stop at a betrothal. It would have been as legally binding, but rather less irrevocable. As it is, I see no other course open to us but to ensure that your lovebirds come to care for one another."

"How, Letty? The boy's on the continent until further notice, and Cecilia is a child."

"By the time he gets back from his travels, she will no longer be a child. We simply put them in each other's way. But first, I want you to give me your daughter. Let her live with Ketley and me. We're fixed in London for the time being. We may go to Paris or Versailles in the next year or so, which will interest her and broaden her experience of the world. Of course, she would return home to Sawards frequently, as would I, but let the child get some town bronze."

"She is still very weak."

"I am not suggesting that we leave on the morrow. Let her convalesce for a further month, and then she and I may go up to town, say for six weeks. She needs clothes in any case, and more importantly, she needs distractions from her thoughts. I can promise to fill her days to the point of exhaustion. She will meet people. I have friends with daughters just her age. She needs to giggle and make foolish schemes and learn how to fit into the world."

"How should you introduce her?"

"As Miss Marchmont. We need not advertise your folly. However, I will drop a hint or two that there is a long-standing betrothal. That will ward off any fortune-hunters."

"And when she encounters Ormiston again? What then?"

"Let us worry about it when it happens. The likelihood is that we have no need to concern ourselves for at least two years, and probably four, given the attractions of the Continent to any red-blooded male."

"I am not sure that Cecilia will feel comfortable with such subterfuge."

"I am quite sure she will feel a deal more comfortable entering Society, as all her contemporaries do, in the guise of an innocent debutante rather than as a child-bride abandoned by her groom. Really, Marchmont, I wish you would try for a little good sense."

Cecilia, of course, knew nothing of this conversation, but she had reaped the rewards of Letitia Ketley's adamant insistence that no one should know of the marriage. She had gone apprehensively to London with Letty, but this trip was very different from the short, disastrous journey she had made to marry Ormiston.

First of all, during her illness, Cecilia had lost much of the bulk that had made clothes such a problem. Her wardrobe might not be up to snuff, but at least she fitted into it. In fact, her dresses hung off her, and besides, she had grown as well as thinned out. Letitia's immediate task was, assisted by a lavish allowance from Marchmont, to dress her niece in the latest fashions suitable for a young maiden.

Her first fortnight in London was spent in a whirl of magazines and fashion plates, laces, satins, sarcenets, crepe and tulle, poplin, cambric and muslin, kid gloves and boots, slippers, gloves, swansdown muffs and Indian stoles. There were decisions of great moment to be made regarding flounces and vandyking, azure blue, blush pink, lilac, sprigs and stripes, pockets, petticoats, and whether amber was too fast an ornament for someone who should still be in the schoolroom. Finally, once the first gowns arrived, Marston poked and prodded and tweaked, without allowing either madam or miss to see, until, at last, satisfied with the end result, she summoned Lady Ketley and at last permitted Cecilia to stand before a cheval glass.

The reflection revealed a slender vision in a sarcenet evening gown the color of bluebells and satin slippers in the same shade. Although the silhouette was simple, rich silver embroidery at the hem, the square neckline, the sleeves, and bodice enlivened the gown. Marston had twisted up Cecilia's abundant head of hair into an intricate arrangement of plaits and silver ribbon, with a diamante pin in the shape of a crescent moon clipped into the dark mass. Her arms were bare, apart from a tulle stole shot with silver thread. Her eyes glowed violet with astonishment and delight.

"Diana, chaste goddess of the moon!" exclaimed Lady Ketley. "The color of that gown, the exact shade of her eyes. Marston, you are a genius. We shall have every aspiring poet in the Ton writing odes to Fair Cecilia."

"Miss Cecilia assisted, although she may not have realized it. She has a fine eye for color, and fortunately, no taste for excessive flounces. It is much easier to dress a girl when she does not care too much for flounces."

"The hair perhaps is a little elaborate for a girl her age, but tonight, it is no matter. We are among friends."

That evening, Lady Ketley had invited around two old friends with daughters the same age as Cecilia. It was her first real encounter with her contemporaries. Any initial apprehensions were soon banished as the girls were first awestruck by her finery and then eager for her acquaintance. By the time her six weeks of London life had expired, she had experienced happy days in the company of her new friends, shopping, dancing, gazing at the Bond Street beaux, even excursions to the circus and theater. Her delight was increased by the receipt of invitations to visit her new friends in the country.

From that time on, Cecilia was not very often at Sawards. She wrote regularly to her family, often sent presents for Reginald and Amelia, and visited infrequently although reliably on high days and holidays. She did not miss a birthday or a Christmas. Initially, Reginald missed her companionship more than Amelia, but Marchmont, chastened by the errors he had committed with regard to his first child, spent a great deal more time at Sawards than hitherto, and was soon taking his son with him around the estates.

Although surrounded by young ladies whose chief object in life was to entice young men with their charms and gifts, Cecilia knew she had no need to attract and thereby proved all the more attractive to potential suitors. Ormiston's scathing opinion ensured that she had no very high regard for her looks, reinforced by both Marston and Lady Ketley, who were sparing in their praise and frequent in their criticism of her bearing, her tastes, and her hoydenish manners. Such faint encomiums as she received from her mentors were generally credited as Marston's triumphs over the odds. She knew she was greatly improved in looks since her marriage, and she understood from all that Marston and her aunt said, that looks were not guaranteed to bind a man to a woman in any case. Looks might do the initial work, but after that, it was accomplishments and charm that entwined a man in a woman's toils. In these spheres, Cecilia strove far harder than anyone suspected.

Knowing that Ormiston was a creditable artist and interested in all things Italian, Cecilia demanded a drawing master and instruction in the language of Dante and Petrarch. With her friends, singing lessons were all the rage, so she followed suit. She noted carefully that the women that men appeared to prefer were generally amusing and witty, well-read but careful to conceal their intellects, competent horsewomen, slow to frown and swift to laugh, but without giggling or simpering. She made sure that she read all the latest poets and understood the articles in *The Times*. This her father had encouraged her to do in any case, although she was quick to see that while he might encourage her to dispute his views when she disagreed with him, most men preferred their female acquaintances to accept their opinions without argumentation.

Her Uncle Ketley was the first target on whom Cecilia practiced female wiles, with some encouragement from her Aunt Letty. He soon pronounced her a sensible puss, and was as eager as his wife to display his pretty niece in Society. He made sure, once he had established that she had good hands, sufficient spirit to manage her horses well, and enough sense not to push them too hard, that she had a neat mare to ride in Hyde Park and a smart curricle to drive with a specially matched pair of gray geldings.

Neither Admiral Ketley nor his wife was aware of Cecilia's

favorite form of riding, which was to perform tumbling tricks learnt from a stable boy at Sawards who had once run away to London. Jem Anderton had found employment at Astley's Amphitheatre and being a small, wiry fellow, found it easy to learn the more acrobatic feats of equestrian display from a resident troupe of Cossack dzigits. After some years, he had wearied of the life, particularly once he had grown to manhood and found himself too large to continue in the ring. Summoned back to Sawards to care for his ailing mother, Jem had found a permanent position in Marchmont's stables and an eager student in Miss Cecilia.

As a child of eight and nine, Cecilia had been fearless, but as her body changed with puberty, she had become self-conscious and unwieldy. Then she had fallen ill and disappeared to London. When she returned, lithe, limber, and more adventurous than ever, Jem had taken great delight in teaching her still wilder antics. It did not occur to him, being unfamiliar with the constraints placed about young ladies making their bow in Society, to ask how she managed to find the privacy and time to practice her skills, but every few months, she would reappear, ready for a new set of lessons. By the time she was eighteen, she could perform handstands or twist beneath a horse's belly and appear in the saddle once more while the beast was in mid-canter. Dancing and deportment lessons had instilled in her considerable grace and she seemed to have gained in strength since her sickness.

In truth, riding was Cecilia's great release. Initially, the concentration needed to perform tricks was the one attribute that drove out all thoughts of Ormiston and his harshness. Then, it became a vital escape from the constrictions of life in Society. Although Admiral Ketley kept a fine stable, he was not greatly interested by horseflesh. His grooms were not kept busy, and preferred it thus. When Cecilia arrived and one of them had to accompany her on all her rides, they were initially resentful. But she preferred to arrange for the hire of a private, indoor school where she could work on Jem's tricks and take bruising rides in all weathers while they waited for her in a dry corner, smoking and relaxing. She regularly spent the first part of the morning in this manner, and found her patience with the constant changes of clothes and largely inane conversational twittering of her companions much increased by this exercise.

Being an intelligent young woman, Cecilia had realized early enough that Lady Ketley wished to promote the match with Ormiston. She did attempt to make discreet enquiries about her legal position, but she lacked gravitas and time to pursue them. What she had discovered indicated that she was more closely bound to Ormiston than her father—or, indeed, Lord Dacre—had anticipated. Much of the time, she was too intent on enjoying herself and diverting her companions to dwell on the future, but as time passed, her friends began to make matches, and fresh crops of young girls entered Society every year. Now she was nineteen, and had been out for three seasons. This year, she had caught from tittle-tattle that in certain circles, she was known as "The Impregnable," and more than one young man had entered into the wager books at Brooks and Whites (and less exalted gaming clubs) his intention of capturing a kiss from the fortress.

When Admiral Ketley was sent to Paris, his wife and niece had been quick to ask whether they might accompany him. Cecilia was unsure whether Lady Ketley knew of her niece's nickname and reputation, but the removal to a foreign country was fortuitous. Or so it had seemed until the chance revelation of one of Lady Ketley's acquaintances that an eligible young English nobleman had recently arrived in Paris and had impressed Madame de Stael and so many others with his address, his elegance, his sophistication. Why, Lord Ormiston was so charming, so well travelled, so monstrous handsome, he had the pick of Paris beauties. It was said his departure from Venice had left the ladies of the Veneto heartbroken, and one particular lady near to death, such was the devotion he inspired. He had some business back in England, something to do with wills and estates, but once he had settled his affairs, he was planning to return to Italy, for he found his native land uncongenial.

Naturally, no communication had passed between Ormiston and his wife in all the years of their separation, but Cecilia was irked by her own ignorance of her husband's movements. Once it was known that he was a guest of the Ferrières family, it was easy enough to track his path through Paris, and Cecilia had immediately determined that she would inspect her bridegroom. She remembered him as a stunning youth, but before she made any decisions with regard to the future, she needed to see him once again.

So she had gone riding that morning. And the hat had come off, and she had made an exhibition of herself and caught only the merest glimpse of a dark young man sitting in a carriage with the comtesse, looking a little bored. It was not enough on which to base any plans. The difficulty would be in encountering him without revealing her identity.

Those distant dreams of subjugating the viscount still resonated in Cecilia's imagination. For so long now, her duties had led her into ways that suited her, and she was used to getting her own way through the exercise of all that she had learnt through her aunt. Finally, all her training would come into play, but Cecilia was not yet sure of the nature of the game in which she would be engaged. Marston dropped the brush. It was time to meet Aunt Letitia and discover what delights the day held.

Five

Of course Letitia Ketley had secured invitations for the Comtesse de Ferrière's great masked ball well before there had been any question of Ormiston attending. Cecilia's imagination had been captured by the collection of plunder that Napoleon had amassed from Egypt, and she spent some hours sketching images of gods and goddesses before devising a costume which she resolutely refused to discuss with her aunt or Marston. On the evening of the ball, Marston came to Cecilia's room and insisted on inspecting the contents of the mysterious boxes that had been delivered earlier that week.

The costume was more demure than Marston had feared, but also more exotic than she cared for. The dress was of fine white muslin with a full skirt, for which Marston supposed she should be grateful, but it was embroidered with gold and scarlet thread in outlandish designs, falcons and cats cavorting about the hem. The bodice was heavy with intricate gold-and-red stitching, and the sleeves were negligible puffs of white material, scarcely there. Cecilia carried a flimsy chiffon scarf with tassels of gold thread. However, the most outrageous item was the mask itself. It was a delicate creation in the shape of a lioness's head, wrought in gold leaf and pleated cloth of gold, leaving her mouth and chin free, but concealing the rest of her head entirely. The shimmering fall of the material reached just below her shoulders.

"It's heathen."

"Intentionally so, Marston. I have taken the likeness of the Goddess Sekhmet."

"I've no idea who she may be, and to be sure, you look seemly and fit to be seen by gentlemen, but there is something wicked about it."

Cecilia laughed and ridiculed Marston's old-fashioned ways, but the woman's disapproval warmed her thoroughly. Tonight, she knew she was alluring. She had taken a step into unknown territory, moving away from what might be suitable for a girl, toward some undefined and infinite possibility.

Marston expected Lady Ketley, on beholding the outlandish costume, to exclaim with horror and send her niece back to her room to change, but the admiral's wife smoothly refrained from all comment apart from an almost approving murmur of "How exotic you look, my dear."

The admiral was more effusive. "Fine getup, m'dear. You'll be all the rage. Must keep an eye on you."

"In that mask, it shouldn't be difficult to track her down should she go astray," commented Lady Ketley dryly as she buttoned up her gloves and fastened her cloak.

The drive to the Hotel de Ferrières was brief, but as the carriage approached the house, it slowed to a crawl as the jam of vehicles gradually inched forward, depositing guests and pulling away. Brilliant light shone from every window of the great mansion, in which every sconce and chandelier appeared to have been lit. Even the garden was illuminated, revealing trees and a box hedge trimmed into geometrically precise borders of knee-height to protect the lawn from marauding feet. The Ketleys and Cecilia stepped out of the carriage and climbed a shallow flight of stairs into the great hallway, where footmen were running to and fro collecting evening cloaks and dispensing glasses of champagne or orgeat for the softer-headed. As soon as he had shed his cloak, the admiral collected his flute of sparkling wine and stood in an unobtrusive corner, promising to wait for the ladies while they retired to repair the ravages wrought by their journey to the ball.

Cecilia helped Aunt Letty adjust her headdress and skirts. Lady Ketley was looking exceptionally fierce, brandishing a spear and a reticule and sporting a horned helmet above her black domino. The admiral had steadfastly refused all entreaties to wear any costume other than his full naval regalia, though he did accept the need to wear a mask.

The ladies rejoined the admiral, who was gazing at the steady stream of eastern concubines, dancing girls, Saskatchewan savages, maharajahs, cannibal kings, bull fighters, assorted gods and goddesses from both Greek and Roman pantheons, and packs of Gauls who strolled through the ornate marble hallway into salons leading to the east and west wings of the house. The waiters in sober black, bearing trays of drinks to and fro, were the most dignified inhabitants of the house.

"Deuce of a lot of houris from Pondicherry attending tonight. They're receiving in the ballroom, so if you're ready, ladies, let us follow the teeming masses."

They walked through a yellow, then a leaf-green, then a rose salon. Pursuing their fellow guests to the strains of a mazurka, they arrived at the entrance to the ballroom. Given the press of carriages at the gates, it was no surprise that they had missed the opening polonaise of the evening. At the great doorway leading into the ballroom, a majordomo was ushering in the guests. Of course, since it was a masked ball, there was no announcement of names, but the Comtesse de Ferrières and her son were greeting their guests and clearly had recognized most as they entered the astounding room.

Once through the doorway and past their hostess, guests found themselves at the head of a shallow flight of stairs, overlooking the huge room. Five huge, arched windows ran down each side. Those on the street side were curtained, but the ones leading to the courtyard at the center of the house were open, allowing air to circulate in the crowded room while also permitting footmen to bring refreshments to those overcome by the press of guests.

The ceiling was heavy with gilded plasterwork, a riot of seashells, cupids, and wreaths. Above gold-and-white wood panelling, the walls were decorated with murals depicting the Muses cavorting with fauns and satyrs. In each window recess hung a great brass chandelier, each capable of holding what seemed to be a hundred candles; the walls were also decorated with matching sconces.

At the far end, the musicians were positioned on a low dais, with doors on either side leading to more rooms where apparently food and drink was laid out. The scent of gardenias from the courtyard filled the air, and Cecilia could just make out the rush of water running over a massive fountain. As the dancers moved, she caught glimpses of the dark wood of the floor.

As she surveyed the guests, Cecilia wondered how Ormiston might look now. He had been tall enough as a youth and might have grown a little more. He would have remained slim, she was sure. His companion, the Scottish artist who had accompanied him to Italy, wrote regularly to Dacre to report on the viscount's progress. The viscount's prowess in Neapolitan swordsmanship featured large in the accounts. So the young man would probably still be slender and wiry, though perhaps a little fuller about the shoulders than when she had last seen him. He had not struck her as a flamboyant type—quite the reverse. Her memory was of a shambolic, almost ragged boy who favored black, emulating Hamlet, taking to mourning on his wedding day. Immediately, her eyes scanned the floor in search of a darkly dressed figure.

She could identify no likely candidate, but her eye was caught by a man leaning against a doorway at the far end of the huge ballroom. He wore the clothes of two centuries earlier, in the style of followers of the cavalier King Charles I.

He was clean-shaven, with long black hair which spilled over a high lace collar onto the shoulders of his pewter velvet jacket, fastened with tiny buttons and slashed to reveal white lawn beneath. His three-quarter-length trousers, tucked into black boots of Spanish leather, were of the same stuff as the jacket. Idly, he swung in his right hand a wide-brimmed hat of black felt adorned with a single scarlet plume.

The fellow reminded Cecilia powerfully of a portrait she had seen, although she could not quite remember where or when. He seemed to be watching her, but her attention was then distracted as another young gallant, wearing lurid, parti-colored hose and a green-and-red-checked doublet, invited her to dance. She stepped onto the floor with her Florentine dandy and in her effort to recall the variations of the quadrille as practiced in Paris, forgot all about the elegant Royalist at the other end of the room.

It took some time for Ormiston to track down his host. Finally, as the flow of guests slowed, he took the opportunity to question his friend.

"The girl in Egyptian dress, with the head of a lioness. Do you know her?"

"I can't remember. Who did she come in with?"

"A Royal naval officer and a Viking lady with a spear."

"I don't know them. The Viking lady was a friend of my mother's, but I can't tell you more than that. I remember the lion-goddess, certainly, but I hadn't realized she came with the admiral and his wife."

"No name, then?"

"No, I'm sorry. She speaks superb French, though, your lioness."

"She isn't French?"

"I don't think so. There is some sort of accent there, although, of course, there was not much time for me to establish where she might have come from."

"And the naval officer really is English?"

"Oh yes! A man of a certain age who is prepared to wear

the domino, but no other form of disguise. I think he may be an admiral. I can inquire of my mother, if you wish."

"No, it doesn't matter. I'll soon find out if she is from England."

"So you are in hot pursuit? What of your lovely *principessa*? Or was she a contessa? No pining for the Italian nobility now?"

Ormiston smiled, looking predatory rather than amused. "Since you show yourself so able, I shall leave you to your speculations, my dear friend." He absented himself in search of the object of his interest.

The viscount was certain that the young lady was the same girl who had so captured his imagination in the Bois de Boulogne. There was something in the way she moved, something in the line of her neck and chin, something in the way she held herself that persuaded him of her identity. And some other impulse, quite foreign to him, was forcing him to seek her out against all his instincts and calculations. Buchan would have been astonished, perhaps even delighted, since the Scot felt that his pupil, while apt, would never achieve greatness as an artist until he unleashed his own passions.

Until now, Ormiston had dismissed his teacher's words as nonsense, for ardor had always struck him as beneath a gentleman. Casual insouciance and competent ease seemed much more admirable attributes to the viscount, and he strove in all things for detachment and unflappability. Now, though, he knew he must find the girl, speak with her. If he had followed the thought through, it would have taken him inexorably toward the realization that he must lie with her, too.

The musicians were tuning up for the opening bars of a new melody. The restored monarch of France had banned the waltz at his court, but the Ferrières were prepared to defy the ban, since His Majesty had arrived at the ball and left within half an hour, accompanied by the attractive Comtesse du Cayla, his favored companion, and her own particular friend, an unprepossessing man called Villele who, it was rumored, wrote all the letters the comtesse sent to the king. It was widely believed that the ban on dancing the waltz owed more to Louis's uncertain health and excessive girth than any doubts regarding the suitability of the dance.

The viscount wound his way through the crowd in search of his Egyptian goddess. He was determined to dance with her. Finding her proved harder than he expected, for several ladies were wearing white and gold, and from the back, it was hard to tell whose identity they had assumed. Finally, he saw the rounded curve of lion's ears and the shimmering veil concealing her hair. She was choosing between two aspirants for her hand, one in the dress of a courtier under Francis I, the other in the yellow embroidered coat of a Cathay emperor. Ormiston bowed deeply and said, "The lady is promised to me." He took her outstretched hand and whirled her away as her two attendants stood dumbfounded by his audacity.

"Have I offended?" He spoke in French, but had to wait some moments for her reply.

"Rather you should ask if you have sinned," Cecilia replied faultlessly in the same tongue. She knew it was Ormiston as soon as he spoke.

He gazed down into her beguiling eyes. "For you are a goddess, and I am instantly in your thrall."

"How easily you pledge yourself." She smiled, but her eyes were cold. Quickly, she veiled them before he could see that his words had angered her. "To how many others have you made pledges so lightly?"

Ormiston did not check, although his hands tightened around her. She looked up again, once more mistress of her emotions. His eyes searched hers, and she returned his gaze without wavering. He forced himself to relax. He only remembered his child-bride because he was on his way to England to sever the farcical ties which bound him.

"I have made one pledge which will be dissolved. And then I shall be free to worship you as you deserve."

"What if I choose not to wait until you are free?"

"A goddess may rule as she pleases. But she cannot prevent her worshippers from thronging to her altar. But tell me, what do you govern?"

"I am Sekhmet, with power over sunsets and sorrow. In my fury, I will bring down destruction on my enemies, but I can also heal what I hurt."

A frisson of discomfort shivered through the viscount, but instantly he dismissed it. She was simply a woman dressed in a costume, playing a game. Well, he would play at her game and see where it would end.

"And what of your lovers? Are they all ashes?" As he whirled her around the dance floor, he was assailed by her jasmine scent.

"I cleave only to my consort."

"Does he attend tonight?"

Cecilia chuckled, giddy with the dance and the folly of her dancing partner.

"He may be close at hand. If he were, you would never be able to distinguish him in this crowd, in any case."

"Is he complaisant? Does he stand idly by while your worshippers beg for your favors?"

"He has no need to be complaisant. He has never been betrayed by me. As for those who follow me, their reward is their worship. They require no other favors."

He longed to shatter her equilibrium, her air of amused unavailability. She was all enticement and elusiveness. He would be the one to lead her into betrayal, and it would be tonight. The strains of the waltz gave way to a more exuberant polka and as couples jostled and twirled, he managed to spirit her into the courtyard where guests more intent on conversation were strolling or sitting on stone benches. There were areas of deep shadow where the light spilling from the thousands of candles gleaming in the house failed to reach. Exclamations and bursts of laughter punctured the rush of water from the fountain as anecdotes were exchanged and gossip passed on. Ormiston drew his dancing partner to a seat just beyond a crescent of light.

"You wish to monopolize me, sir?"

"I wish to know if it was you I saw playing at circus tricks the other day."

"What sort of tricks? Acrobatics? Walking the tightrope? If I were a circus performer, I would hardly have secured a ticket for the most exclusive ball of the Season."

"Riding tricks. You were with a party. A woman lost her hat. You galloped to the rescue."

"You seem very certain that it was I."

This oblique response confirmed her identity to Ormiston. If she had not been the same woman, she would have been baffled, perhaps even outraged by the possibility. He determined to find out more about her. "Where do you come from?"

"I thought we had established that I am a goddess from Egypt."

"You speak French almost like a native, but there is a faint accent. Not German. Perhaps Dutch."

"Why is it so vital? We shall be unmasquing before dawn. Why not wait? What does it matter?" Cecilia strove to keep her voice level and her manner insouciant. It was far too early to reveal herself to Ormiston. In fact, it seemed to her that keeping her identity concealed from him altogether would be her wisest course.

"Why are you so secretive?"

"Because this is a masque, a night of revels without fear of revelation, a night for mystery, a night for secrets."

"Bright-shining goddess, share your secrets with me." He leaned toward her and brushed his lips against hers, then withdrew as swiftly as he had advanced.

"I am no Lesbia, to be abused in your lyrics." Her voice carried a nervous edge.

"I write no poetry. But I did not know that an Egyptian goddess would recognize the words of Catullus."

Cecilia was silent, well aware that her slip had revealed more than she intended. It was unladylike enough to admit to reading Latin, let alone a poet as notorious as Catullus. But his works had been there in her father's library and Marchmont's policy had been to allow his children access to any book he owned. And then, there had been the kiss, gentle as a butterfly's touch, but more potent than champagne. Which was, she realized later when reviewing the events of the evening, her downfall. A waiter was passing and she half rose from her seat to summon him. He stopped, lowered his tray, and deftly removed a glass to hold it before her. She reached for it, but failed to grasp it before he moved away. The glass slipped, its contents splashed her, and the glass itself rolled into a flowerbed. She stood upright and her cavalier exclaimed, "Quickly, I'll take you inside and you can sponge it dry. There'll be no harm done."

He grasped her hand and whisked her into a quiet passage and then up a short flight of stairs into a circular room lit by a single candelabra.

"Wait here—I'll fetch a cloth and some water."

She sank onto a chaise longue and looked about her. The sounds of the ball had quite faded away. It took some seconds for her eyes to adjust to the dimness. Then she began to make out strange shapes and what appeared to be great boxes scattered on the walls. A few more seconds and she had identified the shapes as several globes and an astrolabe, and the boxes as glass display cases holding fantastic creatures: the elongated limbs of a huge crab, longer than the arm span of a man; a twisted ivory horn attached to a small white whale; the vertebrae of something she guessed was a giraffe; a tiger's head; and several stuffed owls. On a cluttered desk, she could perceive the shadows of a sextant and a quadrant. Standing in a corner was a telescope. Dimly, she could identify the constellations which decorated the domed ceiling and she could hear the faint ticking of several clocks not quite keeping time in unison. She was in a *cabinet des merveilles.*

Ormiston returned bearing a bowl and cloth. She began to dab at her skirt. He took the candelabra and set it on the floor near the head of the chaise longue so she could see what she was doing. Fortunately, she had chosen champagne, and the wine had scarcely discolored her skirt. He sat at her feet.

"This is an amazing room. Is it the work of the current Comte de Ferrières?" asked Cecilia as she dabbed at her skirt.

"He has added some items, but I believe most of it was collected by his grandfather. A gentleman of a scientific bent, I am told." He reached out and held the hem of her skirt to make it easier for her to dampen the stain.

"I wonder whether he travelled in search of his treasures or simply bought them in Paris. Such a wonderful collection. My father tried to build up his own on Linnaean principles, but we have no room really suitable for specimens of any sort."

"You sound disappointed."

"I was the chief taxonomist. It was a delightful occupation." She shook her skirt out and dropped the cloth into the bowl.

"Latin and Linnaeus. Unusual fields of expertise for a goddess." Instantly, Ormiston realized his gaffe. For those brief minutes, she had spoken without calculation. Now he sensed the restoration of her social mask, far more impenetrable than the golden whimsy she wore to conceal her identity. "What is your favorite species?"

"It cannot matter. It is time we returned to the ballroom. We may be missed."

"Just tell me. Perhaps we can find your favorite creature in these drawers." He gestured to the cabinets surrounding them.

"I must remember to apply to the comtesse for a full inspection at a more convenient moment."

"Will there be a more convenient moment? Who knows, our lives may be swept away in an instant."

"You hear the winged chariot of time hurrying near?" Cecilia could not control the skepticism which colored her query. "It is a vehicle that many men feel approaches when they find themselves secluded with a lady."

"Always with great rapidity." Ormiston could not help laughing at his goddess's astute reading of the male sex. She laughed, too—a friendly, complicit laugh. He fell silent. He did not wish to appear predictable or simply another importunate suitor. But she was delectable. Subtle. Desirable. Eminently desirable. He took her hand. She wore only a delicate bracelet of gold filigree. No rings. He brought her hand closer to his mouth and turned it so he could kiss her palm. Her breathing was shallow.

His fingers trailed up to the spot where her garnet eardrops brushed against her neck, then along the line of her jaw until he drew the outline of her lips. He looked into her eyes, as if that would help him see through her mask before leaning forward until his lips hovered over hers. Her lips, so lustrous, so full; the scent of her, so heady; the feel of her, so tantalizing. He gave way to temptation and kissed her.

It was his slow tenderness that trapped Cecilia. If he had pulled or mauled her as other young bucks had tried to do, she might have had the strength to push him away, to bring them both back to their senses with a caustic set-down. But his gentle coaxing lulled her into believing that she was almost unaffected until he pulled back slightly—perhaps to take air, perhaps to end the kiss—and some uncontrollable urge pushed her forward to take his lips with hers this time.

Cecilia abandoned all clear thought as her instincts overcame her reason. She reached for Ormiston, pulled him closer, and in so doing, broke his self-control. His hunger for her was matched by hers for him as their kiss deepened. Her tentative, unquenchable ardor inflamed him. He strove to tug her mask away, but her hand came up to his wrist, gentle but determined.

"No. Let me remain masked."

"At least tell me your name."

"My name is Alice." They still spoke in French and she whispered it in the French style. It was her middle name, her grandmother's name.

"Alice, I long to see your face. I long to run my fingers through your hair, and trace the curve of your brow and the line of your nose. Please."

She shook her head. He took her lips with his once again, and his kiss was one of acceptance. But it soon deepened into something more dangerous. Cecilia knew there was no turning away. . . .

Afterwards, they lay together, silent, gazing into one another's eyes in wonder, sated for long minutes as the trance of passion dwindled and faded. She shivered, suddenly chilled. Ormiston reached for her and held her shoulders.

"Alice, please, I beg of you, let me see you, let me know your full name. After what we have shared tonight, I cannot bear to lose you." His voice was shaking.

She shook her head, mute, afraid, as the consequences of her actions sank in. Aunt Letty had been quite clear. If there were to be an annulment, there would have to be medical examinations. Now, there would be no annulment. Now, there would have to be an Act of Parliament and a divorce. Even though the man who had released her from her virginity was her husband.

Breathing was suddenly a great effort. She had been so foolish, so impetuous, so rash. She pushed Ormiston away, scrambled up, and began to tug at her clothes, shake them out, struggle, fumble to put them on. Dazed at first, Ormiston watched; then he sat up and pulled on his own smallclothes. She was in an adorable tangle of muddled buttons and tangled laces. But he could not read her features, only her impatient, angry gestures and the trembling curve of her generous mouth as she attempted to ease the knots and straighten her hems. He stood and helped her. Too soon, she was ready, her costume almost immaculate, the faint stain of the champagne virtually invisible, all other signs of disarray banished.

"There may be consequences." Ormiston broached the silence and she started as he used the very word that had beaten at her brain.

"That is not your concern." She was brusque and poised for flight.

"How can you have been married and yet a virgin?"

Cecilia quashed the impulse to laugh and ask him whether he thought his wife was still a virgin. Giving way to irony would simply prolong this difficult interlude.

"That is between me and my husband."

Ormiston saw that she would say nothing more. There was a desk in the corner. He crossed to it and rummaged through until he had found paper, a pen, ink. He wrote his name and the address of both the London and country homes of the Dacres. He looked down at his left hand and tugged at the signet ring on his smallest finger. When it was off, he wrapped it in the screw of paper and knelt before the woman who had been so generous and was now so dangerously silent.

"I will not plead my cause further. Please believe me when I say I am your servant always. If ever you call on me, I shall come. If ever you need me, you have only to send this ring to the address on the paper and I will be found. I swear this. I will wait for you."

"You do not know me. Don't wait for me, don't look for me. I will not be found."

The viscount swallowed as she spoke with finality. Then he pressed the paper into her hands with a warm kiss. She was trembling still. She pulled away and hurried from the room. The door clicked shut and Ormiston finished dressing. By the time he had made himself presentable enough to rejoin the dancers, she had vanished. He could not stop himself from looking, from scanning the ballroom continuously for her, but he knew that she was no longer there. It took him some time to identify the hollowness of that knowledge as loss. He had never lost anything before.

Six

The better sort of chaperone has an unerring instinct if a charge goes astray, but also has the discretion to wait for a private moment before tackling the errant maiden and her misdemeanors. After a life of guarding young naval wives from untoward entanglements, Aunt Letty excelled in all aspects of chaperonage. Despite Cecilia's best attempts to evade her aunt's scrutiny, she could not sidle off to bed without an interrogation. While Marston was removing the bulky headdress and combing out Cecilia's hair, Lady Ketley entered her niece's room in full deshabille.

"What an evening! We must exchange notes before the night is out, or I shall toss and turn all night. Which of the guests did you manage to uncover?" She began to help Cecilia out of her clothes.

"We know so few people in Paris, I can hardly say."

"That did not stop young men from wishing to dance with you. I wonder whether Lord Ormiston was present." Lady Ketley helped Cecilia out of her dress. She noted that her niece did not react, avoiding her instead by retreating behind a screen to remove her corset and smallclothes. "Quite a success, your costume, and surprisingly original, too. I had thought that half of Paris would have taken up the Egyptian mode, but it seemed that the reign of François I was a more fashionable choice."

"Or the flowers of the Orient," responded Cecilia as she returned in her negligee to sit at her dressing table.

"Mmm. One thing, my dear." Lady Ketley paused and

watched the tension in her niece's shoulders increase. "I do not wish to hound you or be forever insisting that you dangle about me, but it would make me easier in my mind if you did not disappear for what seemed to be hours. Were you quite well?"

Cecilia explained about the spilt wine, and how she had found some water and slipped into the room full of curiosities, then knocked the bowl, and what an age it had taken for the dress to dry, and how she had by then been so entranced by the wonders in the room that she had lost all track of time. Sticking relatively close to the truth should have been easy enough, but never having dissembled to her aunt before, Cecilia felt uncomfortable. The ring, still wrapped in its twist of paper, sat bulkily in her reticule, and Cecilia felt sure that her aunt's gaze was drawn to the lump in the fine silk where before there had been only a silk handkerchief, dancing card, and pencil.

Aunt Letty went up to the dress and held out the skirt. "The stain is not too bad. Marston will know how to get it out. Thank heavens it was champagne, not claret. It would be a shame were you never to wear this ensemble again."

"I could not wear it in Paris, but I suppose if I were to attend a masque in London, it would be acceptable."

Lady Ketley gave her ward a shrewd glance. "You seem very weary, my dear. I shall leave you, but prepare yourself for a good coze tomorrow morning."

Cecilia expected to toss and turn, reliving the night's events, but she was more tired than she had realized and fell asleep almost immediately. The threatened dissection of the ball never took place, however, for Cecilia was awakened by a rather stern Marston, followed by Lady Ketley, brisker than usual.

"My dear, Lavauden has written with news of your father. He is not well and she advises us to return to Sawards promptly."

"Papa! He is never sick. May I see the letter? What does she say?"

"Briefly, Marchmont has had some sort of seizure and is confined to his bed. She says little more. Here, you may see. But I know that you will not rest until you have been home, and I shall be much easier in my mind if I accompany you. However diligently you and Lavauden might correspond about his case, I should never believe anything about his progress."

Lady Ketley wrote a reply to Lavauden to be sent off that day, and Marston chivvied the French girls in the house to launder and press and pack so that the following day, the three women were ready to depart, accompanied as far as Calais by one of the admiral's assistants.

For Cecilia, the hours in the coach seemed to lengthen as anxiety for her father alternated with bitter self-condemnation for her folly at the masked ball. The wanton enthusiasm with which she had given way to Ormiston's touch and taste and scent was a dangerous quality to discover at this point in the game. But now, the game had become a more serious affair altogether. All those foolish plans for revenge on Ormiston for his cruel words five years ago seemed no more than childish nonsense. Who could say in what state she would find her father, and who could say what the future might hold? As the hours cooped up in a carriage passed, as she boarded the packet bound for Dover, Cecilia's honesty forced her to admit that she wanted Ormiston more than ever, that the boy she had detested had become a man she might love. Yet, her own wayward nature had made it more difficult than ever to bind him to her.

He would soon discover that the wife he had left untouched was now unchaste. If he ever found out that she was Alice, her deception would anger him, justly. He had sworn that rash oath to come to Alice when she called. If she used the ring and the letter, she would incur a deserved wrath. There seemed no clear course open to Cecilia and she repented her arrogant assumption that deceiving Ormiston would bring her any satisfaction.

The Channel crossing was timed so that the packet entered Dover with the early tide. Lavauden had set a watch for Lady Ketley and Cecilia at Dover: Cecilia's old favorite, Jem Anderton, was waiting at the dockside. He confirmed that Marchmont remained confined to bed and that Doctor Groves was visiting daily. Jem had hired a carriage to bring the ladies back to Sawards, and once they were installed, he galloped ahead so that their imminent arrival might bring some cheer.

Some four hours later, the chaise pulled up before Cecilia's home, and there on the front steps stood Reggie and Amelia, waving strenuously. Amelia dashed up to the carriage before the post-boy had a chance to climb from his perch and was calling out her relief at seeing her aunt and sister.

"We're so glad you're back. Papa has spoken for the first time in days—Lavauden even allowed us to go up and see him. There's food waiting for you, but it is all cold. Lavauden is nursing Papa, but she'll be down as soon as she knows you are here."

"Get back, Amelia—give them a chance to come down from the carriage. You will have to take her in hand, Ceci. She has run wild since Papa fell ill." Reggie sounded rather peremptory.

Cecilia climbed out first, then turned to help Lady Ketley. It was not until the bags had been handed down and they had all entered the hallway and started to unwind themselves from cloaks and bonnets that she had a chance to speak.

"How ill is Papa?" Cecilia asked Reggie directly. His facade crumbled as he rushed into his tall sister's arms and hugged her fiercely, hiding his face against her as he finally gave way to the fear he had been suppressing now for over a fortnight. He always bore himself so proudly and strove so hard to learn all that was told him, it was easy to forget that he was only eleven years old.

Holding the convulsing boy to her with all her might, Cecilia looked over at Lady Ketley. Immediately, the admiral's wife took her youngest niece by the hand and demanded to be shown to her rooms. Amelia led her to the first floor, casting an anxious glance back at her brother and sister. Cecilia guided Reggie into the morning room and closed the door. Embracing him still, she dropped a kiss on his forehead. Slowly, steadily, the sobs tailed off until Reggie gave only the occasional hiccup.

"Tell me."

"Oh, Cecilia, we were in the garden with Squire Hislop and, quite suddenly, he gave a strange cry and then threw back his head and made such strange gurgling sounds. Lavauden chivvied Amelia upstairs immediately, but by the time she ran down again, Papa had fallen silent and we could not rouse him. The Squire and Jem and two other fellows carried him up to his room, and they summoned Doctor Groves, who simply shook his head. He has come every day, and found men to visit from London, but Papa has been lying still and stiff as if he were dead already."

"But Amelia said he had spoken today."

"Yes, he has. And Mademoiselle did allow us up to see him. But he is so changed. He did not move—he lay there like a log and his speech was more like moaning than words, Ceci. I am terribly afraid. What if he dies?"

"I am here to care for you now."

"But what if you go away again? Why, Aunt Ketley may need you and then what is to become of us? You will go to her and we shall be left all alone."

"Oh, Reggie. I cannot make you any promises, but this I can swear. Whatever happens, whether Papa lives or not, you will be cared for and loved and nothing here at Sawards will change. Lavauden would never leave us, and there are so many other dear people here. None of them will desert us. We must pray with all our hearts that Papa gets better, but you must think carefully. How will he be happiest? An invalid, unable to see to his land, or at peace and at rest, knowing that everything here will continue as it has done for as long as he has been the keeper and caretaker of these lands."

"Ceci, do you think he will die?"

"I cannot tell until I have seen him, Reggie. You must let me go up now. Rest assured, I shall hide nothing from you. I hope and pray that a recovery is possible, but let me go to him now and see for myself."

The young boy drew back and nodded, still stiff with the misery of fear and uncertainty and loss. Cecilia held his hands still and gave them a final squeeze, taking as much reassurance as she gave from her brother's blotched, teary countenance. Slowly, she climbed the familiar stairs and walked the corridor to her father's room. She knocked softly at the door. Mademoiselle Lavauden slipped out of the room and gave her pupil a swift, fierce hug.

"Thank God. Perhaps he will rest a little easier now that you are here. But you must be prepared for a grave change in him, my dear. I will leave you. It distracts him if too many people are about him."

Cecilia nodded and steeled herself to enter. The room was surprisingly airy, with the curtains and the windows open, and her father propped up on a bank of pillows in the middle of his great bed. But the fresh air did not entirely disguise a stale odor, and the light pitilessly emphasized the hollows in Marchmont's face. Always a spare man, he now appeared cavernously gaunt, his eyes rheumy pools of blue sunken into his skull. Accustomed to spending long hours in the saddle overseeing his lands, he had always sported a healthy color, but this had now faded and his skin appeared sallow and parchment-thin. His hair was lank, and his hands against the white sheets were curled like the claws of a pigeon.

But it was the ruin of his voice—once so full and musical, now a slurred mutter—that caused Cecilia to close her eyes to hold back the tears, to swallow and to stiffen with the determination not to give way yet.

"Ceci. Is that Ceci?"

"Papa. I am here." She went over and sat on the bed, taking

his restless fingers in her own before bending over to kiss his brow.

"Time is short, daughter."

"Don't say so, Papa."

"We must face the truth. There is much to be done. Much to be said. I must be brief. I haven't the strength. But you must be strong for us all, Ceci." He paused and looked at her expectantly. She gripped his hands again.

"I will be, I promise."

"Ketley and Dacre are the executors and guardians. But I have named you as guardian also. You are the one who will be able to stay close at hand."

"I will stand by them. You know that."

"I know that. All at Sawards must be managed closely. There may be time. I shall explain the ledgers if you bring them up. We will meet with Kitson. He is a good man. But we have many decisions to make—I have so many unfinished plans. If you discuss them with Reggie and Kitson and Dacre, I think all will be well. If Letty can be brought to stay for a while, she knows the workings of the place. But she should go to Ketley. It was good of her to bring you."

"She loves you dearly. She could not have borne to lose you without seeing you once again. But are you sure, Papa?"

"The quack has had all his friends from London here, at what cost I cannot imagine." The acerbic comment brought a smile to Cecilia's lips. "It's good to see your grin, girl. That will do me more good than all the physic they can conjure out of their cauldrons. They speak fine words, but my body speaks to me with greater eloquence." Marchmont closed his eyes and gathered his strength once more. "There is little pain. Every day I simply seem to be weaker. We have a little time. A few weeks."

At this, Cecilia could hold the tears back no longer. Remorse consumed her. "I should have been here. I shouldn't have been gallivanting with Aunt Ketley. If only I'd spent more time at home."

"Leave off your waterworks, Ceci, my dear. Could never bear a watering pot for a daughter. If we had known, perhaps I might have kept you by me. But we didn't know. Besides, you needed the polish, and now you are a fine lady, perhaps better able to understand the world beyond Sawards. Let us make the best of what we do have. Leave me now, child, I must rest a little more. Come see me after you've dined. Bring Letty with you. I must sleep before I see the children."

Lavauden was waiting outside the door. She gathered Cecilia to her and held her until the stifled sobbing had subsided and she dried the girl's cheeks. It was not long before Cecilia was able to ask quietly, "How long do the doctors give him?"

"They do not know. One says it is a matter of weeks, another gives him some months, a third suggests he could live into next year. I trust Groves most—he is honest and says he cannot tell. He has seen cases like this and there is no fixed rule, and certainly no fixed remedy. There have been signs of improvement. His speech is better than it was a week ago. But he still cannot move his right side at all. But now, you must go to your aunt."

The governess pushed Cecilia down the corridor to the finest guest room, where Lady Ketley waited. Amelia and Reggie were both with her.

"I have tired Papa out, but once he has had a little rest, he wishes to see you, before you sup. You must be prepared—he is not at all strong, but do not be frightened, and run up and give him a warm kiss when you see him."

"Is he going to die, Ceci?" Reggie's anxiety could not be quelled.

"I do not know, darling, nor does he. We must all die sooner or later. Even if he doesn't die, he is very weak and it will take a good deal for him to get any strength back. But you will see for yourself very soon."

At this, the children returned to the schoolroom, leaving

Cecilia with Aunt Letty. After repeating the little that Marchmont had said, she shook her head.

"I know my duty. When you return to Paris, I will stay with Reggie and Amelia. Between us, Reggie and I must learn how to manage the estate. But I want him still to have some freedom, some time to run wild and do foolish things as young men seem to need to do."

Letty laughed. "Clear-sighted even in adversity. Of course your duty is here. But it need not be so very gloomy. You have scores of friends who will wish to visit you, and there can be no great difficulty in coming up to London during the Season. We have fallen into the way of thinking that our home is your home, and so it is and will continue to be, whenever you need it. But you are by no means alone, as Marchmont has pointed out. Dacre has been a constant visitor here in recent years, according to your father's letters, and he knows the ways of Sawards better than I, I'd wager."

Lavauden later put it more poetically, as she came to Cecilia's room just before supper, intent on keeping her former charge in spirits.

"Your father is a wise builder. He has been a support in this world, but he has made sure that his family has plenty of other supports. When we come to look at the building, we miss the pillar—we know it has been there, but the whole structure will not come tumbling down with the loss of one column."

Cecilia grinned, as Lavauden knew she would, at this extravagant flight of fancy, but she also acknowledged the underlying truth of the governess's words. So the next day, she sought out Kitson, who had acted as steward and bailiff on Marchmont lands for as long as Cecilia could remember. Together, with the assistance of a footman, they took the ledgers up to Marchmont's room and together they sat for twenty minutes or half an hour at a time as the invalid's strength waxed and then waned again.

Whether it was Cecilia's return or the need to pass on his knowledge and intentions, Marchmont did rally for some weeks. The family made his sick room the hub of the house, but throughout the estate, all were conscious of living in a state of suspended animation. While none expected great changes with the death of their lord and the accession of the young master, tenants and domestic staff, as well as the family and its intimates, kept catching themselves asking only about the latest news from the big house. The daily round continued, tasks were set and completed, but there was an unsettling sense of impermanence that infected them all.

For Cecilia, constantly attending the sick room and immersed in the minutiae of running the estate, time seemed to sink into an abyss. The more she learnt about the lands and their governance, the more she was conscious of needing to learn. In her spare moments, she prayed earnestly for her father's recovery, and failing that, for him to remain alive and available for consultation, but these were rare interludes now that she was actually taking the reins of managing the estate.

Lavauden had sent a letter to Dacre only a day after the first seizure, since he stood godfather to Marchmont's children and was his closest friend. But the marquis had been travelling in the north, according to a letter from Powell, his secretary at Hatherley, and although he had forwarded Lavauden's letter to the marquis, Powell did not expect it to reach him before the end of March. Sure enough, some six weeks after her return, Cecilia found herself opening a letter from the marquis and reading it to her father. It was brief, recounting only that Dacre intended to meet Ormiston off the boat and then repair immediately to Sawards to visit his old friend. While in Kent, the marquis thought it was time to decide the future of their children. Cecilia folded up the letter with trembling hands as she considered this ominous postscript.

The letter cheered Marchmont, although it reminded him of his daughter's unresolved affairs. For the first time since her return, he addressed the question of her premature marriage.

"Ceci, what are your wishes concerning this match?"

"I hardly know, sir. If you wish it, and if Ormiston accepts it, I am willing to make the marriage public."

"You are a good girl, Ceci. Let us see what happens when they get here." But Marchmont was destined never to see his old friend again. A few days after receiving Dacre's letter, he slipped away in his sleep, and was found, at peace, by his valet, who summoned Letty and Cecilia immediately. Although she had fully expected her father to die soon, now that the time had come, Cecilia felt bereft, adrift and nauseous. When Lavauden and Lady Ketley pressed her to eat, she could scarcely swallow her food and it came up almost immediately. So they sent her to her bed, adamant that at this time, she must regain her strength and support her orphaned brother and sister.

In bed, Cecilia for the first time since her return home considered some feminine mathematics. Suddenly chilled, she counted again and again and came to the same unalterable conclusion.

[illegible]

[illegible] willing to make the marriage public.

You are a good girl, Lucy. Let us see what [illegible]

[illegible]

[illegible]

Seven

At Dover, Dacre waited for his son's boat with some anticipation. The prospect alleviated the grief of hearing from Letty Ketley about Marchmont's untimely death. Speculating about the possible alterations in Ormiston's bearing and beliefs distracted him from the worry of managing the Marchmont brood, including his lovely goddaughter, who was, more pressingly, his daughter-in-law. He did go down to the quay to meet the packet that carried his heir from France, and distinguished Buchan's burly figure without difficulty. Beside the Scot stood a trim, elegant young man, almost dapper. Dacre schooled his expression into unconcerned calm, despite the leap of excitement that far exceeded the interest any female had managed to arouse in him. But then, reflected Dacre, it was always lunatic, unrequited love which led to trembling and palpitations, according to the poets, and if any love had been unrequited in his life, it was his tender affection for his son.

Dacre took the opportunity of his son's arrival to draw the young man into an embrace as soon as the travellers were on dry land. Ormiston did not immediately recoil. The old man had never before shown him much affection, and while the warmth of his greeting astonished, it did not offend.

"Come along to the inn. They have ale, coffee, chocolate, even some decent port. Then we must be off. A stirrup cup and away."

"Off? Back to Hatherley?"

"No, alas. Welcome, Buchan. I'll explain all at the inn."

As they passed the yard, Ormiston noted that his father's great landau was being readied for departure. Once in the parlor, he asked for tea. Once it was served, Dacre began his explanations.

"Marchmont has died. As my letter told, he was taken with a seizure some months ago, but the trouble ran too deep and now he has died. From here, I go to Sawards to attend his funeral. I hope, Ormiston, you will attend it with me." Dacre paused uneasily. "I must speak of that which will cause you anger, I fear, but it must be done. This would be an apt time to discuss your future with Cecilia, your wife. I am named an executor by Marchmont, so my ties with the family will continue, but once you have made this visit and you have both settled on the most suitable course of action, your connection with the Marchmonts may be allowed to dissolve."

"Sir, is this truly the time? When she is newly an orphan?"

"Your feeling does you credit, sir, but it was Marchmont and she who requested such an arrangement. I believe she wishes to free herself, provided you are in agreement." Dacre was intrigued by his son's attitude.

"I have heard it is a most complicated and undignified process."

"Do you wish to remain leg-shackled?" asked Dacre, astonished now by his son's hesitation.

"By no means. Certainly not if she does not desire it."

"Well, I shall see what I can arrange that will minimize the indignities. We are fortunate in that the whole business has been kept so private. She has made her debut in Society but as a maiden, of course."

"How has she been received?" Ormiston tried to keep his query casual.

"You show an astonishing interest in a young woman you professed to loathe."

Buchan could not suppress a broad grin. The marquis had only voiced what he had been thinking himself. Ormiston smiled thinly also, then murmured, "Curiosity merely, sir. She was over-endowed in many areas, but sadly not in looks or demeanor. I only hope she was not mocked or ridiculed."

"She has a good enough name to hold her head up high whatever her looks. I believe she did no better and no worse than any of the other chits. Marchmont did say he'd had to refuse her hand on more than one occasion."

"No doubt her dowry was thought to be sufficient to compensate for her appearance."

Dacre quirked an eyebrow and replied, "No doubt."

The arrangements were soon made. Buchan was to travel by stage to the London house, while Dacre and Ormiston travelled the few hours between Dover and Sawards in the landau. They would all meet up again in London once the obsequies had been performed and the next step in unravelling the viscount's marriage decided upon.

The marquis did not talk once they were en route. Ormiston was glad of this. It gave him time to consider his own future.

Since the masque at the Comtesse de Ferrières's mansion, he had spent all his spare time searching for Alice. But she had vanished, effaced from the city as though she had never been. He had not wished to question the servants too closely, nor to pique the interest of the comtesse, who would, he knew, if he made inquiries, press him to reveal his reasons for inquiring about the identity of her guests. He had tried to identify the English admiral, but there seemed to be a flotilla of admirals in Paris that Season, all involved in some delicate negotiation between the French and the Americans, intended, so far as he could gather, to scuttle the expansionist plans of the Spaniards in the colonies. He could not remember which admiral it was he had seen accompanied by the Viking lady, and after several tedious encounters with his fellow countrymen, he dismissed any further time spent with them as being entirely wasted.

Ormiston could not tell why he could not forget Alice. He had spent just over an hour with her, but the memory of that time was indelible. While his common sense told him that he would never see her again, that she was a light-skirt, a faithless wife of a foolish husband, that their interlude meant nothing, some other part of him could not dispel the enchantment she had woven about him for the brief time they had had together. She had been a virgin. How? He no longer cared. Having lost her, he ached with wanting, with solitude, with longing. Now everything seemed empty and worthless because it could not be shared with that strange, elusive creature, and instead of making her his by making love to her, she had enslaved him. Those moments in the *cabinet des merveilles* made a bitter mockery of the years he had spent courting Giugliana, believing he loved her, plotting how to be with her and how to remain with her. That love seemed insubstantial now, and the memory of that chilly letter informing him of her future with Prince Vergara more a cause for wry amusement at his own folly than heartache for a lost love. But how could he love someone whose face he had never seen, whose name he did not know, whose whole existence seemed as fantastic as a fairy tale constructed by Perrault? This conundrum gnawed at Ormiston, although he did his utmost to conceal it from the world, and even from an intimate as close as Peter Buchan had become.

In this state, he wondered whether it would not be better to settle for the marriage that fate and his father had arranged for him, for he could imagine no union satisfying him unless it were with Alice. If Miss Marchmont—the viscountess—had formed no lasting fondness of her own for any beau, it might be best for her, too. She had been prompt enough to do her duty five years since, thought Ormiston. She might as well fulfill her duties to her husband now she had no father.

Somber in mind and dress, Ormiston arrived at Sawards prepared to deal with his wife fairly and frankly. But he was not to encounter her immediately. Marchmont's sister, Lady Ketley, a spare, austere-looking woman, greeted Dacre and Ormiston, glancing at the viscount with a shrewd eye which alerted him to the understanding that she knew of the secret marriage.

"I must make Cecilia's excuses. She is unwell. She has pushed herself too hard since returning home, and I fear that exhaustion has overtaken her. I felt that she needed rest if she is to comport herself creditably at the funeral, so I packed her off to bed."

It was with some sense of anticlimax that Ormiston went to his room and waited for someone to bring hot water and a change of clothes. The Italian who had accompanied him to Paris quite happily had decided that England was too barbarous a destination to remain with the marquis. Ormiston imagined that up in London it would be simple to find a replacement from one of his father's household. In the meantime, Lady Ketley had mentioned that Marchmont's man was available to assist either Dacre or his son. It seemed that Ormiston was to be the fortunate recipient of this man's attentions, which he imagined would provide an opportunity to discover more about this family. However, it was clear that the man was half distracted with grief for his late master. Quizzing the fellow about Marchmont's daughter would lead nowhere other than to make Ormiston appear unfeeling and lecherous.

The funeral was scheduled for the following Monday. Ormiston hoped that Cecilia would make her appearance before then. It was not to be. Her siblings, Reggie and Amelia, he did meet, and to his astonishment, liked immediately. Despite their recent loss, they were lively and polite to their guest. He first encountered them in a music room, where he had wandered by accident.

The room, pale in the sunshine of early spring, seemed empty and dusty. He picked a few notes on the clavichord, then saw a grimy lute and lifted it onto his lap. But as he started picking at the strings, the catgut split and sprang back at him, whipping at his cheeks. He gently replaced the lute and began searching about the room for something with which to replace the worn strings. Behind a curtain, he heard a furtive, smothered giggle. He drew back the heavy damask and saw there two bright faces, slightly smudged with the grime of playing in deserted corners of the house.

"Where can I find some spares to restring this blasted instrument?"

"In the bottom drawer of that bureau, under the music."

"Who played? Your sister?"

The impish faces creased up in amusement. "Not in an eon. I think it was our mother. But we never heard her, for she died when we were very small." The boy scrambled from the windowseat and stood, his hand outstretched.

"I am Reginald Marchmont. But you may call me Reggie. This is my sister Amelia. Come, Amy, make your curtsey. Are you Lord Dacre's son?"

"I am. Who has spoken of me?"

"No one properly. They only mentioned that you would be coming with Lord Dacre. Is it true you have been in Italy these many years?"

"It is."

"I have heard they have very fine fencing masters in Italy. The best in the world. I should like to see that. Not that swordplay is of any use nowadays. We may not duel and in war, I believe that cannon and muskets are of more value." As Reggie spoke, Amelia harrumphed and went over to the bureau, where she started rummaging.

"I've heard it said. But if you are interested, we may try a few passes, you and I?"

"May we?" The boy's eyes were incandescent with delight.

"Is Italy where you learned the lute?" inquired Amelia. She was kneeling now, a sheaf of music in one hand, catgut in the other.

"A little. I am a better swordsman than musician. But I like best to paint." Ormiston came over, took the various rolls of catgut, all of different densities, and found also a little tin of resin to oil the strings. He set about restringing the lute. It was a laborious process. Amelia's nimble fingers were more successful at the task than his. Finally, the instrument was ready. They all three took turns at plucking at the strings, and then Ormiston began picking out some of the simpler tunes which Giugliana had taught him. Amelia hopped onto the seat at the clavichord and began accompanying him. They drew their music-making to a close and he looked on the child in some awe.

"You have a natural ear."

"It is what Lavauden says. She was going to ask Papa if I might have a music master. But then he fell ill." All three fell silent, and the girl swallowed and Ormiston could see her jaw clench with the determination not to cry. But it was too late, for the tears had welled up and then trickled down her cheeks. It was Reggie who went to her, pulling out a great handkerchief from his jacket and mopping her up and holding her close.

"There, there, Amy, it will all come out right. Ceci has promised it will."

"I know, and I am sorry to be such a big baby, but I do miss him."

"As do I. But Ceci spoke true when she said it was better this way than him lying in bed for years and years, never properly better again."

"But what if Ceci goes away again? What shall we do then?"

"We must all try to see that she never has to leave you."

The two children looked up in surprise as Ormiston's determined statement sank in. They did not ask what business it was of his, but he was conscious of his own presumption. He could not tell from where sprang this passionate desire that these children should have certainty and stability in their lives, but it was suddenly there, decided, intent, resolute.

That night, as he lay awaiting the oblivion of sleep, he reflected on his words to Reggie and Amelia. The firmness of his resolve that despite their loss, they should be allowed to enjoy the remainder of their childhood, had surprised him, for it meant that in some corner of his mind, he had accepted the need to remain married to a plain and ungainly frump. There was in his mind no doubt that someone must supervise the Marchmont estate until Reggie was ready to come into his responsibilities. It did not occur to Ormiston that his own wife might be capable of managing this without his assistance.

Memories of his own childhood began to plague Ormiston. His father's prolonged absences in London, the stern and unbending governess, the occasional visits Dacre made, accompanied by an ever-changing series of brazen and raucous companions, male and female, playing through the night, emerging from smoke-filled rooms as day broke, the sight of his own father tipsily cursing his confounded ill luck as he stumbled past the lonely child waiting in the anteroom, hoping against hope for some sign of affection.

Only at school had Ormiston discovered that rather than being a nuisance, some might consider him likeable, and once his skill with the small sword was discovered, even admirable. He recalled the look on Reggie's face when they had discussed fencing: at eleven or so, the lad was just at the age when he needed a wise Nestor to guide him through the shift from boyhood to manhood.

However, it seemed foolish to tie himself to a dowd of whom his only memories were unpleasant, purely for the pitiable state of these two children, left in the guardianship of the father he felt had already failed one lonely child. If only he had been able to see Cecilia, then he might have some hint of her character and bearing. In all the years of his travels, Dacre had refrained from mentioning her in his admittedly brief letters, a delicacy Ormiston had appreciated, but now regretted. He resolved to quiz the marquis the following morning.

When Ormiston went down to breakfast, he found himself alone with Dacre for the first time since their arrival. The marquis was reading a note, which he folded up on his son's entry.

"Morning, Ormiston. Cecilia has asked me to ride out with Kitson, the steward, and approve certain works Marchmont had in mind. Would you care to accompany me?"

Ormiston agreed, seeing a prime opportunity to interrogate his father further. But Dacre refused to answer any queries about his goddaughter, saying only, "You must make up your own mind when you see her. This folly has gone far enough without any attempt on my part to prejudice you further. You and Cecilia must decide for yourselves. I shall abide by that decision."

Then Kitson joined them in the stableyard and the chance for any further questions disappeared.

The estate was in an impressive state of maintenance. Both Dacre and Ormiston had expected some signs of neglect, given that Marchmont had been laid low for over two months before his death. But Kitson averred with pride that Miss Cecilia had already taken a hand and made sure that all was kept bang up to the mark. Whatever else she might be, it was clear from the laconic but admiring observations of the steward that Miss Marchmont was an astute businesswoman. Ormiston saw that his own contribution to the management of Sawards and its outlying lands could only be minimal. Hoping to be able to congratulate his wife on her abilities, Ormiston was eager to return to the house, but there was no sign of the lady. He spent most of the afternoon with her brother and sister instead.

Although delightful company, neither child spoke much of their sister. She had been largely away with Lady Ketley in recent years, and there was much talk of her generous and thoughtful birthday gifts. Reggie led him around the house, which had everything in its place, including a small armory and gun room where they found foils of various sizes. Ormiston was able to fulfill his promise to the boy, and they made a few passes. Reggie showed promise although, the viscount noted, was virtually untaught. Ormiston contracted to set time aside on the morrow for a serious lesson, causing the boy to beam with delight and anticipation.

Later, they all sat down to dinner, apart from the invalid Cecilia, by which time it was clear that Reggie and Amelia regarded Ormiston as their property. They had slipped their hands trustingly into his as they led him in to dinner and out again to the drawing room, and teased him as he ate and played at spillikins with them, crouching down on the carpet and losing gracefully. All the while, Ormiston had felt his father's eyes upon him, and from time to time, Lady Ketley's shrewd glance.

Alone in his room, he mused over the way he was entangling himself with this family. However charming the children were, it was ludicrous to tie himself to someone he had not seen for five years. Unless, he thought, he was throwing himself into this circle, onto the mercies of a woman he could not remember in an attempt to efface the memory of a young woman he could not forget. Ormiston decided that he would broach with Dacre the possibility of making something of this marriage, provided his bride was in agreement, and to take on himself the care of her father's estates and the guardianship of the children. But he suspected that the trust which the Marchmont children had already shown him was signal enough to the marquis, who, it was now clear to his own son, was an astute reader of other people's intentions and actions.

Two days later, he caught a glimpse of his wife, shrouded in mourning veils, as she was helped into the first carriage of mourners, along with her aunt and siblings. Rather than the dumpy figure he remembered, he gained an impression of height and slenderness, though concealed in the heavy serge cape she wore against the unseasonable chill. She sat stiff and still, like an automaton. He half expected music to pipe from the carriage and to see her move jerkily from one position to the next, like the great dolls he had seen in Venice and Paris, life-size models animated by a clockwork mechanism.

Dacre and Ormiston followed in the next carriage with the lawyer and the doctor from the nearest town accompanying them. A train of mourners followed, the yeomen and servants of the estates joining the procession in dog-carts and traps, wagons and carts. The church was overflowing and the singing of the hymns rousing and heartfelt. Sitting some pews behind the family, Ormiston noticed his wife's shoulders convulse once before she squared them and raised her head to sing out her responses and to sit, solid and straight, as the vicar eulogized his late benefactor.

Afterwards, it was Lady Ketley who performed the honors as the mourners gathered in the big house. Cecilia had once again retired. Ormiston found his father and demanded to know whether Dacre had managed to speak with Miss Marchmont.

"Of course. I saw her before the service this morning so that she might secure my approval for certain works to be carried out. Do you wish to see her? I can mention it tomorrow when we meet again. She pushed herself too far in nursing her father and taking on the burdens of the estate. I think she will be in circulation following the reading of the will tomorrow, but for now, she must rest."

"Should I attend the reading of the will?"

"That depends on your intentions toward the family. If you think you will be involved with them in the future, it would probably be best for you to be there. However, if you wish to sever your connection, there is really no need for your presence." Dacre forbore to mention that because Ormiston had so willingly allowed himself to be thoroughly monopolized by the younger Marchmonts, it would be cruelty to withdraw from their lives now.

The next morning found Ormiston still undecided about his future. He dressed, dismissed Marchmont's man, who had proved efficient and unobtrusive, and took up a charcoal pencil and sketchpad, determined to lose himself in the one constant he knew would never pose him any imponderable questions. He sat himself in a window embrasure overlooking a formal knot garden to the east of the house. There were two black-clad figures pacing the walks, one stout and relatively short, the other slender. The shorter lady wore a bonnet and cloak, while the slim one wore a stylishly cut pelisse and simple mourning veil pinned onto a luxurious fall of ebony hair. Ormiston watched them and strangely, the slim woman moved, he was sure, as he remembered Alice having moved. Paper and pencil fell from his grasp; he reared up and threw up the sash window and shouted her name, but the breeze whipped his words away and she was too far away to hear. He hurtled out of the room and down the stairs, nearly overturning a maid polishing the Italian marble demi-lune sideboards in the hall. He stopped and asked her who was in the garden.

"It is Miss Cecilia, with Squire Hislop's widow, I think. Do you wish me to take a message to her?"

"No—no, I will join them."

Ormiston had time to collect himself before he encountered the ladies. They were making their way back to the house. He went forward to greet them along a brick walkway bordered with lavender. They stopped walking as he approached, and when he had reached them, he stopped and bowed, then took up the hand of the shorter woman and dropped a kiss on it, saying, "Miss Marchmont, a pleasure at last to see you up from your sickbed."

The ladies exchanged a glance, and Ormiston, looking up and into their faces, perceived his mistake at once. The woman whose hand he had kissed was mature in years, by no means unattractive, but certainly not a maiden. The taller, slighter figure threw back her head and gave a throaty chuckle before holding out both hands to Ormiston.

"Come, let me greet you. That is the best joke I have heard for days. You must know, Mrs. Hislop, the last time Ormiston saw me, I was a child of fourteen, so he is paying you a great compliment." Ormiston bent over her hands and released them swiftly, mortified by his error. The squire's widow leapt into the deepening silence.

"And a greater insult to you, my dear," replied the widow, "for if he thinks a nineteen-year-old is as stout and steady as I, he is a sad knave. Nonetheless, I am pleased to make your acquaintance, sir, and I've no doubt if you've not seen Miss Ceci for five years, you've plenty to discuss, so I'll be on my way home."

"We'll see you to your carriage, Mrs. Hislop. You left the horses standing by, did you not?"

"Yes indeed, missy. Now, you must know, my Ned will do all that Mr. Kitson requires—you have only to ask and he'll be happy to assist. I'll send him straight to Mr. Kitson for he's so bashful of you now you're grown into such a fine lady, and for all he's squire now, he's still a cub with more height than sense. If he sees you, he'll be hemming and hawing and before we know it making a cake of himself. It'll be more use if you don't see him, and I know you won't take offense, as you're a good girl with a fine enough head on your shoulders."

By this time, all three were at the front of the house, where Mrs. Hislop's trap awaited her. Ormiston helped her alight, and her driver removed her with a smart crack of his whip. Cecilia turned to him. For the first time, he looked at her properly. Her hair was dark, with a gentle wave in it. It was caught back from her face, but not fully dressed. He thought that under the veil, it must reach her waist. Her forehead was high, her cheekbones good, her nose elegant, her chin definite, and her eyes large, long-lashed violet pools. Her eyelids dropped as his steady, evaluating gaze discomfited her. A rosy flush rose up her fine skin. She breathed in, as if gathering her strength, and looked him in the eye once again.

"Item, two lips, indifferent red; item, two eyes, with lids to them; item one neck, one chin and so forth." Shakespeare was a refuge against that intent gaze.

"Olivia was not so lovely as you. I will make me a willow cabin at your gate."

"There's no need, you're already installed in our second-best bed," replied Cecilia crisply. "In any case, you are more Orsino than Cesario." The viscount's flirtatious air grated on her. Once it would have been all that she desired, but now, her fears for the future confronted her and his flippancy rankled.

Ormiston could not reply as he wished. He knew that every bed would be second-best unless he could share it with this exquisite creature. His wife. His hostile wife. He saw mistrust in those eyes, more intense than the finest amethyst, and hard, he deduced, as diamonds. He frowned in puzzlement. She had reminded him of Alice, and now she did again, of that moment when Alice had mocked him for making pledges lightly. She made him feel uncomfortable and gauche. But now to business.

"We must talk, you and I. Will you take a turn with me?" He offered her his arm.

"Certainly, sir." She ignored his outstretched arm and decorously, delicately, turned back to the gardens. Ormiston was obliged to follow.

He took a deep breath before launching into speech. "We are still bound to each other. If we wish to part, we must be prepared for an intrusive and indelicate inquiry under the full gaze of Society and those members of the fourth estate who make it their business to publish the affairs of Society."

"Yes." Cecilia thought this was a fair assessment of their situation, although she could not tell where Ormiston's thoughts were tending.

"However, we could avoid this spectacle, if we so chose."

She stopped and faced him. "What do you propose, sir?" Wary. Waiting.

"We could, if you wished," continued Ormiston hesitantly, "commence a courtship which would lead naturally to a suitable match."

"Are you suggesting that we marry a second time, in public?" She turned and walked on, determined to hide her astonishment. Ormiston stepped forward, his hands clasped behind his back as he walked on.

"We could, if you preferred, elope or effect a private marriage or blessing at the chapel at Hatherley, which we could then announce to be the start of our marriage. We might say that because of your father's death, it would have been inappropriate for us to arrange a grand ceremony."

They had reached a walled rose garden. Cecilia led the way through the ornate iron gate. "Sir, you may feel I am lacking in modesty, but I must ask what has brought about so great a change in your own attitude to our marriage that you wish to make it public?"

"I feel it might suit us both," Ormiston responded hesitantly, gathering speed as he gathered conviction. "It was clearly the dearest wish of our fathers that this match should be made, but that is no reason to disavow it. I have returned from my travels with no taste for the 'marriage mart,' as I have heard it described. I must provide an heir, you would find it easier to manage your responsibilities to your brother and sister with a husband, and I am willing to assist you in those responsibilities. In short, it would certainly benefit me and may well benefit you to consider making our union public."

"Did Reggie or Amelia put you up to this?" Cecilia frowned in perplexity. "I know they have quite fallen under your spell in the shortest possible time. I find your reasoning extraordinary, I must say, unless it is that you have been bewitched by the children. I know that people do marry for convenience or by arrangement, but we were married because of a wager, a drunken impulse, and both your father and mine have done nothing but assure me ever since that it was their dearest wish to separate us as soon as we were both in the same place at the same time because they understood that their behavior was abominable and the outcome unenforceable." She swung away from him, and he once again was following her like an importunate suitor. It occurred to Ormiston that he *was* an importunate suitor. He tried to trump her.

"What do you mean, with all this talk of spells and bewitching? Reggie and Amelia are fine children who need a firm hand. A masculine hand."

"Let me assure you, Lord Ormiston, that should my brother and sister require discipline, they have a firm enough hand in my feminine one to ensure that they behave in a manner which is wholly exemplary. As for masculine influence, I may trust to my Uncle Ketley, who as an admiral has more than enough experience of applying a 'firm hand' where necessary, not to mention a plethora of godfathers, including your esteemed parent, Lord Dacre. There is no need for you to concern yourself with their upbringing."

Ormiston's exasperation could no longer be concealed. "Well, you did not have to agree to the match. If you had refused, they would not have made us go through with it."

"I was fourteen," spat Cecilia. "A child, with no understanding of the world and its ways, and a great deal of love for a father who was acutely embarrassed. I had no notion of refusing and sullying his honor. In any case, if I could have refused, so could you."

"I was told very firmly that it was a choice of you and Europe or no marriage, no travel. What should I have done?" They were now standing beneath a pergola, hidden from all eyes by the mature vines twined above to form a green roof.

"This is folly. Neither of us was in a position to make any sensible decision at the time. But that does not mean we must be trapped by a mockery of the matrimonial state."

"We must be trapped sooner or later." Ormiston folded his arms and leant back against one of the wooden posts supporting the vines.

"I do not see it as entrapment. I prefer to see it as an opportunity to spend my life with a person who has realized that I am essential to his happiness, and whom I find equally indispensable." Cecilia did not glance his way as she spoke. Her hands were clasped so tight her knuckles shone white.

"After a few evenings of country dances and a couple of glasses of champagne? How is any man supposed to know whether a woman is indispensable to his happiness? The whole notion is preposterous."

"There you are. That is why we must arrange an annulment as soon as we can. I could not possibly marry a man with so dismal an opinion of the married state." To Ormiston's ears her voice was preternaturally calm. He had done his best to provoke, but she sidestepped him at every turn.

"You have married exactly that man. But let me tell you, nine out of every ten of us holds the same beliefs as I do, and the tenth is a mutton-headed fool such as no woman in her right mind would wish to marry." As he heard his own words, Ormiston wished them unspoken. They were the product of frustration and uncertainty coupled with a certain bitterness about his disappointment with Giugliana. But Cecilia was not to know that.

"Then how is it that there are happy marriages? For I have seen them. And I will not accept anything less. Where you are concerned, Lord Ormiston, now that we have renewed our acquaintance, I can safely say that there is nothing you could do or say that could alter my view that remaining married to you would be utterly intolerable." Her composure was tinged with scorn as she turned on her heel and swung away from the viscount. He watched her stride briskly back to the house. He closed his eyes and let out a long breath, only now realizing that he had been holding it. Then he followed her. The reading of the will was due to start within the half hour. He would not miss it. He would not allow her to dismiss him, however woefully he had handled this unfortunate encounter.

Eight

In the servants' hall, a bell rang with prolonged energy. A footman looked up from the silver he was polishing at the array of brass and raised his eyebrows in surprise as he called out: "Dorcas, it's coming from Miss Cecilia's room."

A flustered girl jumped up from a table where she had a pile of mending before her and brushed her skirts off before bustling away through the baize door and up the back stairs. In all the weeks that Miss Cecilia had been back from France, she had never rung her bell in so agitated a fashion. When she finally reached the young lady's apartment, Dorcas found her mistress pacing the floor, her jaw set firm, her eyes flashing.

"Good, you're here, Dorcas. Help me with my hair, please." Cecilia took a seat at her dressing table and waited while the maid gently extracted the pins holding her veil in place. Dorcas then reached for the silver-backed brush Miss Cecilia held out and worked her way through the mass of dark curls. She could sense the tension draining from her mistress's shoulders and neck as she rhythmically stroked the bristles through her hair. At last, it had been tamed into a sleek rope which Dorcas twisted and plaited and pinned. Cecilia sighed and thanked the girl, who bid fair to become a worthy successor to Sukey.

It had been some years since Sukey had caught the eye of a tenant farmer at Sawards, but it was only on Ceci's return from Paris that she had asked to be released from her duties. In fact, it was Sukey who had identified Dorcas as a possible replacement. She was young, but very able, and under the fierce tuition of Marston was promising to become a most competent personal maid. The girl finally arranged a small confection of black ribbons on the crown of Cecilia's scalp, brushed down her skirt, and stood back to examine her handiwork.

"You do suit black, miss, and it's not all of us can carry it off."

"Thank you, Dorcas. You've done splendidly."

They did not know one another well enough for Dorcas to venture any query as to her mistress's state of mind, but she noted that Miss Cecilia now appeared calm and composed, more her normal self.

"It's nearly time for the reading of the will." Cecilia drew a deep breath, as if fortifying herself for the ordeal. Many of the household would be attending, as well as tenants and local notables, since Marchmont had left numerous bequests to the people who had served him so faithfully despite the difficult times. Afterwards, refreshments would be served, and she would have to speak with a multitude of persons wishing to condole and comfort. Dorcas watched as Miss Cecilia visibly stiffened once more, ready to go forward and demonstrate her resolution to continue her father's good work.

"Please tell Lady Ketley I shall be down directly." Thus dismissed, Dorcas left Miss Cecilia to compose herself.

Lady Ketley had taken in hand the management of the event, to Cecilia's relief, since she did feel peculiarly unwell. The sickness had by no means passed off, but if she continued to lie abed, it would undoubtedly occasion comment now that Marchmont's death was receding into the past. It was ten weeks since the fateful masked ball, and while Cecilia knew that sickness was a concomitant of her interesting condition, she had no notion as to the duration and intensity of this malaise. If she continued to take to her bed, however, Lady Ketley would summon a doctor and her secret would be out.

Since she had completed her calculations, she had turned over in her mind various alternatives. She could confide in Lady Ketley. She could seek out a certain woman in the village reputed to have a particular knowledge of certain herbs. She could speak with Dacre.

Finally, she had concluded that she must confess all to her husband. After all, she had her costume, his ring, his address ready to present as proof of her role in the encounter. Yet, some small, still voice had whispered in her dreams that he would, on seeing her, recognize that she and Alice were one and the same, that he would take her and hold her and reveal that he had been combing the streets of Paris until summoned here by his father, that he wanted her and her alone. Instead there had been a humiliating interview in which he had made it abundantly clear that marriage was a state he despised and love an emotion he ridiculed. He had not recognized her, but she had recognized the flare of desire in his eyes as he took in her face, her figure, her physical charms, making a mockery of his passionate protestations to Alice. How many other women had he seduced in the interim? He had told Alice that he would wait for her, that he could not bear to release her, and yet, weeks later, he was gazing with cool lust on what he thought was another woman, a virtual stranger.

A chill detachment, exacerbated by the cruel dissipation of her fantasy, coursed through Cecilia. The childish anger she had felt at his distaste for the marriage five years before was as nothing compared to this sensation which did not boil, but rather made her want to torture him for long years. One moment, she wished the baby away; the next, she rejoiced, for it would enrage him and make him believe he had been cuckolded. Then she wished it away again, so that she could lead him on and on, never releasing him from his vows and never giving way to his importunities. But now, it was time to face the lawyers and the myriad folk gathered to hear where Marchmont had made his bequests. Slowly, implacably, Cecilia went down to the drawing room.

Waiting for her were Dacre, Ormiston, and Lady Ketley. Together, they entered the grand ballroom, which was full of familiar faces, all of whom turned to gaze upon Cecilia, appearing in public for virtually the first time since her return from France. Dacre guided her to a seat and took the chair beside her. The lawyers looked at the marquis, who nodded in response, and the will reading began. It was most efficiently done, for no bequests were to be given that day, but rather collected from the lawyers' offices on the next market day in Tonbridge. Recipients of legacies were ushered gradually into the dining room, where Lavauden, flanked by the younger Marchmonts, had stationed herself.

Finally, Battersby, the head of the solicitors' office, announced that the will reading was complete, bar one codicil which concerned immediate family only. The few remaining guests were ushered toward the funeral baked meats, leaving the solicitor to suggest that Dacre, Cecilia, Lady Ketley, and Ormiston withdraw to a more private location.

"We may be interrupted here and I think it best that this delicate matter be dealt with promptly and with the utmost discretion."

Cecilia was not sure whether she appeared nervous, but a great pit seemed to have opened up below her diaphragm. She stood and led the way to the music room, which was in a wing separate from the great formal rooms at Sawards. She sat on the piano stool, leaving the more comfortable seats for the others. Dacre and Lady Ketley sat together on a loveseat while Battersby settled in the chair Marchmont had used when playing the cello. Ormiston stood near the fireplace, his hands behind his back, his head bowed as he seemed to examine the toes of his extremely shiny shoes.

"This codicil," began Battersby, "concerns the portion allotted to Miss Marchmont. You have already heard how Master Reggie and Miss Amelia are situated. Miss Marchmont's affairs are somewhat more complicated.

"Two years ago, Mr. Marchmont asked me to make some

inquiries on this matter of securing an annulment. He chose at that time to take me fully into his confidence regarding the match between Miss Marchmont and your son, Lord Dacre. My task was to investigate the cost and full legal procedure of such a course.

"I have to say that my findings were most disappointing. It would take several years and a great deal of money for the marriage to be dissolved, not to mention both parties having to participate in what I can only consider to be rather humiliating and public medical, spiritual, and legal examinations. I reported my findings to Mr. Marchmont.

"While he accepted my view of the rigmarole, he felt that he owed it to his child to ensure that she might release herself from her marriage if that was her earnest wish."

The lawyer looked carefully at each person in the room, as a schoolmaster might inspect the understanding of his rather dimwitted charges. He then continued.

"May I say that if the parties are prepared to let the marriage stand, it will be much the happiest outcome. Otherwise, all England will come to know the business of both your families, your names will be as common bywords in the tattiest of news-sheets, and all your past and future laid bare the length and breadth of the country."

Cecilia and Ormiston looked at each other, then swiftly glanced away. The solicitor's orotund voice seemed to echo around the music room.

"My piece is said. It only remains for me to reveal Mr. Marchmont's instructions." Slowly, he unfolded the parchment and read aloud:

> *"To my daughter, Cecilia, I leave the sum of two hundred thousand pounds. This sum must be raised through the sale and mortgage of certain properties which are not entailed to the Sawards estate, listed in full below. If the annulment proceeds, Cecilia will need all these funds to finance the business. If the marriage*

to Ormiston stands, title to the properties will remain in the Marchmont name, with the income serving as her marriage portion and the estates to pass in the first instance to any children of the union. Should the union prove unfruitful, the title will revert to her sister Amelia. A decision must be lodged with the offices of Battersby, Battersby, and Pattinson within six months of my death."

"There follows a list of six properties which came to Mr. Marchmont from his mother's family. The choice, Miss Marchmont, lies with you and your husband."

There was silence. Then Cecilia stood, holding the piano, her knuckles white against its ebony.

"Tell me more of the conditions of the annulment, Mr. Battersby."

"First, my lady, we must lay a suit before the Archbishop of Canterbury. Provided he accepts that the suit is sufficiently substantial, he will approve it. Then there must be solid proof, medical proof, that the marriage is unconsummated. Once this is secured, a reason for the nonconsummation must be identified, usually the inability of one of the parties to fulfill the normal obligations of the marriage contract. You must understand that whichever party admits to this inability has little or no future chance of—" Battersby broke off as Cecilia buckled at the knees and slowly crumpled to the floor in a dead faint. Ormiston started forward. Lady Ketley kept her head.

"Battersby, fetch Groves at once. I know he is present—he was one of the last named in the will and he is forever hanging on Lavauden's arm. He will be in the dining hall."

By this time, Ormiston had swung Cecilia's limp form into his arms. He carried her over to a chaise longue underneath the window and laid her down. He pulled away and gazed down at her. It was, he realized, his first real opportunity to examine his bride since he had arrived at Sawards. She was unquestionably a beautiful girl. Once she attained womanhood, Ormiston knew she would appear stupendous. But this was not the appropriate time to assess the charms of his unquestionably unwell wife. He stepped back and took a deep breath. In came the doctor. Groves looked around and raised his eyebrows at Lady Ketley. She jumped a little and hustled the three men from the room.

Cecilia was already coming around when she felt a damp cloth on her forehead.

"Miss Marchmont?" Her eyelids fluttered open. She looked up at Dr. Groves, then sighed. He left the handkerchief on her brow as he took her wrist and discovered the steadiness of her heartbeat. He then checked the glands about her throat and neck, asked her to stick out her tongue and say "ahh".

"Any stomach ailments? Any disorders or irregularities?"

Cecilia nodded.

"With the bowels or with the menses?"

"Dr. Groves, I think I know why I fainted." The doctor looked at her expectantly. "It is a feminine problem. Well, it is a condition which affects women rather than men."

"You are in the family way?" He sounded curious, with no trace of censure. This gave Cecilia the courage to nod her assent.

"Ah. Is the young man aware of your condition?"

"By no means. I met him in France."

"So you will be some months advanced. Is there no prospect of marriage?"

"It is all very complicated. But the father of my child is my husband. He—we—it has not been made public." Cecilia sat up gingerly. "You have done do much for us Marchmonts recently. Now I add to our debt with a secret I must ask you to keep."

Doctor Groves looked almost offended. "Miss Cecilia, I've known you since the day you first took breath. If you cannot trust me by this time, I do not know how I can do more."

"I did not mean to offend, Dr. Groves. Forgive me." She held out her hand to the old man.

"Of course. My advice to you is to confide in the marquis. He will see that all is settled between you and your husband."

Ormiston was surprised to find himself summoned by a hesitant Dorcas to attend Miss Cecilia in her private parlor a half-hour after the doctor had left her. He went into the room to find his wife silhouetted against a window, a slender column draped in black.

"Please be seated." Cecilia paced the room, then picked something up from her desk and came forward. She held out her hand, clearly intending to give him something. There dropped into his palm a ring he had not seen for months.

"Where did you get this?" Even as he spoke, he knew the answer to the question. He had found Alice. More accurately, she had found him and played him for a fool.

"I was given it by a young man in a suit of silver silk in a small room in Paris. He told me to contact him through his father, the Marquis of Dacre, if I ever needed help."

"What sort of help do you need?"

"I need a father for my child."

"A child. You are with child."

Ormiston was, naturally, dazed by this revelation. He thought back to Paris. Alice had been a married virgin. It had been February. It was now April. The girl did not look large. But she would be nearly three months with child. If it was his child, it was due no later than November. Perhaps she would not necessarily be large. He knew nothing of childbirth or gestation. There could be no annulment. He smiled. Alice was his. An echo from five years before rang in his ears. Cecilia Mary Alice Marchmont was his. No further need to woo or cajole. The maddening creature was irrevocably his.

"Well, it seems that the prospect of marriage to me has become tolerable to you."

"Rather say inevitable. You take this very calmly, sir."

"Yes, I do. I astonish myself." Ormiston evaded Cecilia's

glance by taking a deep interest in the state of his cuffs. As he straightened them, he continued speaking. "I do not wish my father to know of this development just yet. We will now go down and announce that we wish to make our marriage real. We will travel up to Hatherley and there we will have a blessing. And there we will stay until the child is born. Naturally, your brother and sister will accompany us."

"I was hoping to return here to Sawards."

"I see no need for that. Kitson is an exemplary steward, and you must acquaint yourself with your future demesne. You will be marchioness one day. Hatherley will be your home. It has had no mistress in many years. My father has always made it clear to me that on my return from Italy, it would be my task to take on the management of our lands. My heir will be born in his future home."

"To uproot Reggie and Amelia at this time would be cruelty. They have endured enough these past few months."

"They will be well cared for at Hatherley, and we will visit here regularly. But you, my dear Lady Ormiston, will live at Hatherley, make no mistake about that." Ormiston stood and held out his arm. "Now, I suggest we return downstairs to inform our family that we have decided to let the marriage stand."

Cecilia tucked her hand in the crook of his elbow and allowed him to escort her downstairs. They entered the drawing room to find Dacre and Lady Ketley struggling to instill the rules of whist into Reggie and Amelia's weary brains while Lavauden was deftly adding eyes to several embroidered cats that Amelia had half-completed.

Ormiston led his lady to a sofa near the fireplace, then sat beside her. The card table was abandoned and Lady Ketley asked whether Cecilia was sure she should be down.

"Yes. I am quite well. And there is something we need to discuss. Reggie, Amelia, you remember, a long time ago, I told you I was to be married."

"I remember," responded Reggie. "But you never said

anything further about it and you never seemed to have a husband or a wedding ring. So I thought it must have been a hum."

"It wasn't. Lord Ormiston is the man I married, and . . ." Cecilia faltered.

"I saw your sister, Reggie, when I came to your father's funeral and realized that I wanted above anything else to take her to my home at Hatherley, with you and Amelia."

"Why did you never wish to take her to your home before?" demanded Amelia.

"I was away, visiting France and Italy and other lands."

"Did you forget all about Ceci?"

"No, not at all. I came back to England just to see her." Ormiston suppressed a twinge of shame at his manipulation of events. Dacre's lips twitched sardonically and Lady Ketley appeared thoroughly astounded by this sudden announcement.

Cecilia continued into the uneasy silence: "We shall go to Hatherley and stay there for a little while. It is what Papa would want, I know. He said often what a magnificent place it is, with beautiful gardens, a stable full of the finest horses in the kingdom, and trout streams where the fish are so eager, they nibble at your toes. Do you not remember, Reggie?"

Dacre intervened at this point, elaborating on Cecilia's halting description until the family was summoned to supper. Of course, Cecilia could not avoid a late-night interrogation from Lady Ketley. The admiral's wife swept into Cecilia's bedroom, dismissed Dorcas, and took up the hairbrush the maid had been wielding. She admired the practicality of the arrangement, but required some assurance that her niece was happy with this latest development. Cecilia remained calm. Having unburdened herself to Ormiston, there was no need to reveal anything further to anyone else. But when Lady Ketley had snuffed out the final candle in her room and left for her own chamber, Cecilia found herself unable to sleep as she recalled Ormiston's cool reception of her news. Their uneasy alliance had moved into uncharted waters. Years ago, he had seemed so beautiful, and yet so venomous. He was more beautiful than ever, and she knew from their encounter in Paris, tender and able as a lover. She knew better than to succumb to infatuation. Her suspicion that he was intent on his own revenge firmed, but she could not tell whether she was the target of that vengeance or whether it was another.

Nine

The formal announcement of an alliance between the houses of Marchmont and Dacre was greeted with immediate hullabaloo at Sawards. Dacre wrote at once to Hatherley to arrange a ceremony in the chapel and a tenants' dinner and rooms for the imminent arrival of the Marchmont family. Lavauden and Lady Ketley busied themselves with packing and closing up the house, leaving Ormiston and Cecilia in the still eye of a storm of activity. They still had one week at Sawards.

There were expectations on all sides that the happy couple should appear happy. Not merely happy, but also visibly seeking out each other's company. Dacre was keen to hurry them through their meals and then dispatch them to some corner of the house, provided they were together; Reggie and Amelia expressed their revulsion at the thought of having to view them "being all lovey-dovey" while clearly hoping that it would be an easy matter to see how one went about practicing this state; Lady Ketley and Lavauden were forever dismissing the pair for a walk in the garden. It had been agreed to announce a formal betrothal, and to build the impression that the trip to Hatherley was being made in order to seal the marriage. All Marchmont staff and tenants bent a benevolent eye on the couple, so that Cecilia and Ormiston both found that the only peace they could have was in each other's company.

This was, of course, awkward. Ormiston thought to solve it with the simple expedient of sketching his wife. This allowed them to sit together without having to converse. Events for Cecilia had been so tumultuous that she was, he could see, drained of all energy. She had no reserves, after the sickness and death of her father, or so he surmised. Cecilia herself recognized this, and knew that the discovery of her interesting condition and her worry about how to conceal it had also chafed at her.

At the first sitting, Cecilia brought a book, but once Ormiston had positioned her, she did not open it, gazing instead into the middle distance in a reverie. The next day, she did read and Ormiston spent a good deal of time on her hands, which seemed to him very elegant, although it was harder for him to capture this on paper than he had anticipated. He did ask what she was reading, and she revealed that it was Coleridge's tempestuous ballad, *The Rime of the Ancient Mariner*. She did not say that an albatross hung about her neck, that she, too, was surrounded by a silent sea.

At first, he was engrossed in capturing the proportions of her head and neck and shoulders. As he began to add detail to his sketch, he found it harder to draw, easier simply to look, until he realized that watching her would not reveal to him the mysteries of her thoughts and dreams. He began to understand that lovely as she was, those neat eyebrows, the curve of her cheek, the elegant line of her nose, the sweep of her neck, the soft indentations at its base, the long eyelashes, the fullness of her lips, none of these could impart to him the essence of her being. Try as he might, he could not read the lines of her character. He knew nothing of her. And now, unfurling within him was the desire to discover all he could about her.

"Would you read to me?"

"Don't you know the poem?"

"It is years since I read it. Before going to Italy. I certainly never took a copy with me. It is about a sailor who commits a great crime, isn't it?"

"He shoots a great bird which had led his ship out of danger. All the crew die apart from the mariner and he sees strange visions until his sin is finally absolved."

"What is it in the poem that appeals to you?"

Cecilia thought for a moment. "Everything is so vivid. Even though it is a fantastical tale, it seems real and true." She started reading and completed the first part of the poem.

"I do not know that I see so very much in this poem, but read on." Ormiston sounded wary as he sketched, and Cecilia, a little offended that he did not seem to like the poem better, began to read with more feeling.

"Bravo! I cannot say which I like more, this second part of the poem or your rendition. I find it most compelling: *Water, water, everywhere, Nor any drop to drink.* This captures something real, when there is a surfeit which nonetheless is impossible to use. Will you read on?"

With this enthusiastic endorsement of the verses, Cecilia read on, relieved that at least there would be one topic on which she could find herself in agreement with her husband.

Later, dressing for dinner, Ormiston smiled at the memory of his wife's mellifluous voice and her obvious relish for the somewhat gruesome verse. She was very different from Giugliana, whose only literary interest had been in overflowery tributes to her own charms—which he, Ormiston, was ruefully obliged to admit, had been all too ready to shower upon her. Now, he could not help pondering on the nature of his passion for the Italian: in retrospect, he had been more in love with the notion of love than with his inamorata. Which left him where? With a wife who was a stranger, with a wife he might learn to love. Although, the more pressing question remained: would she learn to love him?

The progress from Sawards to Hatherley required three coaches and three wagons to accommodate not only the family travelling but also menservants and nurserymaids, trunks, valises, and assorted pieces of furniture regarded as essential by Reggie, Amelia, and Lavauden once they realized that essentially, they were uprooting themselves on a permanent basis. Ormiston and Dacre resigned themselves to travelling with the ladies, although both found the confinement of carriage travel irksome. Still, it was only a two-day journey, with the night comfortably broken at Dacre House in London.

The Marchmonts did not terribly take to Dacre House. Reggie broke a vase, Amelia lost herself in the middle of the night, and Lady Ketley's bed was so soft that she failed to sleep. Reggie and Amelia were entrusted to the marquis and his son for the day's travelling, while Cecilia and Lavauden attempted to cheer or soothe the admiral's lady in the great Dacre landau. It was a relief when the coaches finally bowled up the drive to the imposing frontage of Hatherley.

The house was very beautiful both within and without. Built of local brick, its proportions were graceful and its parkland exquisitely laid out. The central section of the house rose three stories high with symmetrical wings and a great colonnade in the style of Palladio. It was of the same period as Sawards, but far grander. Reggie sighed as he took in the elegance and turned to Dacre.

"I suppose you have many more things here a chap must take care not to knock over. I shall go on tiptoe, I promise you."

"There are a great many things at Hatherley, Reggie, but we shall have them all made safe so you may go careering where you will."

Dacre's indulgence toward the child irked Ormiston. It seemed to him that his whole childhood had been hemmed in, and here was his father handing the freedom of the place to a young whippersnapper who had no right to it at all. Then the viscount's natural sense of justice reasserted itself. The cases were very different: where Ormiston had needed to learn the lesson of care for his ancestral home, Dacre's first object was to make this orphaned boy welcome and happy in the strange place that must be his chief residence until he was of an age to manage his own estates.

The sight of Buchan emerging from the great front doors

of Hatherley cheered Ormiston immensely. The carriage had barely come to a halt before the young man was out the door and pumping the hand of his tutor and friend.

"It is very good to see you again. You'll have had my letter?"

"Aye, I have, and good news I think it, too."

Ormiston looked skeptically at the Scotsman, by which time Amelia and Reggie were halfway up the stairs. "Come, meet my new friends. Reggie, I believe, has a real talent, though as yet unformed. You shall not shake us off just yet."

There was a scurrying and flurrying as the travellers decanted themselves into the house and thence to their rooms. Cecilia was aware of surreptitious examination from the staff of the great house. From the moment she set foot in the house to the moment when Dorcas closed the door of her chamber, she was scrutinized by footmen and parlormaids, all engaged on pressing errands which brought them very close to the betrothed of the heir.

"I shall be quizzed at supper, all right." Dorcas grinned wryly as she helped Cecilia off with her pelisse and travelling boots. She went to the cupboards and there, carefully pressed and hung, was the trousseau that had been sent ahead of the travellers. First, she helped Cecilia change into an afternoon gown of muslin, then asked what miss would care to wear that evening. After laying out a suitable ensemble, Dorcas left to sort out her own affairs, allowing Cecilia to stretch out on the chaise longue, hoping that she would be left to her own devices for the rest of the afternoon. Her chief intention was to rest. She knew that Lady Ketley and Marston would be deep in their own affairs, while Lavauden would ensure that Reggie and Amelia were distracted from any homesickness. She had seen Ormiston go off with Buchan, and Dacre had closeted himself almost immediately with his secretary. For once, she should be guaranteed some peace.

The past week had been swallowed up and with it, any independent life. Now she was as effectively pinned down as one of the specimens in her father's study, and she must put her mind to taking on the role of mistress of Hatherley and all the other Dacre domains. She must bear this child and she must strive to be a good wife to a man she scarcely knew. At last, she understood that there was no turning back, that those moments of utter folly in Paris had been the point at which she allowed herself to be swept away in a turmoil of emotion whose result was this strange marriage.

However ill-disposed she had felt toward the viscount before his arrival at Sawards, Cecilia was prepared to admit that he had behaved in an exemplary fashion since returning from the Continent. He had accepted her interesting condition, he had striven to interest and entertain her brother and sister, he had made good his promise of assistance given in a moment of lunacy to an unknown female. But he still filled Ceci with unease. She could not trust him. He was capable of cruel words, harsh judgements, and fickleness in his amours.

It was in this vacillating, wary mood that Cecilia opened the door to her husband an hour later. The appointed time for her tour of Hatherley had arrived.

Dacre, who was to act as guide for both parties, joined them in the Great Hall. This gave Cecilia the opportunity to relinquish her husband's escort in favor of her father-in-law's arm. Ormiston's lips tightened, then he shrugged and accepted his place at his father's other elbow.

Dacre's knowledge of his family home was extensive, albeit idiosyncratic. He was able to tell the stories behind the purchase of marquetry cabinets from Italy, French landscapes, and Greek statuettes; he remembered some of the wilder decorative schemes imposed on the house by his grandmother, and the more restrained furniture and wall-coverings restored by his own mother. He also had an inexhaustible memory for the distinguished visitors who had graced Hatherley, including numerous Princes of Wales and the ominous (and apparently wart-ridden) Lord Protector Cromwell. Dacre did not neglect to introduce and share the family background of several footmen, the housekeeper, and the kitchen staff. The servants clearly held him in high esteem and affection, and the house was run on a well-regulated but not inflexible system of operation.

The gardens were an equal delight, landscaped in a classical model, with a series of walled gardens leading one into another, complete with cascades and shell-encrusted grottoes in the Italian style, which Ormiston pronounced both charming and authentic. There were orchards whose blossom was beginning to bear fruit and glasshouses where a profusion of berries, peaches, and even a pineapple were under cultivation. Once again, Dacre demonstrated his familiarity with his staff and his close involvement with the property. When cornered by a plaintive head-gardener with some lengthy dilemma to be unravelled, he waved away his son and daughter-in-law, saying, "This can only bore you. Walk for a space in the gardens. We will meet up again at dinner."

Hesitantly, Cecilia rested her hand on Ormiston's forearm. He tucked it more comfortably into the crook of his elbow and led away. But he did not escort her directly to the house, instead taking a circuitous route into the Italian garden. He stopped at a bench, indicating that they should sit. She settled her skirts and he sat beside her. For a short space they were silent. Then, hesitantly, he asked,

"Do you think you can be happy here, Cecilia?"

"It is a very beautiful place. But do you think that the marquis is truly ready to relinquish the running of it? He seems so closely tied to the people. And if he does not allow you to take any significant role here, surely the question must be whether you think *you* can be happy?"

"Wise words," Ormiston smiled "but an evasion of my question."

"My lord, I am more concerned to see my brother and sister happily settled. My own happiness is not something I seek. I have renounced any right to happiness through my own rashness. It is my business to make others happy and in that aim,

I hope to find some satisfaction." Cecilia stared straight ahead of her, almost undone by her own words.

"Good God, I have no wish to be married to a martyr. Still less do I think that Reggie and Amelia will be content to see you so subdued. I am not a monster, Cecilia. Let us make a bargain." Ormiston paused, seeking for the right words to frame his proposition. He had once again, he could see, offended his wife. Her back was ramrod straight, her shoulders tense, her lovely features distant and forbidding, uncannily similar to Lady Ketley when expressing disapproval. The shriek of a peacock cracked her stillness.

"What bargain?" Cecilia's voice sounded stiff and unaccommodating.

"Let us live here together for a full twelvemonth. The months remaining until your confinement and then for a space once the babe is born. Let us see if we can rub together and take some pleasure in one another. If, after a year from our marriage, you find it still intolerable, we may make our lives separate. I will not offer you a divorce—that would be worse than an annulment. But after twelve months, if you find we cannot rub along together, I will place no further pressure on you to be a part of Hatherley or the Dacre family."

"What about the baby? If I choose to leave Hatherley, you can have no other legitimate heir."

"How direct you are, Cecilia. If we cannot muddle along together, then we will have to share the child. You may call it Rousseauist and outmoded, but I wish to have a hand in the rearing of any child, legitimate or otherwise."

"Have you any bastards?" demanded Cecilia, astonished as she heard herself speak the words with no apparent control over her own tongue.

"Cecilia, really, it is not delicate of you to speak of such things." Ormiston's amused tone gave the lie to his apparent outrage.

"Now it is you who evade *my* questions." For the first time, Ormiston saw her smile without restraint. No masks, no mourning veils, no social courtesy, but a full, true smile. He felt as though he had taken a blow in the gut. Pulling himself together, he replied: "I shall answer you honestly in this, as in all other questions. As far as I know, I have fathered no children apart from the child you carry."

"You have no doubts that I do carry your child?"

"Why should I? You were a virgin. If you were a light-skirt, you would not have this trouble. I have not fathomed how you knew my identity at the Ferrières's ball, nor why you gave yourself to me, but I do know that I was the husband who was too foolish to treasure you as a husband should. I do not intend to repeat the mistake."

"You are very direct, sir."

"We have been given a chance to mend what started out marred. We cannot pretend this is a love match, but how many marriages in our circle are? Marrying for love is a novelettish indulgence. But we can treat each other with respect and honesty and perhaps some tenderness."

"You are not angry with me?"

"I was angry with you. I was bitterly angered when I could not find Alice, I was angrier still when I discovered that you had played me for a fool. Then I remembered your situation and the unfairness of it. You have been a pawn, as I have."

"We were not pawns in Paris, sir."

"Can you not bring yourself to call me by my given name?"

"It seems so familiar. We still scarcely know one another."

"Life together will seem most uncomfortable if you persist in addressing me as 'sir' or 'Ormiston.' Reggie and Amelia already call me Will. I wish you would do the same."

"Very well, Will." Cecilia rose, unsure of what should come next. Ormiston also stood, looked on her face, and longed to take it in his hands, kiss her lips and her eyes and the dip between her neck and collar bone. He could not conceal the hunger he felt for her and she stood as if trapped in a web by the heat she saw in his eyes. Then she stepped back and it was as though a door had swung shut between them. But she spoke.

"I agree to your bargain. A year at Hatherley. Then we decide on our future."

Ormiston took her hand and kissed it in acknowledgement of their agreement, then escorted her back to the house.

Admiral Ketley wanted his wife back, and Ormiston wished the official wedding to take place without delay, so once again, Dacre procured a special license for his son. The servants and tenants of Hatherley had been apprised of the impending matrimonial before the arrival of the happy couple, so arrangements for a suitable celebration were well in hand, although the cook, a normally sanguine woman, was thrown into confusion over the provision of a wedding cake until she remembered that there were several Christmas cakes soaking up their brandy which might easily be iced. Lady Ketley made calls on the neighboring gentry, many of whom hastily cancelled their own plans so that they might be free for the rare pleasure of a ball at Hatherley. Dacre was not known for elegant entertainment, although his reputation amongst local gentlefolk was generally high. Respect for good husbandry ran far deeper than the lamentations of womenfolk that there was no marchioness to lead local society.

Since their uncomfortable *tête à tête* in the garden, Ormiston and Cecilia had scarcely been given an opportunity to see each other, let alone speak at length. Ormiston could not forget that she had been barely able to speak his name. There was no time to remedy the situation before their wedding. Dacre was intent on absorbing his son into the operation of all his interests, while Lady Ketley and the younger Marchmonts made constant demands on Cecilia. Then there were fittings for a wedding gown which could not be deep mourning, and must be made by the local seamstress since there was no time to send to London, letters to old acquaintances of the Ketleys and her own from London, thank-yous for a procession of gifts which began to arrive at the great house, and decisions to be made about music and flowers and menus for the multitude of guests who found themselves able, after all, to attend the nuptials of one of the most influential families in the county—in fact, in the country.

Familiar enough with the obligations of land and tenantry, Cecilia was still taken aback by the extent of the Dacre interests and responsibilities. Becoming the viscountess officially was a great step, and one that she was not entirely sure she was ready to take. She thought often of Ormiston's words (she could not bring herself to think of him as Will, though she did test the sound of it from time to time with Reggie and Amelia) and whether she would take the escape route he offered. At tea with ladies from the prominent families around Hatherley, she found herself longing for Sawards, and considering which of the smaller houses near Sawards might be suitable for her to settle in, once Reggie had attained his majority, and how she might furnish it, and wondering whether Dacre might lend to her the small but very fine Guardi painting of the Grand Canal she had seen tucked away in a niche in the morning parlor.

It seemed at once an age and no time at all to find herself eating toast and drinking hot chocolate on the morning of her second wedding day while Lady Ketley paced the chamber, counting off the last-minute guests and reviewing the timetable for the momentous day ahead, complete with ball and tenants' dance, at both of which the bride and groom most certainly would open the dancing.

Wearing a simple dress of lilac satin with a mantilla of silver lace, bearing a bouquet of wisteria, Cecilia entered the chapel at Hatherley hesitantly. This time, she felt no less reluctant than on her previous wedding day, but at least she knew she looked her best, a knowledge confirmed by the collective intake of breath that greeted her appearance at the chancel of the Norman chapel where Dacres had commemorated most of their births, deaths, and strategic alliances for some seven hundred years.

The music of Purcell rang out, Cecilia accepted the escort of her brother and sister, and walked toward her husband, past the aisles filled with people giving speculative and supportive glances, past her aunt and godfather, up to the altar where Ormiston stood, cutting, as always, an elegant figure in a navy tailcoat with a white satin waistcoat embroidered with delicate gold thread, his cravat fastened with a simple pearl pin, his cream trousers immaculately pressed and his shoes buffed to a high sheen. This time, she saw no anger or resentment in his bearing or expression. This time, she knew the responses and did not stumble on her vows. This time, she knew, whatever bargain Ormiston had offered, there would be no escape.

Ten

The dance for staff and tenants was held in a great barn, which had been decorated with garlands of greenery and a profusion of white blossoms. Trestle tables were laid with simple trenchers, with bread tumbling from baskets, platters of cheese, ham, and fruit placed at strategic intervals. Just outside the back of the barn, two lambs, a haunch of venison, and a side of beef were being turned over a great open fire whose heat was so intense that the men tending the roast had removed their shirts and were slicked with sweat. Along one wall of the barn were barrels of ale, each manned by a steward. All four were hard at work filling tankards. The great double doors had been opened onto a courtyard, and just inside the barn, three fiddlers, a drummer, and a group of singers were running through a repertoire of lively folk songs as the bride and groom appeared in an open landau. The viscountess threw her bouquet, causing shrieks of amusement as the cook caught it and turned to look sternly at the head gardener. Dacre, Lady Ketley, and the Marchmont children also arrived, along with the vicar, the estate factor, and an assortment of other guests of high degree.

Then Ormiston handed Cecilia down from the carriage and they were swept into the barn. A warm speech was made by the butler, Burden, followed by a raucous toast. The fiddlers started up, and Ormiston took his bride by the hand to lead the assembled crowd in the Sir Roger de Coverly, a venerable country dance.

Once the dance had ended, Ormiston raised his own tankard high and toasted the guests before bidding them a good evening. Burden and a contingent of footmen set off for the house, ready for their evening's work, while Ormiston and Cecilia returned to their carriage, followed by the dignitaries also planning to attend the formal wedding breakfast and ball.

"They look as though they will have a wonderful evening," commented Cecilia almost wistfully.

"I half wish we might stay with them instead of having to shake hands with a parcel of stuffy dowagers. Still, I daresay we should throw a damper on their celebration." Ormiston paused, then said, "You look very beautiful today. I have not had a chance to say so."

"Thank you, my—Will."

"There, that was not so painful, was it? I shall have to give you practice, then my name will slip easily from you."

Cecilia smiled. "I need only talk of the future and your name will trip out as free as it may. You'll see."

"Avoiding the issue, I think. You are most evasive, Lady Ormiston."

"It will take a little time for me to adjust to my new name. I was not sure who they were addressing when they toasted Viscount and Lady Ormiston in the barn. Still, the receiving line will be all too lengthy an initiation."

"We have time first to go upstairs and put ourselves to rights." Ormiston wondered how Cecilia would feel when she discovered that Dacre had moved his son and daughter-in-law to the master suite of Hatherley. The marquis had moved out of it many years before, and it had lain unused as long as Ormiston could remember. The viscount was not inclined to tell Cecilia the news with the coachman in earshot. Somehow, he felt she would not be pleased.

Fortunately for Ormiston, Dorcas was waiting to escort her mistress up to her new quarters, where Cecilia was to freshen herself, remove her veil, and have her hair rearranged. It was as the maid was pinning up the last of Cecilia's tresses, woven with silver ribbons, that Ormiston knocked and entered. Dorcas placed the last pin, then turned to give a little bob to her new master. Cecilia turned and met his eyes.

"Dorcas, you may go. Thank you for all your trouble. The dance at the barn must call—run now and have a wonderful evening. I shan't need you again tonight."

"Goodnight, Dorcas," added Ormiston. The girl bobbed once again and tripped away.

Cecilia stood and walked toward him, drawing on her evening gloves, dyed in the same silvery-purple shade as her dress. She did look magnificent. But she also looked a little bare, for she wore no jewelry at all.

"When we were last married, you wore a diamond necklace and earbobs."

"I did not want to wear anything that reminded either you or me of that day. I have some fine pearls, but Aunt Letty told me that it's bad luck for a bride to wear pearls, for pearls mean tears. Or some such."

Ormiston held out a black leather case. "Perhaps these will suit. They belonged to my mother. The marquis gave them to me for my bride. If you don't like them, don't feel obliged to sport them out of politeness. You need no jewelry. No other woman here can hold a candle to you, my dear."

Cecilia opened the case and gasped. Within was a fine silver necklace of diamonds and amethysts, with a matching bracelet and pendant earrings.

"These are perfect! Exquisite! But I should have kept Dorcas. I am clumsy in gloves and it takes me an age to get them on and off."

"I will be your maid."

She held the case and first he placed the bracelet on her left wrist. Then he picked up the necklace and stood behind her to fasten it. His hands fumbled slightly with the clasp so that his fingers brushed the nape of her neck and tickled against her hairline. She took a deep breath to steady herself. She had not expected to respond to so slight a caress. Next, he picked up the left earring and screwed it into place, his fingers once again shifting against her skin. She stood as still as she could, struggling to suppress the shiver of response his touch drew from her as he moved around and fixed the final earring in place, his breath warm on her ear, his hands now sure. She waited until the heat of his touch dissipated as he dropped his hands and stepped back. Then she turned to face him. His eyes were dark pools, his breathing now harsh.

"How . . . ?"

"Don't be coy. You must know the effect you have on me. Come. We must go down now. Everyone will be waiting, and if we stay here much longer they will be waiting all night."

Cecilia hurried to the door, flustered by his words, now utterly unsure of what would happen later that night. She had not thought past the wedding itself, had refused to think of the wedding night. Did the bargain include marital relations? There was no time to consider this vexed question, for Ormiston was escorting her down the stairs and into position. Dacre turned to his daughter-in-law and said, "Lady Ormiston, you look very well." He called to Burden and the flow of guests began.

It took well over an hour to welcome the stream of well-wishers, but the crowd in the Great Hall was dwindling when the doors were thrown open for a tall, caped latecomer. He threw off his driving cloak in a great swirl of wool, tugged off his gloves, and checked his reflection in one of the great pier glasses before taking a flute of champagne and joining the queue of guests.

"It is Earl Lazenby!" exclaimed Dacre. "Do you remember him, Ormiston? Cecilia's met him in London, I know."

"Yes, I do remember him. The great huntsman, is he not? A hard goer."

"Aye, in more respects than one. He was one of your flirts, wasn't he, Ceci?"

There was no time to respond as a local family drew near, eager to meet the bride and fawn on the marquis. Inadvertently, Ceci caught Ormiston's eye, and he gave her a quizzical look before diving into conversation with Mrs. Selby.

It was not long before Alexander, fifth Earl Lazenby, was lifting Ceci's gloved hand to his mouth and drawling, "Devastated, my dear girl, to see you in this cub's clutches. Hoped you'd make me a happy man someday."

"Earl Lazenby, you never hoped any such thing," responded Ceci robustly. Then indelicacy got the better of her: "You made eyes at me, but your real attentions lay elsewhere, I believe."

Lazenby raised his eyebrows and gave a dramatic sigh. "You wrong me, Lady Ormiston. All I ever longed for was the affection of 'The Impregnable.' "

" 'The Impregnable'?" queried Ormiston, offering his hand so that Lazenby had to shake it and, in so doing, move away from Cecilia.

"Why, yes, Miss Marchmont was thus known. You have succeeded where so many have tried and failed. She was also known as 'The Citadel.' My congratulations on your conquest. I wish you both every happiness."

Ormiston could not help smiling, for he had succeeded far better than anyone knew. His amusement was only sharpened by the knowledge that in truth, Lazenby was planning already on making him extremely unhappy. The earl's reputation as a philanderer interested only in other men's wives had been well-established by the time Ormiston had left England. It came as something of a surprise that he had ever shown any interest in an ostensibly unattached maiden like Ceci. Presumably the unavailability suggested by her nicknames had presented sufficient challenge to Lazenby, and clearly the introduction had been effected in a careless moment by Dacre. Ormiston noticed that Lazenby and Lady Ketley greeted each other coolly. Cecilia's risqué riposte had not gone unremarked, either. It suggested that she, too, was aware of the earl's dubious standing.

As the family was finally gathering before entering the

ballroom, Lady Ketley spoke in a fierce undertone to Dacre, "I am surprised you invited Lazenby, I must say. I know he is a neighbor, but he is not good Ton."

"I've known the lad since he was in leading strings, and there's a solid core to him. He looks after his land, and the odd affair with a bored wife ain't enough for me to cut him. He's perfectly good Ton. His family's older than ours if we were to tot up the centuries."

"It was bad enough him dangling after Ceci in London."

"Aye, Letty, you made it plain you disapproved then. This is the sort of do where he must be invited, and let me be plain with you, he is always welcome in my house. He may not be the thing in the petticoat line, but he's caused no outright scandal. Indeed, he'll be welcome even if he does."

"He'll be after Ceci, mark my words. Warn your son to be on the *qui vive*. If you don't, I shall."

"You will not. She's safe from Lazenby until she's produced an heir. He's quite honorable that way. It's up to my son to keep Ceci happy enough so that she don't feel the need to wander. We must leave the young folk to their own machinations, Letty—it don't do to interfere."

Lady Ketley harrumphed and followed Dacre into the ballroom, knowing that they must be ready to watch the happy couple lead the first dance.

Ormiston had specified that he wished the ball to open with a waltz. He had been careful to direct the music master away from the melodies he remembered from the Ferrières' ball. Cecilia and he were greeted with a cheer as they entered the ballroom, followed by a hush as they took their position in the center of the room, waiting for the music. The first notes sounded and he swept her around the floor, making a full circuit before Lady Ketley and Dacre followed them, formally opening the dancing. Suddenly the ballroom was a whirl of colors, as the music soared and crested.

Cecilia barely had time to think after that, for gentleman after gentleman demanded the honor of dancing with the bride. It was nearly two hours later when she managed to excuse herself from a dance by declaring that her thirst must be quenched. A hand bearing a glass of lemonade presented itself before her. She looked up. Lazenby gave his breezy smile, his blue-gray eyes crinkling at the corners.

"Quite like old times. Lemonade is still your favorite beverage, I hope."

"Old times! Last year, you mean. It was only last year that you deigned to notice me at all. Before then, I was just another chit." Cecilia sipped at her drink.

"Never *just* a chit, my dear, but much too young for me, certainly."

"Why, Methuselah, you cannot be more than thirty. That is not so very old."

"Ah, thirty-two summers have I, fair Cecilia." Lazenby had found some more champagne and was clearly enjoying it.

"The difference between us remains the same. I have been out four years now, and you didn't pay me a jot of attention for the first three. Of course, that was when you were deep in dalliance with . . ."

"My dear Lady Ormiston, it does not become you to remind me of the follies of my youth. As for attention, you have always basked in it. What need to add me to your court of followers?"

"Then why did you join?" Cecilia found herself enjoying the rake's company as much as ever. He had made a great show of reluctance when first flirting with her, assuring her it was only as a favor to Dacre and Lady Ketley, to deter her numerous hangers-on.

"At first, to see what all the fuss was about. And then, my fair Arachne, you trapped me in your web and now I writhe like the rest of your prey." He grinned as she absorbed and laughed at his hyperbole, then became serious. "I have missed you a good deal."

"If you are staying at Edenbridge for long, you will be able to visit us here."

"You have no plans to go up to London for the rest of the Season?"

"No. We are still in mourning for Papa, and we think it best for my brother and sister to remain here. Lady Ketley and I should still have been in Paris were it not for Papa's sickness, so I'd not have been here for the Season in any case."

"I was thinking of coming to Paris." Lazenby sounded reflective. Cecilia looked intently at him, for he did seem sincere. "I was sorry to hear of Marchmont's death. He was a good man. I know that Dacre will miss him dearly."

"So will we all."

"Lady Ormiston—Cecilia. You did permit me to call you Cecilia."

"Yes." Cecilia watched Lazenby as he dismissed his thought without speaking it.

"Nothing. Let us dance."

Lazenby offered her his arm and they joined a cotillion.

Ormiston was watching his wife. He found Lady Ketley at his elbow, also contemplating her niece with the debonair earl.

"Watch that one carefully. His reputation dwindles with every new dalliance and he preys on young wives. Bad enough that Dacre should have thrown him together with Ceci last year, let alone draw his attention now."

"Lady Ketley, Cecilia appears immune to his charms. He may choose to dangle after her, but I'd stake my life that she'll not succumb."

"You are very sanguine. It may not happen now, but he'll keep up the acquaintance and in a year or two he'll come sniffing round. That's his way. We saw it with the Melchetts and the Waverleys."

"We shall see."

"Personally, I don't see Lazenby's appeal. He seems too obvious a flirt to me, but perhaps I am too old to merit his coquetry. Your ways can be just as winning. But I don't see you exert yourself much with Cecilia." Lady Ketley's blunt comment drew a chuckle from Ormiston.

"You may depend upon my affection for your niece, Lady Ketley. But you must leave us to fend for ourselves."

"You are as exasperating as Dacre."

At that, Ormiston could not suppress a guffaw. Never before had anyone compared him to Dacre—and if anyone had been so rash, never before would he have been amused. Lady Ketley's frustration with the tiresome marquis and his still more tiresome son increased and it was Cecilia who bore the brunt of her ire. Once the cotillion had drawn to an end, Burden announced that supper was served and there began a drift from the ballroom to the dining hall.

The supper was a buffet meal, taken standing up. Lady Ketley took the opportunity to corner Cecilia and harangue her soundly for dancing with Lazenby.

"You know his character well enough—why, you were rash enough to refer to it in the receiving line. Yet you dance with him and make eyes at him, in public on your wedding day. It is the height of folly, Cecilia."

"He is a neighbor, he is our equal in Society and in the county. I cannot cut him, Aunt Letty. It would put Dacre in a most difficult position. And I was not making eyes at him. He is amusing and he makes me laugh, but I know exactly what dangers he presents. Stop trying to manage me—I am a married woman now, and unless and until my husband instructs me not to dance with guests in his own home, I will do as I please with whom I please."

"How can you speak so to me? Such ingratitude! I, who have kept your secret and launched you in Society and taught you all you know of the world. Sharper than a serpent's tooth indeed!" whispered Lady Ketley with ferocity.

"Aunt Letty, we must speak now and in private. We cannot leave things between us so. Come with me." Cecilia took her aunt in a firm grasp and led her away from the ballroom into a small music room down the hallway. Once Lady Ketley had settled herself in a wing chair, Cecilia went over to her and knelt at her feet and took her hand.

"Dearest aunt, you know that I am deeply indebted to you and will never forget all that I owe you. But this very morning, you were telling me how I must make my way at Hatherley, and make something of this marriage, how I must now be one of the Dacres and follow their lead."

Lady Ketley made a sound which sounded like "mmpff," which might, Cecilia thought, be taken as an invitation to continue.

"I know full well what Lazenby is—a flirtatious rogue. But I also believe there to be something dangerous in him, Aunt Letty, and I do not wish to unleash that on my family."

Lady Ketley dropped a kiss on Cecilia's brow and smoothed a ringlet back from the girl's temple before reaching into her reticule to withdraw a handkerchief with which she dabbed at her eyes.

"Forgive me, Ceci. We have been so happy since you came to us, Ketley and I, and now we have lost my dear Marchmont and with him, we are to lose you. I am so grieved by this, I was not just. Do you forgive me?"

"Of course. I can never forget what I owe you." She stretched up to kiss her aunt on the cheek.

"Now, tell me, Ceci, whatever makes you think Lazenby is dangerous?"

"Perhaps it was nothing. But you remember my friend Susanna?"

"Yes—Maria Melchett's little sister. What of her?"

"When Melchett threw off Maria, she returned home. Susanna said that Maria gave her father her oath that there had been nothing between herself and Lazenby—it was all a hum. He had put the rumor about because she spurned him. He makes me very uneasy, Aunt Letty. But he is the marquis's friend and I cannot be rude to him."

"Tell Ormiston of this, I beg, Cecilia. Not tonight, but soon. Lazenby has you in his sights—I'd wager your fine amethysts on it. You may trust Ormiston, I feel sure."

"Maybe."

"Is all well between you, Ceci? You seemed to have come to an accommodation with Ormiston very swiftly, but I was too glad to see you settled without any great legal kerfuffle to fuss. Should I have done?"

Cecilia shook her head. "The truth is, we are newly wed, even though we have been married more than five years. We must learn each other's ways."

"Will you learn to love him, Ceci? I pray you will find as much pleasure and passion as I have known with Ketley. But this match has been unorthodox from the start and I worry for you. Another reason for my anxiety over Lazenby."

"I cannot tell. I do know that since he came to Sawards, he has been warm to the children, he has striven to put himself forward as a support since Papa's death, he has made every effort to be pleasant to me. This is not love, but it is an advance on the contempt in which he held me five years ago."

"But what of you, child? He hurt you very bitterly then."

"We were both young and foolish. Hurting me was understandable, if not excusable. He was badly enough wounded by his father. He is a man now."

Lady Ketley was wise enough to go no further. It had occurred to her to ask whether Cecilia felt any frisson of attraction for the viscount, but that seemed impertinent. Besides, she had been told clearly enough on three separate occasions this evening that she should not interfere in the lives of her niece and the viscount. She stood and gathered up her niece and led her back to the ball.

Ormiston came over as soon as they appeared in the doorway of the dining room. He looked intently at his bride's face, but Cecilia appeared calm enough.

"Now that supper has been served, we must cut the cake and dance a final dance. Then we are under no further obligation."

"If it is not too soon, by all means let us complete the ceremonies."

Ormiston led Cecilia over to a confection of five tiers. He took up a great knife and held it out so that Cecilia might rest her own hand on his. Then Dacre called for silence, they sliced down, and a great cheer passed around the room. Ormiston smiled at Cecilia.

"Are you ready for a final dance, my lady?"

"With pleasure."

They took to the floor, no longer the cynosure of all eyes, able at last to concentrate on each other. Ormiston noticed slight shadows of fatigue under Cecilia's eyes. She was avoiding his gaze as well. What could be worrying her? He drew in his breath and closed his eyes as he caught the scent of her, delicately musky, overlaid with vanilla and honeysuckle. He opened his eyes and saw the swing of her earrings and remembered the temptation offered upstairs by her soft skin, her unmistakable frisson of response to his hand against the nape of her neck. He caught her eyes on him, uncertain, watchful.

"We may excuse ourselves as soon as we wish. There will be ribald comments whenever we take our leave. Are you ready yet?"

She tensed as he continued to guide her through the crowd in time to the dance. Now, certainly, was not the time to discuss whether their bargain included conjugal relations or not. Surely, thought Cecilia, it would be better to get the discussion out of the way. If, indeed, there needed to be a discussion. She knew he wanted her; he had made it clear upstairs before the ball, and his dark eyes made it plain enough now that he was ready to fulfill his duties. Honesty compelled her to acknowledge that the sensation of his hands close to her aroused her curiosity.

"I am ready. Let us bid the guests good-night."

Ormiston led his bride to the dais where the musicians were playing. They ascended it and waited until the lead violinist fell silent. There was an expectant hush in the room.

"Dear friends, my bride and I thank you for attending our wedding. We will now withdraw, leaving you to enjoy the festivities still further."

The guests applauded and drew apart, opening up a passage through the ballroom and into the hallway. As they walked down it, arm in arm, the guests, forearmed, threw rose petals before them and over them, as the musicians played a lilting Irish air. To Cecilia, their passage through the crowd, to the foot of the great stairs, seemed to take an age. Ormiston and she paused at the first landing to wave farewell and a cheer went up, with raucous shouts of encouragement from the more castaway of the male guests.

"We should be thankful that it is no longer the custom for the bride and groom to be accompanied into the very chamber," said Ormiston as they made their way to their own room, the racket of the throng fading somewhat as the next dance started up.

They stood before the door to Cecilia's chamber. Ormiston opened it for her, but once she had entered, he waited outside.

"You must ask me in, Cecilia."

Chin up, voice firm, she said, "Will you enter, my lord?"

Eleven

The room was lit only by the wall sconces and a single candelabra, placed on the writing table near the window. The drapes around the four-poster bed were drawn and the counterpane drawn back, exposing an expanse of eiderdown and the stark whiteness of the pillowcases. Cecilia went to the dressing table and began unbuttoning her gloves.

"You dismissed Dorcas. Allow me to fill her position." Ormiston resorted to formality to stifle his impulse to crush his wife in his embrace. She turned and nodded her agreement. She drew her breath as he refastened her glove.

"Later," he whispered. Slowly, he removed the bracelet and dropped it onto the dresser. Then she felt the warmth of his fingers brush against the side of her neck as he removed her earrings. Once they were gone, he trailed a finger along her neckline, brushing the lace and the skin of her décolletage. Her lips parted. She swallowed and closed her eyes.

"Are you sure, Cecilia? I can call Dorcas back still." His voice was uncertain. She opened her eyes and moved away.

"I asked you in. I knew what I was doing. There is no going back, no annulment, nothing but the possibility of separation. But we must try—we must make some sort of effort. There are many marriages with less chance of success."

"How reassuringly you frame things, my wife." Ormiston smiled, his tone dry. "What next, I wonder?" His voice was low and soft and close. She watched him as he came to stand so close she felt she could scarcely breathe. When he was near, every nerve seemed to stand to attention; she found herself expectant, taut. It was an entirely novel sensation. Gently, he propelled her onto the banquette by the dresser. "Slippers, I think."

The viscount knelt before his bride. He unlaced the ribbons of her shoes, unwound them from her ankles, his thumbs tracing the fine bones of her heels and feet. Cecilia's arms were rigid, her knuckles tight on the edge of the stool where she sat. Ormiston abruptly ceased his caresses and knelt back on his heels, accompanied by the rustle as her satin dress slipped back into place.

"Let us not forget the necklace." He rose up onto his knees, skimmed his palms up the length of her arms and then around her neck, which he encircled. Then his fingers stroked up her neck, and along the underside of her chin before reaching behind her to fiddle with the clasp of the necklace, his forehead pressed against hers, the tip of his nose brushing against hers, his lips slightly apart, his breath mingling with hers. The necklace came away from her skin.

"This time, fair Alice, there is no need for haste." She nodded in agreement and uncertainty. "This time," he continued, "there are no masks."

She pulled back. "There will be no more masks."

"Very well, Cecilia. No more concealment."

"I do not believe that you have concealed anything from me. I cannot expect anything from you. You have been trapped into this." She moved away and gazed into the fire. Her husband followed her and turned her so she had to look at him.

"No. I haven't. We could have arranged something, my father and I. I am not trapped. I am here willingly, as I hope you are."

"I am here." She still sounded a little distant.

"Alice, I promise you, I shall always be faithful." Her eyes were still wary. "I swear it, Cecilia."

"Men say these things. So do women. Sometimes they say

them but they find they can't keep the promise. Don't swear anything irrevocable."

"Our union is irrevocable. No woman could compare to you. You bedazzle me. It's rare. Unique. We mustn't be afraid of this."

"I can't help it, Will. I never expected it. I don't know what to do about it."

"Let me show you." He silenced her with his mouth and hands and skin and flesh, helping her shed her clothes, leading her to their bed, until they were together, lost in a conflagration of desire.

Afterwards, slick with sweat, entwined, they returned to earth.

"You called me Will." Ormiston's voice was low in her ear. Cecilia turned and looked at him, raising a hand to sweep the strands of hair from her face.

"You called me Alice."

"Why did you pretend that night?" He pulled away from her, then lay alongside her, his head propped on his elbow.

"I thought I could have some sort of revenge on you. You were so cruel about me when we first married. I wanted to punish you. But in the end, I only punished myself."

"Is this child a punishment?" His hand trailed over the slight curve of her belly.

"No. But leaving you that night felt like torture. It felt wrong and cruel, and I knew I'd miscalculated. I'd been a fool."

"I don't know that we would be here now if you hadn't made that miscalculation. This is no punishment. This feels like a piece of heaven." He kissed her neck and stroked her waist.

Cecilia shivered. "When you say something like that, I feel as though we are about to be blasted by a thunderbolt. Hubris."

"Don't you think we can be happy? Don't you think we are allowed to be happy?"

"I don't know. It just makes me feel uncomfortable."

"I've married a pessimist. This may have been arranged in the clumsiest way, but I believe it is up to us to set things to rights. I believe things between us can be set to rights."

"Do you believe in love, then? You didn't seem to at Sawards. You spoke of expedience and the preposterousness of expecting happiness in marriage."

Ormiston lay back, his arm concealing his face. "I don't know about love, Cecilia. I thought I was in love for several years, and it proved a chimera. I do believe that we have as much chance as anyone else of happiness, particularly if we remain true to one another, tell no lies, and treat each other with respect."

Cecilia could not answer immediately, for if she did, she knew she would cry. This was not the romantic declaration she had expected after the maelstrom of physical passion which had engulfed them both. It was perhaps unrealistic to expect Ormiston to understand that she had teetered on the brink of love with him since she was a child, and since Paris, she had fallen into the brink and was struggling not to sink into a passion that she felt must demean her so long as it was not mutual.

She slipped from the bed and doused the last four candles. When she climbed back into bed, Ormiston took her in his arms and held her spoon fashion, his whole body curved around hers. Soon, his breathing sounded deep and regular.

It was strange to attempt to sleep with another person in the room, after so many years in her own bed in her own room. Perhaps Ormiston had shared his bed with so many women, or one woman so frequently—Cecilia could not decide which was the most unpleasant notion—that he was accustomed to the sensation. For her part, it was acutely uncomfortable. His breath tickled at her neck, his arm was very heavy about her waist, impeding her breathing somewhat; she could not stretch out her legs and her back was slick with perspiration. Altogether, it seemed inelegant and disagreeable. Eventually, she wriggled out of his reach and teetered on the edge of the bed, desperate for some cool cotton against her skin.

Restless and unable to settle, Cecilia rose and fumbled for a tinder box. She lit a single candle and sought out a peignoir. Sleeping without clothing was another thing she was not used to. Once she was dressed, she felt more wide awake than ever, so she took her candle and slipped into the dressing room next door, where there was a chaise longue and a copy of Fanny Burney's *Camilla,* which she was in the middle of rereading.

The next thing Cecilia knew, there was a rustle of material and she was hoisted up in the most alarming fashion. She was too bewildered and befuddled with sleep to put up any resistance as he dropped her back on her bed.

"You thought you could escape me, Cecilia?" Ormiston did not sound very pleased. She could not make out more than a dim outline of his face. Slender beams of light falling on the carpet through the divide in the curtains indicated that the sun had risen, but the heavy damask ensured that the room remained in the gloom.

"No. I couldn't sleep and I did not wish to disturb you."

"Luckily, you left the door ajar. I was not compelled to wander the passage unclothed in search of my errant wife." He joined her on the bed and his hands began to ease the gauzy tissue of her peignoir away. "This is a fetching garment, but I see no need for it." He stroked the bare skin of her upper arms and began to kiss her neck and the tender skin below. Cecilia quelled a brief desire to mutiny against the pull of desire. He may not love her, but at least here, she knew that she had some sovereignty over him.

"We won't be disturbed?"

"We are not expected to emerge from here until midafternoon. The marriage must be seen to be soundly consummated. Particularly given your condition." Ormiston dealt curtly with Cecilia's query, preferring to inspect the curves of her legs, the tangle of hair at the apex of her thighs, the small but significant indentation of her navel. Then she laced her hands in his hair and pulled his head up so she could kiss him and they both forgot everything except one another.

This time, Cecilia did sleep soundly in her husband's arms. She was roused by the sound of the curtains opening, and a sudden glare of light from the windows, which faced southeast. She buried her head under a mound of pillows. She heard Ormiston's muffled voice.

"Cecilia, are you hungry? I'm ravenous, I was planning to ring for some food. Do you care for some, too?"

"Yes, please. And a bath."

"An excellent plan. We may share it. An imaginative wife is indeed worth more than rubies. Move over—I would not frighten Dorcas with my nakedness and she will be here shortly."

Dorcas did indeed come rushing to the room, clearly agog with curiosity over the fate of her mistress, now in the clutches of a ravening male. Ormiston dispatched her promptly, instructing her to bring a dressing gown before she returned below stairs with their request for hot water and sustenance. When she had gone, Will turned to Cecilia.

"Do you wish we were going away on a wedding trip? We could still arrange it if the prospect of constant inspection by our servants seems wearisome."

"Not to mention our families." Cecilia sighed. "It is tempting, but I feel we should remain here until Reggie and Amelia are properly settled. I feel as though I have neglected them grievously, what with nursing Papa and now this rush to regularize things between us. Besides, we have a great deal to learn about Hatherley, both of us."

"Sensible Cecilia. But then, there is amorous Alice, hidden under that dutiful exterior. An enticing combination."

There was a knock and Dorcas entered quietly, laying Ormiston's robe and a fresh set of clothing on the windowseat. She turned back and bobbed a curtsey at the bed, her eyes fixed firmly on one of the wooden columns of the frame, evading any eye contact with its occupants.

"Please, your ladyship, Lady Ketley asked me to pass on a message to you. You are not expected downstairs today. But she did say that Master Reggie and Miss Amelia were pining a little after all the excitement."

"Thank you, Dorcas. We'll inform you of our plans for the day once we're fed and bathed."

"Yes, your ladyship." The girl bobbed and darted off again. Two trays of food arrived soon thereafter. Ormiston and Cecilia withdrew to a dressing chamber while a procession of maidservants and footmen organized the water for their bath. Ormiston commanded Cecilia to read to him, but soon pronounced *Camilla* to be a tiresome girl and declared her troubles with her arriviste family insignificant.

Ormiston had hoped that the bath would provide an opportunity to reacquaint himself with the pleasures of his wife's body, but she was anxious to see her siblings and brushed his hand aside when he attempted to sponge and rinse her. He withdrew and watched her instead, and was compelled to call for a fresh bath, reluctant to submerge himself in cold, lavender-scented water.

Cecilia did not wait to watch him wash. Instead, she left their chamber in search of her brother and sister. She found them with Lavauden, establishing their schoolroom in an airy set of apartments in the east wing.

The children greeted her warmly, while Lavauden inspected her gravely, as though checking porcelain for blemishes and irregularities. They were surrounded by primers, atlases, and curious-shaped devices for the drawing of angles and curves and were busy tacking up maps of the oceans, the night sky, and various land masses to liven the bare walls.

On seeing her, Reggie began clamoring to know whether he might have fencing lessons and music lessons and riding lessons and swimming lessons.

"We have been here so brief a time, there has been no opportunity to consult with Dacre or Lavauden about your curriculum. It will all be settled shortly, and I am sure that if you wish to pursue all these activities, it can be managed. But I thought you had already learnt to swim at Sawards?"

"I have, a little," Reggie replied stoutly enough, but Cecilia was able to read between the lines to see at once that he was insecure in water.

"There are many other things to do here—there is bound to be fishing and soon there will be shooting and then hunting. Should you like to try your hand at those as well as all the other things you wish to do?"

"Indeed I should, Ceci. It is a spanking place, full of exciting things to do."

"But it isn't half so good as Sawards." Amelia's chin wobbled a little as she spoke, and Ceci went over to lift her sister into her lap and hold her close.

"It is very different. Much bigger, certainly, but I don't think it any better. We always had plenty to amuse us there. But Lord Dacre has a better selection of instruments, and here there is also Mr. Buchan, Amelia, who has been teaching Ormiston to paint these five years. Ormiston did mention that he might have a pair of talented new pupils to study with him."

"The views here are very dull compared with Sawards, Ceci, and the garden is full of twiddly bits, not smooth and rolling like our Downs."

"It is true that the grounds are very ornamental compared with Sawards. Have you seen the greenhouses yet? Dacre showed them to us the other day, and they had the most extraordinary plants and fruit in them, Amy, all ready for painting, not to mention tasting afterwards."

"I am not to be bought for a bit of exotic fruit. I miss home, Ceci, and I want to go back. We don't know anyone here, and there haven't been any children here since Ormiston was small, and that must have been an age ago, for he is quite old now."

"He's only twenty-four. That's not so very old."

"It seems ancient to me."

Seeing that Amelia was not to be drawn from her fit of the sullens, Cecilia turned her attention to Lavauden, inquiring whether she was being treated well by the staff. Lavauden was able to confirm that her every comfort was attended to, her room was pleasant, and her position in the hierarchy unassailed. The governess then suggested they walk out in the grounds, it being a fine, dry day and the children not yet having had an airing.

As the party of four left the house, a cocker spaniel of Dacre's bounded out, immediately occupying Reggie, who began looking about for sticks to throw. Amelia at first shrank a little from the animal, but then joined in with Reggie in chasing after it as it leapt and barked in its quest for branches and twigs.

The shock of realizing that this was the first *tête-à-tête* that she had shared with Lavauden since her father's funeral inhibited Cecilia slightly. But the Frenchwoman, discreet as ever, did not press her former charge with questions, instead winding her arm with Cecilia's and suggesting they discuss a program of study for the two Marchmont children. In mulling over this neutral topic, Lavauden established to her own satisfaction that Cecilia was prepared to remain at Hatherley for the foreseeable future. Gradually, Cecilia found herself revealing the details of the bargain into which she had entered with the viscount.

"So you have agreed between you to remain married for at least a year. Is this the result of reading too much poetry or too many novels?"

"What do you mean?"

"I am a Frenchwoman—we are notoriously practical and pragmatic. You are married to a young man who is certainly handsome, and seems to be good. He is still young, and you may have a hand in shaping him, as he will definitely shape you. But here you are, shilly-shallying. Why?"

"He does not love me."

Lavauden rolled her eyes and murmured in French. Cecilia

spluttered, "I am not a crazed dreamer. I think it reasonable that my husband should love me."

"This is an alliance, not a love match. You haven't made the mistake of falling in love with . . . Ah, I see you have." Lavauden sighed. "I don't know a great deal about such things. I have loved, but it was never returned. I have never had a lover. But I understand that amorous infatuation can often be mistaken for love. Are you sure you are not mistaking desire for love?"

"I'm not sure, Lavauden. I've never loved anyone else." Cecilia could not conceal a degree of petulance from entering her voice. Lavauden might at least have responded with some sympathy. None could be expected from Aunt Letty, but Lavauden, it might have been hoped, was a little more sensitive and a little less worldly. "Even if I am mistaking my emotions, I feel as though I am in love and he does not seem to care for me at all. He has married me because he could not have the woman he loved, and it is a ridiculous tangle."

"Ridiculous, certainly, but not a tangle, as far as I know. He is both obliging and complaisant, characteristics not shared by many husbands. He is capable of inspiring considerable loyalty. Mr. Buchan has spoken to me of his travels and it is clear that he holds the viscount in affection as much as in esteem. I believe that it is your duty to your brother and sister to suppress your own emotions if they lead you to interfere with your judgement. Try to rub along with your husband. If you are a good wife to him, he will come in time to love you, I am sure of it."

With this small consolation Cecilia had to content herself, but it left her resentful and dissatisfied. This was not a state of affairs she could long endure, she knew.

Twelve

Less than a week after the wedding, Lady Ketley was on her way back to Paris. With her departure, the weather broke, and what had been a fine June turned dismal. The clouds, perpetually gray and lowering, forced the household to use extra candles and the temperature was so low that fires were lit every evening in the dining room, music room, and all bedrooms. The trees perpetually dripped with rain, the ground was sodden, and forgotten springs began to well in lower-lying areas of the extensive Dacre lands.

With the rain came Lazenby. He rode over one afternoon to consult with Dacre about a shared land boundary and stayed for tea with Lady Ormiston, accompanied by her sister and the French governess. He renewed his flirtation with the viscountess and charmed her small sister. When Ormiston turned up, he was playing the piano while Lavauden and Amelia sang a pretty little French air. He looked very fine in his riding boots, black jacket, and *eau-de-nil* waistcoat, his still-damp curls swept back from his high forehead, his merry eyes twinkling with mirth as he speeded up the tempo of the song until Amelia burst into a fit of giggles. It was the first time Cecilia had seen Amelia relax and laugh since their arrival at Hatherley.

Lazenby did not outstay his welcome, leaving a few minutes later. As he rode home, he thought of when he should visit again, and how pleasant Hatherley would become with the ladies residing there, and what a shame it was that a dour block like Ormiston had managed to leg-shackle himself to the only intelligent filly to have come out these five years. She was reputed to be warm in the pocket, too—Marchmont had never been a lavish fellow, but everyone knew that his lands were well-managed and he had had other interests, too—coal and cotton in the Midlands, it was said. It seemed hard that the Dacres, who had always had plenty of money, should have nabbed one of the finer heiresses.

Money had always been a trouble to the earl, and what was the use of being an earl without any spare blunt to splash around? His financial woes were the main reason he was rusticating this Season, although perhaps he should have followed his aunt's advice and found a nice little child with a decent dowry and married himself off instead of retreating to the countryside. And the other reason was that rash dalliance, which had ended with Moberley threatening to horsewhip him the length of Pall Mall. The lady had assured him that her husband was complaisant, but that was the last time Lazenby intended to trust a wife's judgement. He had been lucky that Moberley had not taken a pistol to him.

There would be no more flirtations. He was now in the business of finding himself a wife. Lady Ormiston had some charming young friends, and it was no hardship to keep company with her, though it was clear enough that she was besotted with Ormiston. It certainly was unfair when a chap with address and *savoir-faire* such as himself should be pipped by a silent, brooding type with no notion of how to please the ladies. It was clear that the sensible course of action was to keep in with the viscountess and persuade her to invite a party to Hatherley composed of her wealthier available acquaintance.

Lazenby knew better than to turn up too often, but he did manage to call at times convenient enough for wangling further invitations for luncheon or dinner. It was his intention to become a fixture at Hatherley, even if it did mean buttering up Ormiston and his Scots amanuensis, Buchan. He assimilated some of the vocabulary of appreciation and managed to make eloquent noises about their daubs; he amused Amelia and Reggie with juggling tricks and romps and he demanded tuition in the nuances of the French language from Lavauden. He was always game for a round of cards with Dacre and he found himself reading poetry with Cecilia. Meanwhile, the rain kept falling, which made the ride over from Edenbridge deuced uncomfortable.

There also came disquieting rumors about wild groups of travellers roaming the county. Local farmers began to report the loss of livestock, then a lawyer riding between Thrapston and Kettering was set upon, his horse stolen and, to his outrage, his documents burnt. The local militia once again began to train, although they were equipped chiefly with pitchforks and scythes. On investigation, the lawyer's claim to have been attacked by a horde of fifteen men had to be reduced to five, but the furor did liven up the conversation of the stream of callers curious to inspect the viscount and his new wife. Ormiston ordered two grooms to accompany Amelia and Reggie on any excursions by horseback, but the weather imposed a far more effective prohibition on any rambles.

Reggie was less affected by the restrictions imposed on him by the incessant damp than Amelia. Both Buchan and Ormiston were happy to instruct him now that he was moving beyond the rudiments in the art of the small sword, and they managed to practice most days in the ballroom. But this was not regarded by Lavauden as suitable exercise for a young lady, so Amelia was perpetually condemned either to spectate or to practice more ladylike pursuits elsewhere. Gradually there built up in her heart a bitter resentment that she had been wrenched from her home to sit here while everyone paid attention to everyone else and none to her, at all, ever. Even Lavauden bustled about the place, her skill in smoothing ruffled feathers and her direct access to the viscountess's ear placing her much in demand above and below stairs.

While Cecilia tried to spend as much time with Amelia as

possible, the demands on her as chatelaine of Hatherley mounted daily. It was clear that while Dacre's household had run perfectly smoothly, now there was a lady of the house the staff was determined to restore to her an abundance of tasks which they had carried out but which they felt more properly belonged to the mistress. There were numerous petitions for a series of improvements and the purchase of sundry gadgets that had been long desired, from new mangles to fresh preserves pans, which could not be sanctioned by anyone other than Lady Cecilia.

Then there were the visitors, as relentless and regular as the rain. Hatherley was the greatest house in the area, superseding even Edenbridge, particularly now that it looked as though its inhabitants were settling permanently there. Following the actual bridals, the local ladies were keen to lay claim to the viscountess. Once the immediate calls had been received, Cecilia was then obliged to return them, whereupon followed requests to attend supper parties and musical soirees. There may have been a Season in London, but most of the genteel families in the area were quite content to remain within the county, travelling cheerfully from Market Harborough to Kettering, Corby, and sometimes even as far afield as Stamford and Oakham for their entertainments.

So it was that Amelia's general discontent was missed by all those close to her, the first anyone realizing its extent when Lavauden went in to wake her one morning some three weeks after the wedding. Her bed was empty and uncreased, a crumpled but legible note resting on the pillow. It revealed that she missed Sawards and had amassed four guineas which she was sure would be enough to take her there, for though Hatherley was all very fine, it was not home and there was no one left to put flowers on Mama and Papa's grave.

Lavauden went immediately to the master suite, knocking furiously at the door. Dorcas opened it.

"Is Lady Cecilia up yet? We must rouse her immediately, for Amelia has run away."

Although Lavauden was doing her utmost to remain calm, she felt by turns deeply guilty and enraged with her small charge. Within seconds, she was swept into Cecilia's dressing room, where the newlyweds were sitting over their breakfast. To Lavauden's relief, she found them both fully clothed.

"When do you think she left?" asked Cecilia after she had read the note.

"She does not appear to have slept in the bed, but I do not see how she could have left the house without notice. It was locked up very early last night, for we had no visitors for once. And she seemed so cheerful and happy, happier than for some time, I thought. I imagined she was getting used to her new life."

"Do you think she would have been able to saddle up her pony?"

"Not without rousing the grooms, surely."

"Let us go down to the stables without delay. At the very least, they can saddle up my gelding and I can start a search for her. We will get the footmen to search the grounds." Ormiston dropped his hand on his wife's shoulder. "We'll have her back in a trice, Cecilia."

"I cannot sit while you search for her. I will go out with the footmen. Or Buchan, perhaps. He has showed her one or two paths where she might find pleasant views for a study or a sketch. She might have followed those."

The whole house was roused, and the search commenced. Most of the grooms and footmen were enlisted in the search. A tinder box and lantern had gone missing and one of the French windows in the music room had been unbolted. The hunt fanned out from that point. Grooms were sent out to the local towns in all directions to see if by any chance Amelia had succeeded in reaching a point where she might find a stage to take her to London.

Buchan led Cecilia and Reggie behind the house and into the thickening woods to the east of the house, which blended imperceptibly with Rockingham Forest. They walked with sticks, calling Amelia's name from time to time, Cecilia increasingly worried for her sister's well-being. The wood was dense with beech and sycamore trees, its floor carpeted with bracken which concealed rabbit holes and other hazards. Cecilia could not dispel from her mind the image of Amelia trapped in some gamekeeper's deterrent to poachers, or nursing a broken ankle from slipping into some animal burrow. The forest floor undulated, and the rainfall had made bogs of any low-lying dells. They heard the faint cries of other searchers in the distance. Then Cecilia caught a glimpse of a flash of red. She moved toward it silently, forgetting to call to her companions. She quickened her pace and found a scrap of fabric caught on brambles. It was unmistakably from Amelia's warmest dress, which brought a little comfort. She clutched it as she forged blindly on, fighting her way through thickets of blackberry bushes and tangles of ferns, her feet sinking into muddy hollows, her face and hands scratched by thorns, her dress and petticoat dragging as they soaked in moisture from the leaves and ground.

She paused. She had lost Buchan and Reggie. Gradually, her breathing stilled and she became conscious of the deep silence surrounding her. Then just to her right, a twig cracked. She glanced toward the sound, but saw nothing there. A rustling just behind her had her whirl around. And then a hand clamped across her mouth and an arm swooped across her waist, hauling her backwards against a huge chest. She was picked up and turned bodily around and around until she was dizzy and disoriented. Then she was dropped.

When she looked up, she saw three men, their hats drawn low over their eyes, scarves muffling the lower halves of their faces, their coats worn and shabby, missing buttons and frayed at the sleeves, their legs and feet wound in rags above great nailed boots.

They spoke, but she could barely make out their meaning, their speech obscured by thick dialect as well as the woollen mufflers. One lost patience and grabbed a handful of leaves and threw them in her face.

"Art thou lookin' for the young lass?" shouted the largest, enunciating each word.

"Yes. You'll be paid for your trouble. And given shelter and a meal."

They laughed at that, but one of them started wheezing and then a racking cough bent him double. When he was finally calm, another held out a hand to her to help her to her feet.

"Come." One led the way, the other two flanked her. She now had no idea where she was being led. She only hoped that they would leave a trail sufficient for one of the Hatherley keepers to track them down. But the men were moving quite quietly and easily through the forest. It was only she who made any noise, she noticed.

The walk seemed endless, but cannot have lasted more than thirty minutes. Finally, the little group reached a clearing where a narrow drift of smoke signalled a small fire on which sat a dented kettle. There was a makeshift shelter of a couple of tarpaulins tied between several trees. Beneath it sat a woman nursing a baby, a toddler fiddling with a pile of buttons, and Amelia, looking bedraggled, grubby, and woebegone, tear-trails streaking her muddy cheeks. The little girl clambered to her feet and ran toward her sister.

"Ceci, oh Ceci, I'm so glad to see you." She started sobbing as she reached her sister and threw her arms about Cecilia. "They've been as kind as they can, but they've nothing to eat and the little baby is so hungry, it keeps crying. And I don't understand a word they're saying."

"What did you think you were doing?"

"I don't know. I wasn't thinking at all, and I'll never do it again. I was so frightened, and I didn't know what they were going to do with me."

"I'm here now, and everyone at Hatherley is out looking for you, so it is only a matter of time before we are found and we can thank these people properly."

"That's just it—I don't think we will be found. We've moved already from where they found me last night. I believe they are fugitives, Ceci, and they don't want anyone to know of us. They made me walk for ages this morning."

"Perhaps now I'm here, they will leave us and just disappear. Or take us somewhere closer to a road and leave us far from their camp. I confess, Amelia, I have no idea where we are or how to get back to Hatherley. But there is such an army on the hunt for you that I am sure that we'll be home by nightfall."

But Cecilia's confidence was dented as time passed and the forest seemed as silent and looming as ever, apart from the low murmur of the men playing at cards and occasional peeps from the baby. The toddler was silent, either asleep in a small bundle of tattered blanket or playing incessantly with its collection of buttons. There seemed to be no food in the camp. After a little while, the woman went over to the small fire and slopped some hot liquid from the kettle into a battered enamel cup. She walked over to Ceci and offered it silently. Her hair was matted, her face was beginning to wrinkle like a walnut, and her hands were bony and worn.

Cecilia took the cup and sipped at it gingerly. Then she offered some of the weakened, stewed tea to Amelia, who also sipped on it, grateful for any warmth and wet. So they sat on, huddled together against the dripping rain, the damp slowly rising to engulf their clothes and limbs, their ears straining for the sound of any approaching movement.

Much later, when the sky was darkening, Cecilia finally heard what she had been waiting for. A dog barked and was answered by another baying howl. The travellers did not stir, even when the sounds of men and hounds crashing through the undergrowth were nearing the dell where they had settled. Cecilia stood up and went toward the center of the dell, Amelia following tentatively behind. A compact missile hurtled toward them, throwing itself about Cecilia.

"We've found you at last!" exclaimed Reggie. "Ormiston sent for Lazenby's hounds—it was a capital idea, and they picked up your scent easy as can be, even through the rain. Who're those men? What are they doing here?"

The men were now standing, heatedly but incomprehensibly arguing. The woman had also risen and placed her hand on the toddler's shoulder.

"They found me last night. I was lost and I was crying and the big one found me and then they made me walk for miles and I thought I should be lost forever until Ceci came, and then it was just damp and horrible."

"You are the stupidest girl to put us all to so much trouble."

"I'm not stupid. And I didn't mean to put anyone to any trouble."

Just then, Lazenby, Ormiston, and Buchan, narrowly followed by two exhausted handlers half-dragged by a pair of mastiffs, arrived in the clearing to find the Marchmonts reunited and Amelia clearly in fine fettle.

No one subsequently remembered the exact sequence of events which followed. The toddler started moving at about the same time as one of the dogs shook off its handler. The woman screamed. Cecilia shoved Reggie and Amelia behind her and then made to grab at the dog's leash. She caught it and tried to halt it, but the animal was so strong that it seemed to wrench her arms from their sockets. She was clinging on when she was tugged over onto her front and dragged by the dog along the hummocky ground as it still hurtled toward the child. It was going at full pelt for nearly thirty yards across the clearing, hauling Cecilia over roots and brambles, rocks and bracken, until it slowed and came to a bewildered halt, only to be pounced on by two of the woodsmen and its handler.

Ormiston hurtled toward his wife, whose grip had finally loosened from the dog's leash with her grip on consciousness. He turned her over on her back and she came to. Her pelisse was ripped and coated with mud, and her nose and chin and right cheek were badly grazed, the blood already starting to well. Her eyes were wide and staring with shock and she began to shiver. A sickening apprehension flooded through the viscount. He strove to suppress the panic welling within him. Softly, he spoke to her.

"Do you think you can sit up, my dear?"

He helped her lever herself up and cradled her in his arms. Amelia and Reggie were looking on with utter terror. Buchan came forward.

"Your sister will be right as rain in a moment. Come with me. It's not far to the road and we've a carriage there. Come along now. Ormiston will help your sister, but we'll all find it much easier if we start the procession. Earl Lazenby, would you be so kind as to offer some reward to those poor souls? We will settle our accounts tomorrow if that is convenient, but I fancy we must get these wanderers back to Hatherley with all speed."

He shepherded the terrified children back to the carriage. Lazenby did go up to the wood-dwellers and gave them the few guineas he had on his person before going toward Ormiston.

"Lud, I'm sorry about the dog. Need any help getting m'lady back to the carriage?"

"I think we'll manage. Go on ahead and get blankets ready for her. Don't worry about the dog. It was an accident."

Lazenby went off. Ormiston released the breath he had been holding and leant his forehead against Cecilia's. "Do you feel able to stand?"

She nodded, still not mistress of her voice. She watched as Ormiston rose up and held out his hands to her. She took them and staggered to her feet. Her eyes registered a flash of pain and her knees nearly gave way.

"What is it?" Ormiston swept her into his arms and held her.

"I don't know. Nothing, I expect. You can put me down."

"No." He started walking, but before he left the clearing, he turned back and called out, "Thank you for sheltering my wife and her sister. If you need food or shelter or work, come to Hatherley. Ask for Ormiston."

The men shook their heads and waved them away. The

woman was still bent over her children. The viscount moved away and with sure steps headed for the carriage. Cecilia seemed to faint in his arms, her body lax and suddenly heavier, her head lolling against his shoulder. It took nearly half an hour to get back to the road. He could hear Buchan encouraging the children forward and Lazenby with his great dogs moving ahead of him, but all he was conscious of was the burning in his arms and shoulders and his great fear for Cecilia. The short seconds of watching her body being pounded against the ground kept repeating over and over in his mind's eye, lasting longer and longer and moving more and more slowly as every thump and pummelling and jolt registered in his memory. His arms tightened about her, even when he paused to rest.

Finally, he saw the welcome sight of lanterns in the dusk, heard the clink of the harness, and saw the dim outline of John Coachman. The tiger was waiting with a blanket ready, and once Cecilia had been wrapped in it, between them, Ormiston and Buchan maneuvered her into the coach where Reggie and Amelia already sat, cowed and silent. Lazenby had already mounted his horse and was waiting to make his farewells.

Ormiston said softly to Buchan, "Will you ride my horse back? I must stay with Cecilia and the children. Do the pretty with Lazenby. We owe him a great debt, for without his dogs, we'd never have found the girls. The rest was a misadventure—tell him he mustn't blame himself or the handler."

"You're more forgiving than I would be, I must say." Buchan was gruff and his expression was fierce as he took in Cecilia's sorry state. "Be off with you. Do you want me to ride directly for the doctor?"

"Yes. Please. I hadn't thought of it, but you're quite right."

Ormiston settled himself in the carriage, holding Cecilia close and Buchan pushed the door to and gave the order to the driver. The journey home seemed endless to all three conscious inhabitants. None of them could bear to break the silence, but Reggie cuddled his sister close as silent tears streamed down her cheeks.

Lavauden was waiting on the great steps as the coach rolled toward the house. She whisked the children away, murmuring comfortably about hot baths and warmed beds and soup, as Ormiston tried to rouse Cecilia. He carried her into the house and up the stairs to her room. A great tub of hot water was being filled as Dorcas came forward to help him remove the ragged, sodden clothes. She was shivering as he eased her into the water. Dorcas washed her hair, then Ormiston took a soft cloth and gently started to clean her face and hands of the dirt that had embedded itself in her skin. She winced and the fog that had descended over her seemed to lift slightly. The room was very quiet. Dorcas was combing her hair and dabbing at it with a towel; Ormiston was dipping the cloth into the water, then dabbing it against the grazes and bruises. The fire crackled and spat in the grate.

The first spasm came. Cecilia cried out in shock as a cramp twisted in her belly and she curved inwards, whimpering with pain. Dorcas shot up, knocking over her stool, dropping the comb and towel.

"Dorcas, is the bed warmed?"

"Yes, sir."

"Then you may go. Mr. Buchan has sent for the doctor. I will stay with Lady Cecilia."

"Yes, sir." She curtseyed and went slowly. "Are you sure you want no help, sir?"

"No, girl, just send up the doctor as soon as he arrives."

She left, and Ormiston helped Cecilia out of the bath and wrapped her in a warm towel. He held her close.

"You know what this may mean?"

"I believe I do," she whispered. He kissed her on her left temple, on one of the few patches of undamaged skin on her face.

"You are a very brave woman. Let's get you to the bed."

Once under the sheets, she curled up into a small ball.

Ormiston removed his jacket and boots. He lay down on his side, his head propped up by one hand, the other hand idly stroking her hair.

"Tell me if you need anything."

"Nothing. You needn't stay with me. Dacre will want to see you."

"My place is here. Does it hurt?"

"A dull ache."

She dropped off and the evening darkened into night. She was roused by another fit of agonizing cramps. Ormiston rubbed at her lower back, desperately hoping the doctor would arrive before long. But it was another hour before he arrived, and in that space, Cecilia was subjected to more frequent pains.

Finally there was a knock at the door, and the doctor was ushered in. He pulled back the covers and asked Cecilia to attempt to stand. She did manage it, but as she was standing, the blood began trickling down her inner thighs, warm, sticky, and final.

Thirteen

For three nights and four days, Cecilia hovered in a feverish state which had the doctor in perpetual, agitated attendance. On the third day, he called in Letty Fourstep, the local midwife. She sent him off, along with a list of herbs and spices to collect and brew together, which confounded all but the cook, Mrs. Caterham. Letty applied poultices, brewed strange teas, and massaged Cecilia's stomach for what seemed hours to Dorcas, who was constantly on the run for hot water and fresh rags to rinse down her ladyship. There was a great deal of blood—it frightened Dorcas, but Letty Fourstep seemed calm enough. The maid was unable to conceal her fear from Ormiston, however, who had been banished by Letty Fourstep along with the doctor. Unable to contain himself any further, just before luncheon he barged in and demanded that the wise woman tell him what was happening to his wife.

"Losing a baby at this stage is nigh as bad as giving birth. Besides, there's the chill she caught waltzing around the woods half soaked. The fever makes things seem much worse, but I reckon she'll pull around. She's bleeding steady now, and should do for maybe ten, maybe fourteen days. I'll stay on till the fever breaks. Hopefully tomorrow, otherwise the day after. I've seen worse cases."

Ormiston nodded. Letty eyed him with speculation. "She's far gone for a bride of less than a month."

"Yes. It's why we married so swiftly, even though her father had just died."

"She might not be able to have children after this. It'll depend on what's settled in her. Some women have a time like this and then no more babies."

"I don't care. I'd rather have her well and barren than lying like this. Get her better, Mistress Fourstep. You'll be well rewarded."

"I always heard you were a blunt lad. If you love her, go and speak to her. It'll help. Tell her your heart. I must see Mrs. Caterham for some broth. I'll be a while. Sit with her and talk. You won't be interrupted."

At first, Ormiston felt awkward speaking to the restless, insensate girl. He started talking about Amelia and Reggie. "They're utterly cast-down. Amelia thinks everything is all her fault, so you must get better. They need you, Cecilia—they have no one left other than you." He hesitated. "And so do I need you. I need you more than I can say, more than I thought it possible ever to need anyone. I love you, Cecilia. You may not believe me, because I have seemed fickle and foolish. I have been callow and cynical, but now that I am in danger of losing you, I realize what love is. I only pray it is not too late. When I saw you reaching for the mastiff, I was frozen with horror, and by the time I reached you, it was too late—you were hurt and suffering. Now I can only think how I must have made you hurt and suffer before, when you were only a child. All I seem to have done is bring you pain."

He reached for her hand and traced its outline against the linen sheets. Her skin was translucent, the veins at her wrist prominent. He stroked her skin and along her forearm. She was frowning in her stupor, as though trying to concentrate hard on a distant sound. He spoke again.

"Perhaps I will be able to make reparation for all that you have endured. Cecilia, I'm going to hold you to our bargain even though the reason for it is now gone. The baby was only an excuse for me. It is you I want, you I will always love. I've never been so helpless before, but Letty Fourstep seems to think that there is some succor for us both if I speak to you.

"How can I conceal it from you? Since we were married here at Hatherley, I have never been happier. You have been mine, you have been the most generous and passionate of wives, and I thought all would be right, that I would never have to profess my own passion for you. You have eased relations between me and my father, you have helped me to love my own home, and with every passing day, I have felt more strongly for you. It seemed inconceivable to me that you would choose to leave me at the end of our twelvemonth together. But now, you might slip away from me, and it would be too late, you would never know the truth.

"I want to show you how much I love you. I do not know the right way. Should I offer you your freedom as soon as you are well again? Or should I cling on and demand that you fulfill our agreement? What can demonstrate my true feelings for you best? What honors my love for you?

"I felt such exultation when you told me about the baby. I saw you faint when the will was read, and I knew then, as clearly as if you had told me. When you explained, I wanted to shout and crow and proclaim the news to the whole world, because you must be mine."

He leaned forward and smoothed the damp hair away from her cheek and stroked the flushed skin. "Come back to me, Cecilia. Come back and let me love you as you deserve. Come back and put Amelia out of her misery. You've been at Hatherley only a month, and you have become its heart. Come back and restore joy to us all." He kissed her brow and stood up. He went to the window and stood there, looking out over the gardens, seeing nothing, his head aching with the effort of suppressing tears.

Letty Fourstep returned and found Ormiston back at his wife's bedside, wiping the sweat that beaded her forehead and trickled into her hair.

"Go and rest, man. I'll call you back in a few hours' time. You look as though you haven't slept in days. There are two children hanging around outside. You might reassure them.

They wouldn't believe me when I said her ladyship would mend."

The Marchmont children were leaning on a side table in the hall, their eyes huge with apprehension.

"She's going to die, isn't she?" said Reggie in a small voice. Ormiston held out his arms to the children. They ran into his embrace.

"No. Mistress Fourstep says she will pull through. She is still unwell, very unwell, but it seems she is no longer in mortal danger. The fever should break tonight."

Lavauden rushed up and tried to relieve Ormiston of the children. He shook his head wearily and begged that he might stay with them. They distracted him from the vision which remained embedded in his mind's eye of his wife either writhing or immobile in their shared bed. He could not escape the belief that it was he who had brought her to this pass. It had been he who had seduced her, without any care or conscience. She might have appeared worldly to begin with, but he had known by the time she touched him in the *cabinet des merveilles* that she was not what she appeared.

He escorted the children to their nursery and remained with them while they were served with their lunch. The door opened and to the general astonishment, Dacre came in.

"Here you are! What's the latest with Cecilia? I had Lazenby here this morning making his inquiries."

"Mistress Fourstep is with her now. She says I may return to Cecilia later. She is quite optimistic."

"I am astonished that a chill should have had so deleterious an effect on her. Warburton doesn't usually call her in for a fever."

Ormiston avoided his father's gaze. Everything between Cecilia and himself had been so fragile that they had not yet discussed the pregnancy. It had been one of those subjects from which both tacitly shied away in any conversation. He had made playful reference to the changes that the condition had wrought upon her body—her magnificent curves and enriched bosom.

But they had not, beyond the brief mention he had made of the child when presenting to her the notion of remaining with him for a twelvemonth, discussed the fraught question of when and how her condition should be made public.

A suspicion formed in the marquis's mind, but he dropped the subject and turned instead to the simpler task of amusing the children. He brought out a pack of cards and played a series of very simple games with them, astonished to discover that Marchmont had studiously avoided teaching his children even the rudiments of which suit was which. Then, as Amelia was enjoying the opportunity of routing her elder brother in a round of Pelmanism, he flushed guiltily at the memory of the drunken wager with his old friend. Perhaps that unfortunate night's play had deterred Marchmont from introducing his offspring to the delights of cardplay. Now here he was, guiding the children toward the path of folly and ruination. But the children were enjoying themselves so much that he could not bring himself to call a halt to their pleasure.

Just after five, Letty Fourstep called Ormiston back to the sick room. Cecilia's state was unchanged. Beneath a sheet, her body was still twisting, her head tossing to discover a cool place on the pillow.

"Do you want to stay with her, or do you wish to leave her with me?"

"I will stay with her."

"That will make things easier. That Dorcas is a sensible girl, but your wife needs to hear the voice of someone she knows well. You must talk to her, peaceably and calmly. Nothing rough or upsetting. Tell her about Hatherley, how it looks in the winter, what you love most, what you wish her to see and do here."

It did not seem possible or sensible to correct Mrs. Fourstep's misapprehension about his relationship with Cecilia. At least he would be with her, whatever happened. It had been far worse to be kept away from her, only able to guess the worst of what was happening to her.

"Do you wish to rest a little? There is food downstairs, or at least tea or ale to sustain you. I will stay with her as long as you permit it."

"I will go downstairs for a little. If you've a mind to, you could watch with me through the night. The fever is easing, but it isn't broken yet. It will be hard."

"If it is hard, at least let me make it a little easier on you, Mrs. Fourstep."

The woman eyed him shrewdly for a few seconds, then nodded her head, as if to indicate that he would do, before stepping out.

She had not exaggerated. The night seemed an endless round of changing linens and nursing their restless patient. Cecilia's temperature and agitation seemed to increase until her sweat drenched the sheets. Letty Fourstep's serviceable gray gown ended up splashed with water as she tried to cool the girl down, while Ormiston dabbed—ineffectually, he felt—at her brow and tried to sustain his low-voiced narrative of the pleasures of Hatherley, his hopes for the future of the estate, his expectations of the role she would fill. Every now and then, Letty handed him a cup of an herbal brew which he tried to trickle into Cecilia's mouth without slopping it all over the sheets and pillows. From time to time, the midwife went around the room, exchanging wax stumps for fresh candles, pausing to cool herself down.

Lavauden came in at one point and sent Mrs. Fourstep to lie down on the chaise longue in the dressing room. She did try to persuade Ormiston to rest, but he could not bear to leave Cecilia. He did not say as much to the Frenchwoman who had known and loved Cecilia longer than he had, but he was not certain she would live and he knew that he must be with her if she should reach the point of death. Ormiston insisted that Lavauden go and tend to the children, but she looked at him in astonishment and protested that it was past midnight, that Reggie and Amelia had been asleep these five hours and she wished to keep watch with him.

While Mrs. Fourstep was dozing, Cecilia's eyes snapped open and she spoke quite lucidly for the first time in days. Lavauden was out of the room, fetching fresh water.

"Amelia! Is Amelia quite well? She hasn't caught a chill. No, Lavauden would have stopped all that. I tried to keep her dry."

"Amelia is right as rain. It is you who have given us a fright." Ormiston's voice quivered slightly with suppressed excitement and fear.

"I've lost the baby, haven't I? I'm sorry. Perhaps you won't mind terribly. You won't have us hanging around your neck after all." Exhausted, she fell asleep, her temperature sinking by stages.

Mrs. Fourstep rose just before dawn and examined her unconscious patient.

"You've done the job, my lad. Between you and that Frenchwoman, you've brought her down and she'll do now. I'll stay until she wakes, but after that, she'll be on the mend."

Cecilia slept for a further eight hours, not waking until early afternoon. Her rousing was not dramatic. She simply opened her eyes and found a strange woman with gray eyes and straw-colored hair sitting by her bed with a piece of tatting in her hands. She looked around the room for some moments, then cleared her throat and asked quietly who the woman was. The matter-of-fact response did little to enlighten her. She thought back to the events in the wood and flashes of memory came back to her. She reached a hand up to touch her face. The skin of her cheek and chin and temple were rough with scabs.

"May I have a mirror?"

Mrs. Fourstep rose and fetched a hand-mirror from the dressing table.

"It's not too bad. We've been putting my elderflower cream on it, but you've been sweating that off quicker than we can layer it on. Now you're quiet and cool, those will mend easy enough. There won't be a mark in a week. You won't be up before then, in any case. I should think you feel as weak as a kitten."

"I do. The baby is lost, isn't it?"

"Yes."

Cecilia turned away from Letty Fourstep onto her side, curled up, and silently, unstoppably, cried for the small life that had flowered in her and was now gone. The midwife came and sat on the bed and pressed a handkerchief into her hand.

"You're young and you're strong. You've a fine man there, and if you sort out the troubles between you, there's every chance of having a houseful of fine children."

"Has Ormiston been here?" Cecilia turned back to look at the woman.

"Ay. Watching over you until he wore himself out. He wouldn't leave your side. That Frenchwoman finally prized him away at seven this morning. I'll just summon Dorcas and she'll fetch him if you've a mind to see him."

"I don't know. How was he? Was he very angry?"

"Whyever should he be angry? He was beside himself with worry, which is more than you can say for most husbands."

"You said we had troubles between us. How can you know that?"

"It doesn't take an Oxford professor to tell you're not at ease with him nor he with you. It's more than newlyweds getting used to each other, too, though that's part of it."

"You see too much, Mrs. Fourstep."

"I may see a great deal, but I keep it to myself. As we'll keep this baby to ourselves. Doctor Warburton knows, obviously, but it's more than his job is worth to tell. Otherwise, it's just you and his lordship that knows. Dorcas has probably guessed, but I'll have a word with her. She doesn't seem the type of girl to blab below stairs."

"Do you think that's best?"

"I do. You make a fresh start with that young man. In your heat, you have said things and he has said things that have made a great deal clear to me. It doesn't matter a hoot to me what has passed between the two of you. Still, it'll be easier for the pair of you if it don't get abroad. You've a chance to make something of your marriage. Don't throw it away out of false pride."

Mrs. Fourstep went to call Dorcas. Within minutes, a dishevelled Ormiston was by Cecilia's bedside. Once there, he was hesitant. Her last words to him rang still in his wounded ears.

"It gives me great pleasure to see you, my lady."

"You stayed with me."

"I did."

"I thank you for it. How are Reggie and Amelia?"

"Eager to see you. Are you feeling strong enough to see them?"

"Oh, yes, unless Mrs. Fourstep thinks I might frighten them still."

"You look less worn than his lordship there. I should let them in, they'll only fret themselves more if they don't see you."

Ormiston went to find his brother- and sister-in-law and so all private conversation between himself and Cecilia was ended for that day. Once she had seen Reggie and Amelia, Mrs. Fourstep pronounced it time for her ladyship to rest again.

The next day, Cecilia was able to walk a few paces within her room. Mrs. Fourstep returned home and the nursing was now principally left to Dorcas and Lavauden. Her strength gradually returned on a diet of fortified soups and frequent doses of Mrs. Fourstep's particular tisane. Ormiston, Dacre, and the children came to spend time with the invalid, but she was never left alone with her husband. The prospect of any intimate discussion was distressing, so she did not dwell upon it. Although increasingly impatient with being confined to her room, she did not wish to talk to Ormiston about the future. The dim memory of what she had said when the fever had broken troubled her a little. She could not recall her exact words, but she was sure that she had absolved him from their bargain in some way. Still, now that she was recovering, now that she could remember the weeks since their wedding and reflect on them, she found that she did not want to leave Hatherley or her husband.

It was nearly three weeks after Amelia's flight from Hatherley before Ormiston gingerly gathered up his wife and carried her downstairs. He seated her on a wicker lounger in the garden. After the rains of June, the lawn, the trees, the flowerbeds were lush and luxuriant. The temperature shot up and parasols were absolutely necessary to ward off a scorching sun.

Shaded by the spreading branches of a great horse chestnut in full leaf, Cecilia sat and watched as her family played at bat and ball on the lawn. From time to time, someone would come and flop into a chair beside her and take a draught of lemonade or ginger beer from the two great jugs on the table near her. She dozed and woke, then went for a gentle walk around the lawn, her hand tucked in the crook of Ormiston's arm.

"You are looking ethereal. The color is not yet back in your cheeks and you look as though you might flit off to some enchanted bower."

"You are fanciful. I am feeling much better. Mrs. Fourstep says I may expect a swift progress."

"Is there any pain still?"

"None. Even the bruising has faded. What happened to the family in the woods?"

"Buchan went back and sought them out. The people are from Yorkshire. They don't wish to go back. I have found them a temporary home in a cottage and they have enough to live on while they make up their minds what they wish to do. I believe they were turned off their land.

They are two brothers and an uncle, as well as the woman and children. They seem to be countrymen, not town dwellers. We can find work enough or land for them here if they wish it."

"Why were they hiding?"

"They had been poaching, and then they heard that the militia was seeking seditionists and pamphleteers. They knew enough to realize that being strangers marks you out in any place, so they retreated to the woods. They had been living there since the spring, but you could see how makeshift it was. But you are turning the subject from yourself."

"There is nothing to say on that subject."

"Cecilia, there is a great deal to say. We must decide on the pattern of our lives. Things have changed."

Reggie yelled with delight as he caught a ball off Dacre's bat, and the viscount turned to watch. He saw the elegant figure of Lazenby emerge onto the terrace steps and wander toward the Marchmonts.

"Damn! I had hoped to speak with you longer, but now we must do the pretty for our guest. Do you feel up to it?"

"Yes, I do." Cecilia's relief was almost tangible. Ormiston sighed and returned her to her seat, by which time Lazenby was upon them, bowing to Cecilia, bending over her hand to press a kiss to it and beg most penitently for forgiveness for his hound.

"It was only following its instincts. I hope you have not harmed it. I had not known that dogs could be bred so huge and so powerful."

"I have not harmed the dog, but the handler has been dismissed. His attention slipped and with it the animal. I am only glad that there has been no lasting ill effect. You are quite recovered, are you not?"

"I am not yet ready for a full night of dancing, but I believe I could manage a gentle minuet."

Ormiston, observing that Lazenby and his wife were

falling into somewhat frivolous conversation, excused himself and returned to the game with his father.

"Does his lordship disapprove of dancing?"

"By no means. I have found him an able partner."

"He seems very dour. I scarcely know him, although we have been neighbors since we were both in short coats. He is very serious about his art."

"And his fencing. He and Buchan and Reggie have complicated discussions about the merits of the Venetian and the Neapolitan schools, which lose the rest of us."

"He does not seem to laugh a great deal. Of course, he has been most concerned for your health, but he has always been thought of as staid. Odd, with a father like Dacre."

"I do not believe that it is quite right to discuss my husband with you, Earl Lazenby."

"Come now, I was Alexander to you before you became Lady Ormiston. Surely we are on terms. Don't come the dowager with me, Miss Cecilia."

"Well, I won't. But I must say, I wonder how you can judge Ormiston to be staid when you also say you scarcely know him. Particularly since he has spent the better part of five years abroad."

"Word seeps back, y'know, even when you are far from home and think yourself free from all of Society's strictures and inspections. Dacre's been baffled by the boy. Never games, you know. No horses, no cards, no dice, no wagers, no boxing. Just the fencing and the painting. Rum."

" 'Rum' you may call it, 'reassuring' is how any wife would find it. How vile, how miserable to find yourself rolled up because your fool of a husband has wagered the family silver on the turn of a card."

Cecilia's vehemence astonished Lazenby. It was clearly just as well that Ormiston and Miss Marchmont had found one another—they must be the only two members of the Ton who had ever felt so fiercely about gaming and its evils. Everyone else Lazenby knew was all too happy to drop hundreds or thousands in their search for some relief from the boredom of balls and soirees. He could not help making a sly bet with himself that he'd seduce one or other of the Ormistons either to a gaming table or into making a wager within a two-month. It would be amusing to tempt the righteous pair into the way of a little speculation.

Fourteen

A wise general sizes up the enemy thoroughly before planning his campaign. Lazenby felt that he knew both his quarries well enough, but it never hurt to study one's prey closely. He resumed his regular visits to Hatherley, noting carefully that Ormiston and his lady seemed subdued and not entirely at ease with one another. He continued to make a great favorite out of Amelia, who delighted in his manner. He knew the opposite sex well enough to understand that there is nothing so charming to a young girl than to be treated as a mature and attractive woman.

Occasionally, Cecilia's rather sharp scrutiny did cause the earl a little unease, but on the whole, he was well satisfied as July passed into August. He gave himself until the end of August to tempt his targets to the gambling tables.

At first, he tried a direct approach, inviting the viscount and his lady to play at faro or whist. When he was soundly brushed off, he decided that Cecilia, being of the weaker sex, would be the more susceptible. The object of his wager was not to bet against her directly, but to lead her into a situation where she must gamble or appear ill-mannered and foolish. If he had still been accepted at the houses of the local gentry, all would have been child's play, but he was perceived to be dangerous and unacceptable to those ladies who fixed with one another on who was to be invited to a rout and who was most assuredly unwelcome. Lazenby had not minded the ostracism until now, but he began to think it might be worth attempting social rehabilitation. Apart from anything else, it was amusing to be greeted as though one were a cat that had learnt the trick of opening the canary's cage.

Truth to tell, he was bored. He could not afford to go to London, he did not wish to jeopardize his estate any further by the deep play that he would inevitably encounter there, and he was a little weary of the Cheltenham tragedies that had been enacted as a result of his more libertine propensities. He did not really intend to toy with the family of one of his strongest supporters, but the temptation to cause mischief began to overwhelm his scruples. He craved amusement and spice. At the very least, he hoped to jolt the viscount and viscountess from the stupor of respectability that was descending on Hatherley with their prolonged residence, so heavily centered on the interests and activities of the Marchmont children.

The earl found his opening with Mrs. Selby. Her husband was a solid man with few pretensions. He was one of Lazenby's hunting cronies. Out in the field, a firm seat and good hands were more important than the color of one's money, and Selby, who had earned a fortune in some dubious trade during the late wars, was a very good rider. So good, there were rumors that he had started life as a groom. Mrs. Selby was the daughter of a doctor, but she had pretensions, and made the most of her husband's fortune by adorning herself in the latest fashions, altering the decor of their house at a whim and throwing great parties to which everyone grudgingly came because she did serve excellent food and decent liquor. She was much too old to be one of Lazenby's flirts, but he had always buttered her up, at first to please old Selby, who had loaned him money and never asked for it back, and then because she remained one of the few local hostesses who would admit him to her house.

Mrs. Selby was herself a dashing rider. Despite bearing two children, her spare figure showed to advantage in a riding habit. She had a great laugh and was one of the few women who treated Cecilia with less than reverence. Her days of kowtowing to the nobs were done, she stated firmly. If Lady Ormiston chose to attend a do at the Selbys, all well and good, but it should make no difference to the fun that would be had if she did not so choose.

It was only after Cecilia had recovered fully from her illness that she developed a friendship of any sort with Mrs. Selby, and that was fostered by their mutual enjoyment of horseflesh. Dacre ensured that his daughter-in-law was mounted on a spirited gelding. After a week of schooling him to her ways, she took to the bridle paths around Hatherley and it was on a beautiful afternoon that she met Mrs. Selby properly. She had been riding through woodland with her groom when they came upon a rise of common land with a track that begged a rider to put his horse to the gallop. Eager to try out Phoebus's paces, Cecilia warned her groom that she was about to go flat-out, dug her heels into the chestnut's flank, and urged him on until the wind had plastered her veil against her face and both she and the beast were panting with exertion. It felt wonderful.

As Phoebus slowed down, she heard another rider coming toward her at a considerable rate. She slowed her mount, edged him to the side of the path, and waited. There appeared Mrs. Selby, who, on seeing her, hauled in her horse and came to chat.

"A pleasure to see you out and about. How tiresome to be ill so soon after your wedding. You've a fine fellow there. One of Dacre's?"

They talked of horseflesh and the pleasures of a lively mount and Cecilia felt her ever-present reservations about her own life melting away in this simple, straightforward discussion. She invited Mrs. Selby to call soon, laughing when she saw that lady's eyebrows rise up.

"Are you sure? I'm not quite the thing in these parts. Too loud, whiff of trade and all that. You'll make the tabbies sit up and yowl if you take up with me, my girl."

"What is the use of being a viscountess if one can't choose

one's friends? What nonsense. Of course you must come up to Hatherley and we may talk of sensible things instead of embroidering cassocks for the parish church."

A couple of days later, Daphne Selby did call on the viscountess and did find herself taken up. Her forthright manner and her age, close to that of Lady Ketley's, were great advantages. So many of the local ladies who came to call giggled and skirted around topics like nervy greyhounds, bounding forward, then recoiling and sniffing fastidiously if they felt a subject was veering toward indelicacy. Mrs. Selby arrived in Cecilia's drawing room sporting an exuberant bonnet and a quizzical air which wore off after fifteen minutes had passed and the pair of them had established that they did not wish to discuss the provenance of last week's flower arrangement for the altar and whether Bessie Makepeace was pregnant by her husband the publican or her lover the apothecary. Instead, they spoke of affairs in Europe and whether Britain might actually complete an alliance with her foe and former colony, the upstart United States. Finally, they started speaking of horseflesh and bloodlines, competent farriers and poultices, saddlers and stamina, suitable bits and hunting country.

It was nearly two hours before Mrs. Selby left, and when she did go, she could scarcely credit how swiftly the time had passed. The viscountess was a definite addition to the neighborhood. The marquis had always been a fixture at her parties, but here was a lady of high degree showing every sign of wishing to cultivate her acquaintance. It was a heady prospect for Daphne Selby, all too accustomed to accusations of being a mushroom.

It was not long before Lazenby heard of this unusual friendship. He at once set off for Mrs. Selby's house and spent a fruitful hour there listening to the woman extol the virtues of the viscountess, virtues which most women would not have acknowledged as such.

"She's a thoroughly sensible young woman. She rides

well and she favors a martingale for that gelding, which I can understand. She'll certainly liven us all up."

"I believe so, too. But do you know, Mrs. Selby, she don't play."

"What do you mean? Why, everyone plays, and when she comes here next month, I am sure she will take her turn at faro and anything else we decide to offer."

"She won't, you know. Dead against all games of chance and wagers. Viscount's the same, you know. They're not prosy about it, that's certain, but they don't play and they won't play. Not for anything."

"Lady Cecilia might play for the right stake. If I offered up the next foal from Jasper as a stake, she'd jump at the chance, mark me."

"She won't. She'll offer to pay, and a handsome price, too, but she won't play. I'd wager my last groat on it."

"That's all you have to wager, or so I've heard."

This injudiciously familiar remark infuriated Earl Lazenby. Without delay, he bade farewell to the overdirect Mrs. Selby and rode off, muttering about her tendency to try to cap one's comments and get the upper hand and have the last word in every conversation. But it had been useful to discover that the viscountess had a taste for horseflesh. A taste! A positive passion. Another mark in her favor. She really was most delectable and intriguing. How Ormiston might take this new friendship Lazenby would give a great deal to know. Perhaps, if he stuck close by over the next few days, he would hear whether the viscount approved or not.

It turned out that, according to Dacre, Ormiston was so delighted to see Cecilia revive that her new friend might have been Beelzebub himself, provided Lady Cecilia was in good heart and good health. To Lazenby's astonishment, it was the marquis who was less enthusiastic about the developing friendship.

"She's a good woman, Daphne Selby, but coarse and fast. I wouldn't like to see Cecilia too closely associated with her, although as a viscountess, I suppose she may do as she pleases." He took another swig of port as he made his pronouncement before his son and his neighbor.

Lazenby did not accuse the marquis of hypocrisy: however *laissez-faire* Dacre seemed to be in relation to his young friend, the earl was well aware that any such comment would overstep the bounds of their friendship. But it did surprise him that the marquis should be so precious. Somehow, it added piquancy to the notion of fostering the friendship, which Daphne Selby's blunt comments had nearly quashed.

Inadvertently, Mrs. Selby had reminded Cecilia of an activity she had not indulged in for months. In the course of her riding, she soon identified an isolated paddock at the edge of the Hatherley estate where she might practice once again the art of standing in the saddle or swinging from side to side of her mount. Of course, she was out of practice and her muscles were loose and unready for any advanced maneuvers, but once she had found this secluded and well-shaded spot, protected from any casual observer by trees and hedgerows, it was too tempting not to try a trick or two with Phoebus. She did tumble from the saddle, but it was worth it for the exhilaration it evoked. To attain once again her former standard, she would have to draw on considerable reserves of concentration and strength. It was a challenge that Cecilia could not refuse, a small chance for rebellion, for control over her own environment and behavior. As the summer progressed, so did her skill. Besides, Phoebus was the most responsive and eager horse she had ever had the pleasure to ride. He seemed to enjoy the early mornings of cantering steadily around as much as she did.

This rediscovered recreation was a valuable distraction from the boulder-strewn path of her relationship with her husband. He had not joined her in their marriage bed since her illness. He did not speak of his withdrawal from marital relations, so Cecilia could not bring herself to mention it, either. Yet she knew that he had not willingly left her side during the miscarriage and her fever. It was as though since her recovery, he felt that she needed him no longer. She had a vague memory of his voice—tender, constant, pleading—but she could not recall the substance of his words. She tried to remember if she herself had said anything which might indicate to him a distaste or rejection. Meanwhile, they seemed never to be left alone. It was a strange reversal of that difficult time following the announcement of their betrothal and up to their marriage.

Ormiston did wish to speak with his wife, but found himself continually thwarted. He had felt so easy before her accident in visiting her room. He had allowed Dorcas time to help Cecilia with her clothes and then he had left his father to his port and climbed the stairs with anticipation not only for the physical delights she shared with him, but also for the talk, the opportunity to explore more about the workings of her mind, to discover her view of the day at Hatherley and how life there might be improved for its inhabitants, however humble. She had an awareness of the importance of everyone who contributed to the well-being of the house and its lands and an unerring instinct of how to ensure that well-being. In only a few weeks, through Dorcas and through other conversations, she had made it her business to discover all she could about the servants and the economies of the household. From trying to soothe the cares of the humblest maidservant, to showing concerned for a tearaway brother, to the vexed questions of setting wages and supervising the household accounts, the new viscountess had proved herself more than equal to the position of chatelaine.

Better still, she was able to recount to him her doings in a light and entertaining way, while informing him of the concerns and preoccupations of the people who would one day call him master. It was so tempting to forswear all responsibility for the estates, so tantalizing to consider a return (this time with Cecilia) to Italy, where he could dawdle and paint to his heart's content, without the ever-present demands and decisions of the marquisate. However firmly he told himself it was his duty to learn the ways of his lands and his people, the urge to abdicate still ran strong in him. His relations with his father were still uncomfortable, although undeniably closer than he had imagined possible. Cecilia continued to act as a vital conduit between the two men, still so ill at ease with one another, both so anxious for her well-being and general contentment.

But since the night when she had roused from her fever and spoken so frankly, so openly, assuming that he had no care for her or for their child, even after he had poured out his heart to her, he had felt broken inside. He had tried to broach the impasse between them that afternoon in the garden, when she had finally seemed strong enough to discuss their future, but her relief at the interruption caused by Lazenby had been almost tangible. It made him believe that any conversation between them would lead inevitably to her departure from Hatherley. That he could not countenance, so he avoided her.

Ormiston knew this state of affairs could not persist indefinitely. With every passing day, Cecilia seemed to be gaining in energy and health. She was beginning to look better than ever, her hair glossy, her eyes bright, a spring in her step as she went about her business, her fresh, flowery scent beguiling. It was a torment to be in her presence, so he retreated by taking up painting again. He found himself glancing through the sketches that he had completed at Sawards, and it came to him: he could paint Cecilia from the drawings. She need not sit for him. The task so occupied him that he became more withdrawn than ever.

He did venture out to the local market town to order more paints and paper from a stationers there. As he came out of the shop, he bumped into Miss Bennett and Mrs. Baxter, two ladies of the town who considered themselves arbiters of taste and decorum in the county. He made his bow to them, but before he could slip away to the inn where his horse was quartered, they engaged him in conversation, asking after the viscountess and her dear brother and sister, inquiring whether any summer entertainments were planned at Hatherley, recalling the grand days when the marchioness had arranged picnics, country dances, and boating trips.

"We have not yet fixed on any such diversions. Lady Cecilia is still in mourning for her father, and the children are still settling into their routines."

"I must say," commented Mrs. Baxter, "her mourning does not seem to prevent her from racketing round the countryside with Daphne Selby. Not the most judicious of acquaintances in a young wife."

The viscount stiffened. "Mrs. Selby is a good friend to my father and myself. She was also known to Mr. Marchmont, my wife's late father. It would be injudicious indeed for anyone to question such an acquaintance." He bowed crisply and withdrew before any further comment could be made by either lady. Mrs. Baxter tossed her head and pronounced the viscount top-lofty, while Miss Bennett did her best to soothe her companion's ruffled feathers.

Ormiston rode home seething. He was not sure who angered him more, his wife for her rashness, Mrs. Selby for her reputation, or the biddies from town for their petty malice. Fortunately, the first person he encountered on his return was Reggie, who wheedled him into a bout with the foils, distracting the viscount from his temper. Then at dinner, vexation returned, for Dacre announced that he had accepted on behalf of the viscount and viscountess an invitation to a party at the Selbys' home for the following week.

"Is it wise to be seen too much at the Selbys'? We shall be tarred with the same brush, pronounced spendthrift and careless of our responsibilities, if we mix too much with them."

"An evening in their company is hardly an endorsement of riotous living, and it will be a damn sight more lively than an evening at Mrs. Baxter's, with her tedious daughters and those insipid young men she seems to drag up from London drooping about in search of respectable wives. Daphne Selby knows how to keep her guests up to the mark. It will be amusing and her entertainments are never in the common way. No watered punch and stale cakes for her. It'll be champagne, turtle soup, and fire-eaters, at the very least."

"It has been months since I've been to a lively party." Cecilia rued her words as soon as she uttered them. Her eyes met Ormiston's and he raised his eyebrows, knowing as well as she that the last party she had been to, other than their own recent nuptials, had been the masked ball at the Ferrières' in Paris. Her gaze dropped to her lap. "Still, if you don't like it, we needn't go."

Feeling like an ogre, Ormiston retracted swiftly, pronouncing himself ready for any frolic dreamt up by the vivacious Mrs. Selby. He said nothing to Cecilia about the deepening friendship, but he kept a more careful eye on her daily activities, and soon discovered that she disappeared regularly before breakfast. It had escaped his attention, since he no longer spent his nights with her. Then he went to her room early one morning, having spent a restless night longing for her, finally determined to settle things between them, only to find that she was out and had been since dawn. Dorcas's tone was carefully neutral, but he sensed that she could not understand how the rift between her mistress and himself had opened and deepened so drastically.

"She rides every morning, you say?"

"Yes, my lord. She is generally back in time to change before going down to breakfast."

Like an actress arriving on cue, Cecilia appeared in the doorway. She wore an ancient, grass-stained riding habit and there was mud on her cheek. Her face was flushed and she was breathless with the rush of hurrying up from the stables. She stopped short as she saw Ormiston.

"My lord."

"My lady."

"You have been riding?"

"I go out most mornings. Phoebus needs the exercise."

"Did you fall?"

"A slight tumble. Nothing to concern yourself over."

"You take a groom with you." His tone hovered between statement and query.

Cecilia was trapped. She did not take a groom with her, of course. She would not lie. First of all, it would be beneath her, and second, it would be easily found out if she did. But she should be accompanied, she supposed. She delayed her answer by dropping her gloves and crop on her dressing table, unpinning her hat, and fussing with her hair.

"I stay in Hatherley grounds. I don't see the need for a groom here. If I were travelling further afield, naturally I would ensure I was accompanied." She looked pointedly at the steaming tub of water which awaited her. Ormiston came further into the room.

"I have seen you bathe before. Please, continue." Ormiston settled himself in a chair.

Cecilia rolled her eyes and retreated behind a lacquered Chinese screen with Dorcas from whence various rustlings indicated that she was undressing. She emerged swathed in a towel and lowered herself carefully into the water so that barely a flash of skin was visible. Ormiston shifted uncomfortably. Perhaps pressing the issue now was unwise. He watched silently as Dorcas washed Cecilia's hair, dried it with a towel, and began combing it out. Once the worst tangles had been smoothed out, he rose.

"You may go, Dorcas. I will see to the rest of her ladyship's needs." The maid grinned cheekily as she bobbed and left the room.

"I have a great deal to do this morning, Ormiston. If you wish to speak with me, perhaps we may arrange to meet later in the day."

"I do not know that speaking is my main object." His voice was deep and amused.

"Sir, what can you mean?"

"Oh, Cecilia, perhaps this is what I should have done six

weeks since." He leaned forward from Dorcas's stool and his tongue ran along the length of her collar bone and up the side of her neck. He shifted forward and took her mouth with his. They kissed softly, tenderly, and it was as though all the words they could not speak to one another were distilled in that kiss. All confusion and awkwardness between them dissolved. Cecilia turned in the water and they both stood so that she was twined about him, her soaking body pressed against his, his hands running freely about her waist and hips and back, her fingers laced in the thick darkness of his hair. Finally, the kiss gentled and they each took breath. He released her and picked up her towel, wrapping her in it. Then he picked her up out of the bath and laid her on the bed.

"I am drenched from head to foot, Cecilia."

"You will have to change. Perhaps I might help." She began undoing the buttons of his waistcoat. He captured her hand and raised it above her head.

"First, we must speak." He kissed her. "I wish nothing more than to give you pleasure, to take pleasure from you. But I cannot continue as we have been doing. I must know your intentions. Do you wish to stay at Hatherley or are you planning to return to Sawards and settle there?"

"What of the twelvemonth bargain?"

"I consider, Cecilia, that we are back where we started before I knew of the baby. At that time, my mind was clear. I wished to seal the marriage and attempt to live as man and wife. That is what I still wish. More ardently now, because we have already, however briefly, managed to live in harmony."

"Why did you not say so? I thought you wished to be rid of me. I feared that you only wished to see whether I could produce an heir and then put me aside." She sat up, confused, a little dazed. "Everything between us always seems so havey-cavey. We never seem to be frank with one another. We must try to be honest." She winced and bit her lip. It was not yet time, she felt, to admit that she was busy practicing horseback tricks as she had as a girl of fifteen and sixteen.

"Yes, we must. And the truth is that I wish our marriage to stand, that I wish to be a good husband to you, that I wish that you felt the same as I do." Ormiston did not study to avoid any mention of love, but still, he held back. He lay there, winding a lock of her hair about his finger, evading her gaze. "When you ride, you really must take a groom. You fell today, and it was nothing serious, but what if you were out and fell and were pinned beneath your horse, or your skull were damaged. We both know such things happen. I could not bear it if you were hurt. Not again." He loosed her hair and stood up, the memory of his fears for her vivid, quenching any lust he had felt. He walked briskly to the window so that he need not meet her eyes. He did not want her to know how frightened he had been, how much he cared for her. He wanted her to be vulnerable to him, not to divulge to her his own lack of defense against her charms. All very well to speak of honesty, but he was not yet prepared for it.

Sitting swathed in her towel, Cecilia watched Ormiston's back. Neither of them was prepared to risk everything with the other. It might be a matter of time, or it might be that they never could trust one another, not after the way they had been married in the first place. She could not entirely dispel the suspicion that he was arrogant and self-centered; he could not fully believe that she was no longer an impressionable and unattractive child. There was undeniably lust. He was more beautiful to her eyes now than he had been at eighteen. He had filled out, his features had matured, and his travels had taught him to dress well and bear himself with ease. He was now like a finished gemstone, where at eighteen he had been rough, uncut. The warmth in the pit of her stomach increased as she thought of his hands on her body, of her wish to caress his body. Whatever secrets they each concealed from the other, at least they could enjoy their marriage bed. She slipped from the bed and stood behind him.

"Turn and let me see whether you must change your clothes."

He smiled as he faced her. Water had marked his coat of superfine, his fine trousers, and his sateen waistcoat. She helped him out of his clothes, revelling in the scent of him, the smoothness of his skin, the neatness of his limbs, the contained strength of his arms. She let her towel fall and led him to their bed. For the moment, lust must suffice to bind them together. Surely, love would follow.

Fifteen

Everyone knew that Daphne Selby had planned something extraordinary for her grand party to mark the start of the shooting season. In past years, she had recreated Venice by the side of her ornamental lake and insisted that everyone come dressed for Carnival; she had found Egyptian dancers who had, to the delight of the gentlemen, gyrated about wearing immodest and diaphanous garments; she had presented a Jacobean masque; and she had directed a troupe of whooping natives from some corner of the lost colonies to replay the massacre of a pilgrim village. Her entertainments could not be considered tasteful, but they were widely acknowledged to be most authentically and convincingly carried out.

On arriving at the Selbys' mansion, guests were bidden to join a throng on the terrace. The crush was great, producing a swell of chatter and laughter, the whole gathering taut with anticipation, ready either to congratulate or to disapprove. Cecilia was flanked by Dacre and Ormiston, who protected her from the crowd. They fought their way through to a suitable vantage point, and Dacre then went in search of refreshment. In the press of bodies, it was easy, Ormiston found, to position himself so that Cecilia could lean back against him, providing him with access to certain sensitive curves without anyone observing his caresses. She looked up at him as his knee nudged her legs apart and he was able to make quite clear to her his interesting state. He leaned forward to whisper in her ear.

"Perhaps we should adjourn to a more secluded spot. I am sure we could find an unoccupied bedroom from where we might view this grand spectacle from above, in far greater comfort."

Unfortunately, Lazenby appeared at the viscount's elbow, inhibiting Ormiston's more amorous inclinations. Almost immediately, there was a thundering sound, which Cecilia recognized as hooves on damp turf. In the distance, some eight or nine flickering torches appeared and accelerated as they approached the house, glowing orange and red against the darkness of the night. One after another, the riders swooped toward the house, first one, then the next, planting flaming lances into Lady Selby's turf. Once free of their torches, the riders began cantering steadily in the round until they had created a great circle, forming an instant arena for themselves. They whirled their horses around the ring, whooping and shrieking over the drum of the horses' feet. One after another, they stood in their saddles until all nine were upright as their horses evenly pounded around. The riders began a series of tricks, dropping and collecting handkerchiefs from the ground, riding in tandem and swapping from one horse to another, jumping from one side of their mounts to the other, somersaulting off their mounts and hopping back on as the horses steadily pounded around the circle. As a finale, they created a great pyramid, with four men standing on their saddles, supporting three more men who bore aloft a pair of curvaceous young women in breeches.

With every trick, the audience gasped, cheered, and applauded until the riders disappeared into the dark and the company returned indoors to exclaim over the display as they ate their supper before preparing for dancing and the next installment of Mrs. Selby's entertainment.

The squeeze of people was immense. Dacre was keen to use this occasion to introduce his son to as many of his neighbors as possible. This meant neither was at hand when the dancing started. Lazenby had stuck to Cecilia as feathers stick to felt and begged to lead her onto the floor for a country dance. She refused as prettily as she could, aware that being still in half-mourning, she certainly should not be dancing with anyone other than her husband. Lazenby's persistence put her out of charity with him, but she was careful to couch her denial in general terms. He inspired wariness and it had occurred to her that his appearance on the scene all too often coincided with moments of particular tension between Ormiston and herself.

"So what did you think of the Cossack riders?" enquired Lazenby.

"They were amusing, but nothing so very out of the way, I thought. I have seen such tricks before, although it did not take Cossack riders to perform them."

"How blasé you are, Viscountess! I wish I might ride half so well. I'd have every eligible heiress swooning over me if I could bounce on and off my horse like India rubber."

"I believe it is not so very difficult to learn such tricks. You must practice regularly, of course, and the less weight one carries the better. But I don't believe that heiresses are so susceptible, and certainly, their trustees would be far happier to see some skill which is less flashy but more lucrative."

"Such cynical advice. How do you come to know so much about trick riding, my lady?"

"I know very little, other than what I was told by a groom we had at Sawards. He worked in a circus for a time after finishing his apprenticeship and before settling down on the estate."

"Did he teach you any tricks?"

"He tried, but I was much too clumsy ever to master any of them."

"I cannot believe it, Lady Cecilia."

"Well, you may believe it." Cecilia's eyes flashed with irritation, indicating her clear wish that Lazenby drop the subject. He was intrigued by her discomfort; it was always amusing to bait a friend. Especially when one had in mind a little set-down. He smiled as an idea began to form, the sort of idea which would certainly prove entertaining.

When Ormiston reappeared, Lazenby relinquished his spot at Lady Cecilia's side with good grace and wandered off to inspect what games of chance were already under way. The viscount noted his wife's exasperated expression.

"You seem a touch piqued by our friend Lazenby. Does he pester you?"

" 'Pester' is too strong a word. He seems determined to challenge me where possible, as if he is wishing to put me to some test or trial." Cecilia glanced provocatively at her husband. "If we lived in medieval times, I might believe he is sent by you to test my honor and probity."

"If I wished to test what I know to be sound, I would be a fool indeed. But if I were such a fool, I hope I would do the testing myself, rather than through an unreliable proxy." Ormiston raised his wife's hand to kiss it before continuing. "He is playing the same game with us both. He is forever presenting me with a prank or a wager and tries to make me feel foolish or cowardly for failing to take him up on his wilder suggestions. I believe he wishes to use us for his amusement because he is bored. It is petty malice—if we stand firm against it and seem not to let it trouble us, he will soon give way and seek some other amusement."

"You read his character most perceptively. I wish we could be done with him but he is your father's friend and we cannot deny him the house."

"If I had known you felt so strongly, I would have made representations to my father before this. I thought he amused you, but now I find that he irks you, we can easily avoid him and discourage his visits."

Cecilia was about to reveal to Ormiston the tale of Maria Melchett, who had been pursued by Lazenby and then had her reputation shredded for daring to refuse his advances. The next entertainment was announced, however, and the company fell silent. There followed a tumbling act accompanied by fire-eaters and sword swallowers. It seemed that Mrs. Selby had purchased the complete services of a Muscovite circus. Cecilia enjoyed these tumblers far more than the riders, for she gauged that their skill and dexterity was far greater than that of the horsemen, although the impact was inevitably less, being indoors and enacted under the light of numerous chandeliers.

Afterwards, Cecilia wound her way through the mass of people in the ballroom in an effort to find Mrs. Selby and pay her compliments. She found the lady with Lazenby and steeled herself for further teasing, which duly came. Smiling sweetly and intent on disarming the earl by refusing to rise to his barbs, she offered her compliments on the evening's excitements.

"So you preferred the tumblers to the riders, Lady Cecilia?"

"I did. Their entrance was less dramatic, but their contortions and tricks were far more demanding. They were very fine indeed."

"That is not the last of our entertainments. I hope you will enjoy our finale as much, my dear. I am sorry to hear you did not think much of the riders. But perhaps their horseflesh was not to your taste."

"By no means. They had excellent mounts, very well trained. There lay the greatest talent of the troupe."

"You consider it is all in the horse, then, such riding?"

"By no means, Earl Lazenby. Of course you need a good horse, but it is the rider who performs, using the horse as a stage." Invited to speak about horseflesh, Cecilia could not resist and was soon carried away by her enthusiasm. "You cannot have a slug of a pony, nor yet a flashy stallion for this sort of riding, but provided you have a middling piece of cattle, well-trained and able to canter steadily for the duration, it is up to the rider to make what he can of these stunts."

"She sounds most knowledgeable, Mrs. Selby—so much so, I'd hazard that our viscountess has practiced such tricks herself."

"If I had ever done so, it would not do to admit it in public." As soon as Cecilia uttered the words, she wished them unsaid. Lazenby immediately took them as confirmation that she was able to do such tricks, and she knew she would now have no peace from him. So it proved.

"But you might be prepared to admit to it before your friends, surely. A demonstration before a select group could do no harm."

"If there were anything to acknowledge, perhaps there would be no harm in it. But I am an indifferent horsewoman." Cecilia knew well enough this would not serve to quell Lazenby.

"Now there, Lady Cecilia, you are talking nonsense, as you well know." Mrs. Selby robustly prevented her from quashing the subject. "Why, anyone who has seen you on horseback knows full well what a fine seat you have and what delicate hands. We have all of us at one time or another sought to make the most of our skill, and what is any different in this case?"

Disingenuous as Mrs. Selby's comment was, Cecilia strove to defuse it with grace. "Pranks practiced by young girls are one thing, Mrs. Selby, but when we marry, we put such nonsense behind us."

"Which makes us much the poorer for it. I would give anything to see you ride to the best of your ability—why, I'd even offer Jasper's next foal. What do you say to that?"

"A handsome offer, but I could not accept."

"Whyever not? I tell you what—let us find Dacre and see what he has to say on this matter. He'll not turn down a chance at one of Jasper's offspring."

Cecilia felt that to protest any further would be to make too much of this foolish plan. She was confident that Dacre and Ormiston would back her in withstanding any pressure to perform before a group. A foal from Mrs. Selby's prize stallion was certainly tempting bait, but she was well aware that the discretion of neither Mrs. Selby nor Lazenby could be relied on, and any display of her hidden talent was likely to be bruited around the county and even as far as London before a week was out. It was not a risk worth taking. Of course, she could weather any storm, but she could not help feeling that any escapade, however minor, would draw unnecessary attention to Ormiston and herself, not to mention bringing a certain reputation to her brother and sister. She did not wish to seem staid, but neither did she want to be known as an exhibitionist.

Naturally, Mrs. Selby was accosted by guests and by her master of ceremonies requiring further instructions, so her quest for Dacre was mercifully diverted. Cecilia also attempted to melt from Lazenby's side, but he held out his arm and tucked her hand firmly into the crook of his elbow.

"You shall not escape me, Lady Cecilia. We will find your menfolk and lay our plan before them. All will be well."

Naturally, they found Dacre before they found Ormiston. Lazenby began by discussing the possible appearance and quality of Jasper's next crop of foals, setting Dacre to a wistful daydreaming of what he would do with his own collection of hunters and steeplechasers if he could infuse it with the blood of Jasper. Up came Mrs. Selby, who amplified on Jasper's antecedents, which included the Godolphin Arab, or so she claimed.

"We have three mares in foal to Jasper, and I've a mind to keep one of them and sell the other two. Would you be interested?"

"Naturally."

"What if I were to say there was a way you could get one of the foals without spending a penny?" Mrs. Selby dangled her bait carefully.

"Now, how might that be? What can I have that you want so badly, Mrs. Selby?"

Daphne Selby was direct as ever. "Lady Cecilia was telling me how inferior my Cossack riders were. She herself has had training in this stunt riding, and I would give anything—even Jasper's next colt—to see her engage in some vaulting."

"Good heavens! Where did you come by such tricks, puss?"

"You may remember our man Jem Anderton. He ran away when he was a lad and spent some years at Astley's Amphitheatre, where they had a resident band of stunt riders. But he had little success with me, I am afraid. Mrs. Selby has quite the wrong idea about my abilities in this area."

"Has she? Then why have you been bringing Phoebus back into the stables every morning quite exhausted? And where, exactly, do you go on your rides?"

Cecilia looked at her father-in-law in astonishment. "I had no idea when I came to Hatherley that I would be under constant surveillance. How do you come to know of Phoebus and the hours at which I ride?"

"Since your illness, both Ormiston and I are reluctant to allow you too free a rein, my dear. We nearly lost you then, so now we watch over you where we are able."

"It is over two months since my misadventure. I am quite recovered."

"In that case, you can have no objection to setting a date to share with us your groom's secrets." Mrs. Selby was quick to pounce.

Cecilia looked around in vain for her husband, who would surely put a stop to this ridiculous business. But Ormiston was nowhere to be seen.

"Very well. I will ride for you. But, Marquis, there must be no audience other than yourself and Mrs. Selby."

"Now, now," drawled Lazenby, "Mrs. Selby will not agree to the wager without my presence. There must be an uninvolved party to adjudicate. Let us set the date immediately. A twelvenight hence?"

"Very well, Earl Lazenby. If Mrs. Selby is intent on this arrangement, a twelvenight hence. But only if my husband agrees to my making a spectacle of myself."

Just then, the musicians rounded off their latest dance and withdrew for a brief rest. Ormiston escorted his partner back to her escort and rejoined Cecilia, who was still simmering beside her father-in-law. Dacre lost no time in discussing the proposed trial with his son, who glanced over at his wife with a quizzical air.

"If Cecilia is ready for such a display and you are intent on this foal, who am I to gainsay you?"

"If you think it unseemly, you must say. I would not wish to do anything you might consider to be improper." Cecilia's pleading gaze spoke volumes to Ormiston, but he chose to ignore the message she sent him so speakingly.

"A private exposition before a select group of friends is hardly unsuitable. I myself should be intrigued to see you ride. After all, my notice was drawn to you when you rescued your companion's hat while riding in Paris."

Cecilia looked sharply at her husband before turning to Lazenby and Mrs. Selby.

"You have your wish, then. I shall do what I can to earn a foal from you."

Ormiston reminded her that she had agreed to dance with him and removed her from her tormentors' presence before she could be further provoked.

"Why on earth did you agree to this? All you had to do was cut up stiff and the matter would have been dropped and then forgotten."

"You misread our hostess and our neighbor if you think that would have been an end to the matter. This is containable, but allow their baiting any further rein and we shall all become a public spectacle."

"But I am not a performer. Once in a fit of ridiculous exuberance, I lapsed and collected up Louise de la Trémouillère's hat. Otherwise, I have never performed in public and I am hideously out of practice. Since our return to Sawards in February, I have scarcely drilled at all."

"But you have been out every morning for the past six weeks, I believe."

"I am weak and out of condition."

"Frankly, Cecilia, I believe you need do very little to impress. It will be a little like Dr. Johnson's views of dogs walking on their hind legs and women preaching."

"Not done well, but surprising to find done at all. You may be right, but I don't wish to appear a charlatan. It is true—those riders were nothing out of the way, but neither am I at the moment. At one time, I could have done all manner of fine maneuvers."

"At least now you need not conceal your practice from all of us. You may take more time to train. What if we summon Jem Anderton from Sawards? He could be here in three days if we send for him at once."

"You would do that for me?"

"It is scarcely anything at all, and the very least I should offer, having placed you in this position. But do you see my point about Lazenby? Mrs. Selby is a different kettle of fish—you need only hint at withdrawing your friendship and I am sure she will come around. But I am uncertain about Lazenby. I feel he could be an unpleasant enemy, and this is so simple a way to defuse his mischief."

"But what if it gets out?"

"Dacre and I will ensure that it don't. You may rely on us for that at least. And once this is done, we can dismiss him from our circle of intimates."

"Perhaps it will work. But only if Dacre can be brought to see how untrustworthy he is. That I must leave to you."

"Very well. Now, are you ready for more dancing or shall we call the carriage?"

"We must wait for the final round of entertainment from the Muscovites, I think."

The viscount and viscountess withdrew soon after the finale to Mrs. Selby's party, which was a somewhat dismal display of tumbling and dancing by a troupe of rather mangy bears who clearly would have preferred to sleep and were only sustained by the promise of sustenance and excessive prodding from their two ringmasters. There were whispers of a livelier show on offer to gentlemen only in the small hours, but Ormiston was far happier to return home in the carriage with his wife.

True to his word, the viscount summoned Jem Anderton and within three days, the groom arrived at Hatherley. Cecilia trained on a barrel for a couple of hours before climbing into the saddle for up to three hours each day and her strength and suppleness increased markedly. Jem harrumphed over the business of the wager, but after speaking with the local men, he had established that the official stake was worthwhile. Ormiston, meanwhile, put it about that Cecilia was suffering from overexertion after illness, thus excusing her from numerous calls upon her time.

Once he understood that Cecilia's antics had not brought any disgrace on him, Jem Anderton was an eager coach.

"We must work on the movement, for laymen are more impressed the more you move about. They don't realize that the real skill lies in holding a balance on a beast. So plenty of vaulting, some roll-ups, and a couple of *obryvs* if you've the flexibility. Lots of scissoring and an arabesque. Can you still do a shoulder-stand?"

"I can try. I can't hold it for long."

"Don't need to. Short one on either flank and that'll please the gawpers. We'll start with that."

Jem soon worked out a routine that did not demand excessive strength, but did require a great deal of flexibility. He was complimentary about Phoebus and the way Cecilia had built up a rapport with her new mount and this increased her confidence. On the eve of her appointed exhibition, Dacre, Ormiston, and the children demanded to watch her training session. Jem was dubious and laid down strict rules for the viewing. He stood the group, which included Lavauden, of course, at a certain point in the paddock, out of Phoebus's eyeshot, gave them strict instructions not to clap, whistle, or whoop, and indicated to his pupil that it was time to perform.

As Cecilia brought Phoebus into the ring at a trot, the first shock for Ormiston was that his wife wore the uniform of a Zouave, which had clearly been tailor-made, for it fitted to perfection, exposing her long, slim legs, her high waist, her straight back. Her hair was drawn back from her face in a tight plait, every fiber of her being concentrating on controlling her mount. Phoebus bore a strange-looking saddle with additional straps passing under his belly, extremely short stirrups, and a very loose rein hooked round the pommel, which Cecilia did not touch at all. She eased the horse into a canter and when the gelding was moving smoothly around the ring, she rose until she was standing, feet securely in the stirrups. Then she fitted her boots into toe loops on the saddle and stood as Phoebus steadily increased his speed to what seemed to be a full gallop. Ormiston's mouth was dry with fear for what she would do next.

She knelt down, her knees together, then began to vault first to one side of the animal, then the other, very evenly. Then she slipped down and rode a circuit, hanging first from Phoebus's right flank, then from his left. Then she directed her mount to gallop down the middle of the ring, alternately picking up first a ring from his left and then one from his right until she had amassed six rings.

Once again, she stood in the saddle and threw the rings one by one to Jem, who caught them neatly and nodded. She began a series of balances, kneeling, lying back with her legs in the air, performing arabesques like a ballet dancer facing both forward and backward, and finally balancing entirely upside down, her shoulder and head balanced against Phoebus's neck, facing backward as the horse continued in his steady canter. Then she swung back into the saddle and, quite suddenly, dived under the horse's belly, disappearing entirely from the spectators' view for heart-stopping seconds until she reappeared, climbing back into the saddle. With a broad smile, she eased Phoebus down to a trot and then to a walk before bringing him over to Jem. She slipped from the horse's back, patting him fondly and bringing out a handful of carrots to reward him for his steadiness. Then the viscount came over and embraced her, as though to check that she was still in one piece.

"And this is *out of condition*!" exclaimed Ormiston. "I cannot tell how long this took to perform. To me it seemed an eternity, yet now you have finished, it seems too short for such grace. Mrs. Selby will see at once that her Muscovites were small beer."

"Do you think it will quell Lazenby?"

"That I cannot tell. I fear it may inflame him further, but Dacre says he will deal with the earl. Our more immediate problem is likely to be your brother and sister."

It proved as Ormiston indicated. The Marchmont children were hopping with excitement, desperate for lessons from Jem and eager for him to stay forever at Hatherley that he might teach them. Cecilia had to be very firm with them.

"Before we initiate any program of training, we must have approval from both the marquis and Jem. It is no good having the approval of one without the other, and I have no idea whether Jem will be prepared to remain at Hatherley. Certainly, if he will not stay, we may try to find another trainer, but it will take some time."

"You could be our trainer, surely, Ceci."

"No, Reggie, I could not. I am still learning myself and you know how busy I am here. There are always callers to be received and people to be seen on the estate and all sorts of functions. I cannot promise to give you regular instruction."

Lavauden calmed the children and escorted them back to the house, leaving Cecilia with Dacre and Ormiston. The marquis was looking extremely pleased.

"What an asset you are to the family, Lady Cecilia! Why, if we are ever on our uppers, we need only hire you out and our fortunes will be remade in an instant. The Vaulting Viscountess!"

Cecilia rolled her eyes in exasperation. "You are not meant

to be pleased by such nonsense. If that sobriquet ever becomes known in Society, I shall know where to look, and I warn you, I will have my revenge."

They returned to the house, where Cecilia changed into regular clothes before spending a quiet afternoon with as few distractions as possible, followed by an early night. Somehow, she felt that Lazenby would not allow his strange campaign of action against Ormiston and herself to rest after the morrow's display. A more permanent means of distracting him or avoiding him altogether must be found, but in the meantime, she would play her part.

Sixteen

Early in the afternoon, Mrs. Selby arrived with Lazenby in her carriage. They were welcomed by Dacre, given refreshments, and taken to an open-air ring behind the stables where seats had been arranged for them. They commented on the absence of both Cecilia and Ormiston, but the viscount soon joined them.

"I have been trying to encourage Lady Cecilia. She is a little anxious this afternoon. But if you are quite ready?"

The guests nodded and Ormiston signalled to Jem Anderton. Phoebus and Cecilia appeared from around a corner at a full gallop, with Cecilia standing tall and elegant on the saddle, eliciting a gasp of astonishment from Mrs. Selby and a sharp intake of breath as Lazenby took in the viscountess's costume, with her jacket tight about her torso, flaring out at the waist, her long legs accentuated by the billowing Zouave britches she wore, tucked into riding boots which reached her mid-calf. Rider and mount carried out their routine flawlessly. Mrs. Selby could not help applauding, but fortunately her hands were gloved, so the sound was muffled and did not distract Phoebus in any way.

Cecilia vaulted from the saddle at the end of the routine. To Lazenby's astonishment, Ormiston, who he had always thought of as such a dry stick, ran to his wife, who was handing Phoebus's reins to Jem Anderton. The viscount embraced her and kissed her soundly before laughing with delight. Then he turned to look Lazenby full in the eye before leading

Cecilia over to their audience. Mrs. Selby was effusive in her compliments, which Ormiston affably accepted on behalf of his wife, his demeanor more than his words emphasizing that this exhibition was private. Cecilia excused herself so that she might change.

As the party walked back to the house, Lazenby was utterly silent. It was difficult to read this silence, which might have been awe, infatuation, or anger. Since Mrs. Selby was in continuing raptures about the display, wishing she might have the honor of presenting a similar act at her next party, yet understanding that it was quite out of the question for the viscountess to perform publicly, Lazenby's subdued response was not overly conspicuous. Tea had been laid out in one of the larger public rooms this afternoon, for Ormiston had decided that it was time to remind Mrs. Selby of the substance and preeminence of the Dacre family. She might affect an insouciance about rank and riches, but if Cecilia so chose, invitations to Hatherley would always have more cachet than her own.

Cecilia joined the party to general congratulations, which she accepted with wry amusement. She suspected that both her guests had hoped to see her make a fool of herself, but she felt that she had acquitted herself with honor and some aplomb. She sat down, not entirely relaxed, but appearing very cool in a gauzy dress of duck-egg blue trimmed with lace, complete with matching fan.

"Why, you look so very elegant, I can scarcely believe that we saw you not half an hour since in your uniform. It appeared to be specially tailored?"

"Yes, Mrs. Selby, I devised it some years ago. It is comfortable and practical without being unduly immodest."

"If you wore such a costume in London, it would be all the rage inside of a week. Most fetching, is it not, Lazenby?"

"Indeed." His eyes were hot as he recalled the viscountess's figure, at once taut and curvaceous. No wonder Ormiston had so proprietary an air. The thought of what other wonders that athletic body might perform in a more private arena inflamed Lazenby and he shifted uncomfortably in his seat. He wished to go, but he was also reluctant to leave Cecilia's presence. She seemed to become more entrancing by the minute.

Lady Ormiston then asked about the arrival of Jasper's foals, which flustered Mrs. Selby, for she leapt up and declared that she must go, but that she would consult her chief groom and write with full details in the very near future. Naturally, Lazenby had to accompany her. As he left, he took Cecilia's hand and made a deep obeisance.

"I seem to have underestimated you, Viscountess. I shall not make that mistake again."

Cecilia removed her hand from his and watched him as he stood tall before her. To her ears, his simple statement was an open threat. She flicked open her fan and fluttered it gently.

"According to some of our writers, it is the fate of all women to be underestimated. I should hope you do not succumb to such an error, although generally speaking, when men do so, we are quick to use such lapses to our own advantage." She snapped her fan shut.

"I am warned. *À bientôt.*" The customary twinkle had left his eyes. "My best wishes to your brother and sister."

In the carriage, Mrs. Selby was very chatty. "We have been thoroughly trumped, you and I. If we make this public, it is we who will appear foolish. At the same time, we have been shown our place most firmly. Still, I do not hold it against them, though I am a little dismayed about losing my horseflesh. That is the last time I shall challenge the Dacres."

"Not much bottom, Mrs. Selby."

"You do not depend so nearly on their good will as we cits. Selby would be very cross if I lost their favor. You had better look out nonetheless. Dacre will not stand for it if you try to make his son or daughter-in-law ridiculous, you may believe me."

"I do believe you, madam." The earl was close to losing his temper. He concerned himself with flicking dust from his pantaloons, evading Mrs. Selby's eye. It had not escaped his attention that Dacre had been markedly cooler toward him this afternoon.

"All very well to speak softly, but I don't like the look of you, Lazenby. I should be sorry to see you lose your last champion. Tread warily, is my advice."

Lazenby smiled, but his eyes were cold. If he did not answer, perhaps she would be quiet. Eventually, Daphne Selby did fall silent, allowing Lazenby to muse on what he had seen that afternoon. Lady Ormiston had made her own position clear. She might not love her husband, but she was no easy target driven to recklessness by boredom. This, of course, made her more desirable. She was beginning to appear in the guise of a worthy opponent. The marriage had clearly been a dynastic alliance. The Marchmonts were connected with half the noble families of England, and no doubt the dowry had been considerable. There seemed to be some affection between bride and groom, certainly, but as to love, Lazenby could not swear to it. They were somehow too courteous, too careful with each other, despite Ormiston's show of affection and pride in his wife's odd accomplishment.

The earl was prepared to play a waiting game. He had plenty to do in exercising his hunters and coursing his hounds, inspecting the brakes and bounds of his lands and generally preparing for the hunting season to come. He did not come to Hatherley for more than a fortnight after the viscountess's triumph.

It was a crisp morning when he did come, the cooling air hinting at autumn. His ostensible reason for riding over was to fulfill a promise made to Reggie to show him a new gun come from Purdey's, the gunsmiths fast superseding Manton's. It was a disappointment to hear from young Marchmont that Lady Cecilia was knee-deep in dreary ladies calling to arrange some dull doing. Worse was to come. Reggie led the earl to a target range he had set up, whereupon Ormiston popped up like a rabbit emerging from its warren. However tempting it might be to shoot him, Lazenby concentrated on the official targets, showing Reggie the new gun, helping him to hold it correctly, for it was much too large for a boy not yet twelve, showing him how to check the sights and load it. Lazenby fired at the targets, picking them off very neatly. Reggie clamored for a turn, but both Lazenby and the viscount said the kick of the gun would be too great for him. The earl offered Ormiston a try with the rifle.

The viscount took it. Lazenby was not sure what he was expecting. Certainly not the smooth, even routine of cleaning, loading, and firing with scarcely a blink until each of the eight targets had a neat, accurate hole at its center. Ormiston might be a dandified aesthete, but he was also a very fine shot.

"What a talented family! With your skills, you might settle in a wilderness and never want for anything."

"Wherever I am, I hope I shall be able to protect and feed my family." The warning was unmistakable, however smilingly it was given.

Lazenby glanced at the viscount and turned the subject slightly. "I do not remember your being so fine a shot."

"I would be surprised if you remembered me at all. I generally have not mixed with my father's acquaintance until now. I was at school, he was often away. We saw very little of each other." Ormiston changed the subject swiftly, inviting Lazenby up to the house for refreshment. In the hope of seeing Cecilia, Lazenby agreed, chaffing Reggie as they cleared up the makeshift shooting range and walked to the terrace. He caught a glimpse of several ladies sitting in a morning room, a flash of black amongst them which made his heart leap. While Cecilia did not wear mourning for informal calls, he had noticed that when entertaining larger groups, she conformed to Society's dictates. She displayed a beguiling mix of rebellion and duty.

"This way, Lazenby," said the viscount, holding open one of the French windows into the gun room. After storing

Lazenby's weapon there, they went to the library, where Buchan was reading *The Spectator*. He willingly left his article to join in a general discussion of shooting, guns, and the prospects for the hunting season.

"Does Lady Cecilia hunt?" enquired Lazenby.

"She has no suitable hunter as yet. Phoebus might serve, but I would be reluctant to see her take to the field on him since she has trained him so superbly for her own purposes."

"But you do not object to her taking to the field?"

"Why should I?" Ormiston's eyebrows shot up, making it clear he found Lazenby's line of questioning intrusive. "My wife would never behave in a way that anyone found ill-becoming in a viscountess, I am sure. Certainly, her skill on a horse is more than adequate to meet the challenge."

"I am sure Dacre will not leave her unmounted for long. Our hunting is excellent—it would be a shame for her to miss the chance to ride out over such fine country."

The door opened and Lady Cecilia entered. "Burden said I might find you here." She saw Lazenby and checked before advancing more composedly, offering a languid hand, which he kissed. "Viscountess."

"Lazenby. I had forgot you were due to show Reggie the wonders of your new gun."

Ormiston stepped forward. "What was it you wished to speak to me about?"

"Nothing urgent. Simply an idea of the ladies which requires our support."

"We are due to ride out this afternoon. We will have an opportunity then to discuss any plans you ladies may be hatching. In the meantime, Lazenby, we must not keep you after your generosity with young Reggie this morning."

Aware that he was trespassing on the borders of hospitality, Lazenby tried to press his host. "I was hoping to see Dacre also."

"I am afraid the marquis is engaged for the day. He has already had to disappoint Reggie and Amelia, so you are in good company." Ormiston's smile of welcome was distinctly frosty. Cecilia had engaged Buchan in conversation and they had moved away. Lazenby gave a slight bow.

"If you will ring and ask for my horse to be brought around, I would be grateful."

There was nothing hurried about his leave-taking, but it was uncomfortable to feel that no one in the room wished him to linger. It was with some relief all around that he made his farewells when the footman came to say the horse was ready for him. Buchan accompanied him out of the room.

Ormiston and Cecilia were left alone. "We were not too blunt, were we?" asked Cecilia, anxiety furrowing her brow.

"You were not, although I may have been. I am certainly no favorite of his. You should have seen his face when I appeared at Reggie's range. I half feared he might turn his gun on me and render you an available widow."

"If that is a joke, it is in poor taste."

"You do not wish to be free of me?"

"Not at present." Cecilia did not appreciate being teased by Ormiston. Also, his intelligence about Lazenby merited more thought and less levity, in her view. "He is not someone to be trifled with, Ormiston." She did not mention how disquieting the earl's gaze had been when she had come into the room. He had seemed to follow her every movement, reminding her of the ball where Dacre had first introduced her to the earl. Lazenby had rather summarily kissed her hand and excused himself, preferring to spend the greater part of the evening watching the current object of his interest, a young wife who was intrigued but not yet entranced by him. His eyes had tracked the woman as she danced with various partners, and he had positioned himself so that he must catch her eye from time to time as she moved about the room. He had eventually danced with Cecilia when it was clear that the young woman had no free dances and he had spent the entire passage of the dance attempting to maneuver himself closer to his quarry.

"My father has said he will discourage the earl's visits. He is planning to ride over to Edenbridge in the next day or two to speak with Lazenby. You know that we have only to say the word and Buchan will draw him off should he come here again."

"He is ingratiating himself with other families here. We are bound to meet up with him again, even if we ourselves do not attend the soirees where he is present."

"I hope that I will be ample escort for you in future."

"You were not to be seen at the Selbys' when he cornered first me and then Dacre into this ridiculous nonsense over the foal."

"I shall not repeat that error. The entire county will say that you have me on leading strings, but I shall not leave your side if I know he is about."

"We will be the laughingstock of the county if we are unable to leave one another's side," scoffed Cecilia.

"So be it. You are convinced he is a threat, and I am not disposed to treat your concerns lightly. I saw how he watched you."

"You did?"

"No need to sound so astonished. Buchan has trained me to be observant, your comfort is my first object, so consequently I keep some watch over you. Lazenby looks like a particularly hungry tiger when he sees you."

"You are teasing me again."

"If you choose to think so." Ormiston turned the subject, for he had revealed more than he wished to concerning his wife and did not wish to pursue this particular conversation any further. "Now, what was it brought you here in such high commotion?"

"The ladies of the parish wish to hold a children's party to celebrate Harvest Festival, which will require the use of one of the public rooms here. I wished to know which you thought the most suitable, and, of course, to ensure that you will be in attendance on that day. I thought it would be a good way to broaden Reggie and Amelia's acquaintance in the neighborhood."

This cheerful plan diverted both Ormiston and Cecilia from the dangerous topic of Lazenby, and they set off at once to determine where to hold the party, what entertainments should be offered, and the best time of day for such an event. Once again, they avoided any overcontentious discussion, for fear that it should lead one or the other into saying something regrettable or revealing. Easier by far to eschew any subject which might tend that way.

Since recovering from the loss of her baby, Cecilia found she had little time to reflect on any aspect of her life. Her list of obligations and duties seemed to increase from day to day. She had never before envied fictional women such as Lady Bertram of Mansfield Park, who managed to escape the endless calls on her time to lie on a chaise longue dallying with embroidery, but Ceci now found herself wistfully recalling the days of her girlhood with Lady Ketley when her most pressing concern had been which dress to put on and which engagement to attend. At Hatherley, there was always someone ready to request her opinion, require a decision, or demand arbitration. There were occasional moments of peace—when she dressed for dinner, for example, a half-hour which she had deemed sacrosanct—but all too soon that time, too, was encroached on, for Dorcas began to arrive carrying messages and revealing grievances borne by the staff.

The viscount was kept equally busy in learning his lands, so it was rare for either of them to see the other during the day, and on those infrequent occasions, the time was eaten up in discussing practical matters, such as this engagement to provide an entertainment for the children. Once they had withdrawn to their chamber, all too often they were overwhelmed by passion or weariness.

On the whole, they continued to avoid, by tacit agreement, any conversation which might lead them into the uncharted waters of their own feelings for one another. At times, one or the other strove to speak, but invariably they were distracted from their purpose, interrupted by some unfinished task or diversion.

To all at Hatherley, it was clear that the viscount and his wife were dedicated and competent in the management of their future demesne. But it was clear only to Lavauden that both Ceci and Ormiston were both being rushed into taking a far greater role at Hatherley than was strictly necessary, given the robust good health of the marquis, and the increasing contentment of both the Marchmont children. She noticed, where others did not, how few the spells of solitude were for both viscount and viscountess. Knowing Ceci as she did, she understood that her former charge must be pining for some privacy, and knowing Ceci as she did, she also knew that the viscountess would not rest until her position at Hatherley was established and her duty fulfilled to the utmost. It was no good trying to ease the burden of her situation, for Cecilia herself would not accept anything less than her utmost. It was no good, either, trying to discover exactly what difficulty Cecilia had with her husband, for the girl—*woman*, Lavauden tried to remind herself—had ever fretted rather than confide her troubles in others.

It was this sense of impotence to alter matters on behalf of Cecilia that drove Lavauden to broach matters with Buchan. They held the same sort of position in the household—neither servant nor master, but some nebulous place in between—where they took meals with the family, provided services and companionship which went beyond contractual obligations, and had through years of service built up an understanding of their respective employers. Lavauden guessed that Buchan felt as warmly about the viscount as she did toward the Marchmont children, for he would otherwise have been quick to leave Hatherley for a new situation once the viscount was returned safely home. But here he was, and she had had cause to consult with him about the younger Marchmonts and their talents. He had seemed so calm and pleasant, his reading of Amelia and Reggie so perceptive and sensible. Surely he would be able either to set her own mind at rest, or to suggest some plan of action to help the viscount and viscountess.

When cornered by Lavauden one afternoon in the room that had been converted long ago into a studio for Ormiston, Buchan initially assumed that the Frenchwoman wished to discuss the progress of their mutual pupils. It was he who inadvertently turned the subject to the newlyweds.

"I do wish that Ormiston were more regular in his art. If the two children could see him, they would learn a great deal, but he scarcely has time to draw breath these days. It is a great pity. You have seen some of his earlier works hanging around the house, I am sure, but his work in Italy gained so much depth, so much in both technique and expression."

"He has not been painting since his return?"

"Nothing that I have seen. He spoke of working on something recently, but only to lament that he had not enough time to devote to it."

"Both he and the viscountess are much in demand around the estate."

"Ay, but Hatherley managed well enough four months ago, before there was any question of their settling here, or so I understand. I have not been here any length of time myself."

"It is a grave obligation to inherit such lands and such a house. Sawards seemed large to me, but now I have been here, I am amazed by the intricacy of running so great a household."

"To be frank, mademoiselle, I do not see why Ormiston and Lady Cecilia need be fretted with such affairs just now. The children are well settled and would be happy to remain here with Dacre and you for support and guidance."

"And you also."

"Well, for a little time, I suppose. But I have it in mind to return to Scotland. I have family there. Ormiston certainly does not need me and though I am fond enough of the little ones, if I am to be honest, I should prefer older students. I have plenty of my own work to form the basis of an exhibition and I have been in correspondence with my old teachers in Edinburgh."

"I am sure that the viscount will not let you leave so easily, Monsieur Buchan. Why, if he remains here, he will need your company more than ever. You are so close to him."

"A newly married man would do better to make his wife close to him. But I think that is next to impossible if they remain here."

"You do not think they are close?"

"They scarcely see each other and when they do, they are beset on all sides by claims on their time and their attention. I am astonished when I see my lord so calmly submitting to the ceaseless clamor of so many. Here is a man who would brook no interruption when working, even for sustenance." Buchan was too discreet to mention that even Giugliana had had short shrift when Ormiston was determined to finish a painting. But he was concerned for his young friend. Here was a man with a passion for his art, expending his every energy on fulfilling his family obligations, suppressing his hunger to excel in his own field, containing his emotions, concealing from himself as well as everyone around him his true inclinations and abilities.

"What can be done?" asked Lavauden, although she had an idea that Buchan and she thought along the same lines: the viscount and his wife must be sent away for a wedding journey of some sort.

"What do you think should be done, Mademoiselle? Can Lady Cecilia be removed from the children at this stage, or are they still too upset by their bereavement?"

"If they know exactly where she is, and there is a promise that they will be reunited with her by Christmas, I think they would be happy enough here. Amelia is settled since her escapade, and, of course, the weather has improved so she has been able to go out and about."

"In that case, I think we should put it into Lord Dacre's mind to send them away. It would certainly remove them from Lazenby's sphere, and they may return here in three or four months, by which time everyone will have realized that they are not indispensable to the smooth running of this place. For they certainly are not."

Lavauden heartily endorsed this plan. She did not choose to explore Buchan's views of the earl, having already been fully briefed on his perfidies by Lady Ketley, but she was well aware that the nature of his interest in Cecilia had altered over the past weeks and not for the better. She and Buchan settled on how they must conduct their campaign to extract their two charges from Hatherley. That very lunchtime, she began to make innocent inquiries about the extent of Dacre possessions, while Buchan made noises about his plans for exhibiting his work, thus drawing the viscount's attention to the inevitable sorting and framing that must be done if his souvenirs of his time abroad were not to molder away.

It took nearly a fortnight of gentle direction and a second brooding visit from Lazenby before Dacre, Ormiston, and Cecilia all managed to conclude that it would be beneficial if the newlyweds took a tour of the Irish estates. Buchan and Lavauden were relieved when the packing and preparations began. There was a chance, after all, that the viscount and his wife might come about.

Seventeen

As Ormiston watched his wife sleeping, he reflected on what he had learnt about her in the past months. She loved to read, she loved to eat apples, she could sew most delicately, but equip her with a pencil and she could not draw a recognizable flower. She was an extraordinary horsewoman and a talented manager of people, with the ability to inspire even an insignificant chambermaid to take some pleasure in the drudgery of her position. She loved to dance but could not sing a note; she adored following the fashions, yet once she was dressed she never fussed and fretted at her clothes or checked her reflection in a mirror. She tried to be kind about everyone but occasionally allowed a suppressed talent for mimicry to emerge when recounting the visits she had made or received that day. She would fulminate and rant against her neighbors if she heard of them behaving with injustice or cruelty, yet she would suavely greet them and maneuver them into confronting their own folly. She was admirable, interesting, short-fused, and engagingly easy when faced with her own failings, always ready to laugh at her own slips of judgement. She had certainly taught him a great deal about himself and about the workings of his fellow men.

The candle on the bedside table flickered beside him, casting a trembling glow over Cecilia's prone body, throwing shadows on her smooth skin and causing highlights to gleam in her dark hair. She was beautiful also, so beautiful that at times he felt he could never have enough of the sight of her, that he wanted to watch her and would be quite content to follow her around the estate like a well-trained spaniel, gazing always on the way she moved and the delicacy of her features and the grace of her limbs. Since her illness, she had filled out once more, so she was soft and rounded, supple and warm.

Why he could not say directly or show her plainly that he loved her, he did not know. He knew that she was rare and precious, that he was fortunate beyond all he deserved to have married this woman. Still, he could not speak. It was not a simple, childish impulse to withhold his profession of love until he could be sure of her feelings, or at least he did not believe it was so simple. He turned the matter over. He was afraid to declare himself because she might feel compelled to stay with him out of pity. He was too cowardly to confess that he was devoted to her because he remembered so vividly the anger that had flashed in her eyes when they were in Paris. Sometimes he thought she was still angry with him. Something he had said or done or failed to do five years before still lay between them, so that even if he did speak his heart to her, she would mock or mistrust his words. Behave as well as she might, play the wife as fully as she did, her essential lack of confidence in him leached into every aspect of their lives together. There seemed to be no remedy but to show her with his every action that she was mistaken in him, that he could be constant and true to her.

Now there was Lazenby to contend with. It seemed as though there would never be a time when he and Cecilia could simply love one another and take joy in that love, without any interference from any outside agency. It was not that he feared that Cecilia could be lured by Lazenby. She had made it perfectly clear that she regarded the earl with deep mistrust and a skepticism which veered at times toward disdain, until she remembered that his tongue and his tales might menace her own family and amended her own behavior accordingly. No, there was no danger of Cecilia succumbing to his dubious charms. But he was a distraction and a hazard, yet another of the increasing calls on their time.

Perhaps a visit to Ireland, as Dacre had suggested that morning, was the answer. It would give him time alone with Cecilia, without the thousand-and-one distractions they both seemed prone to, from his daily fencing with Reggie to her unceasing visits to all and sundry throughout the neighborhood. She had greeted the idea coolly, but perhaps that was because she was innately reserved whenever a proposal was put to her. Ormiston had remarked that since coming to Hatherley, she quelled her more spontaneous reactions.

Ormiston had also noticed that once Lavauden had put the idea into his head, his father had been quick to encourage a visit to Ireland, while on the more uncomfortable issue of barring Lazenby from Hatherley, the marquis had dallied. Dacre's reluctance was understandable, Ormiston supposed, for it was no easy thing to place a distance between oneself and any intimate. Of course, Dacre had become polished at giving his mistresses their congé, but this, Ormiston could see, was different. There was no overt reason to get rid of the man. By every measure, his behavior had been impeccable since Cecilia's illness, for it had been Jane Selby who had pushed Cecilia into the wager of her riding. Whatever one might suspect of the man, he did play his hand with subtlety.

If Ormiston or Dacre could have seen Lazenby at that moment, they would have had ample grounds for casting him beyond the social pale. The earl was in his cups, in a bed, *not* his own at Edenbridge, accompanied by a dashing young woman with a fall of dark brown curls, a kittenish face, and rather watery blue eyes, familiar to anyone at Hatherley as the wife of Mr. Featherton, a local lawyer who had ridden out that day on an errand invented by the master of Edenbridge. Lazenby was not entirely sure that the delectable Sally understood that theirs was a mere dalliance until his other plans came to fruition, but he didn't feel equal to emphasizing the impermanence of his attachment for her. Not just now, when she had demanded a lengthy and wearying amorous performance, not just now when his head was pounding with the port he had consumed. Not just now when all he wished was for silence and sleep and Cecilia. He hauled himself out of bed, reflecting that he was getting too old for this kind of adventure.

"I must go now, Sally—otherwise your servants will find me out."

"Stay a while, my lord." She did not yet dare call him Alexander, although he was free enough with her name. And to her mind, to call him Lazenby sounded cold and still a little familiar.

"No, girl, I must be gone."

"But when shall I see you again?"

Lazenby muffled his prevaricating response by dragging on his shirt and casting about beneath the bed for the rest of his clothes. He hauled on his trousers, wrenched on his waistcoat and jacket, and continued groping for his stock and boots.

"When shall we meet?" asked Sally again.

"I will send you a note. Good night, little vixen." Lazenby, carrying his boots, slipped away in his stockinged feet, his stock dangling about his neck, his head pounding, and stifling the impulse to tell Sally Featherton that she was mistaken if she imagined he would be returning to her bed.

But it was Mrs. Featherton who had the good fortune to break the news, nearly a week later, to Earl Lazenby of the forthcoming bride journey of the viscount and his wife. Mischievous Daphne Selby had invited the Feathertons to a small supper party—only twenty around the table, noted Lazenby—and seated him next to Sally. "How elusive you are, my lord."

"Closeted with my man of business, I am afraid. A dull stick, intent on quelling my every pleasure. What excitements have transpired during my brief retreat?"

"None whatever, and fewer are likely. We were so hoping

for a ball at Hatherley, but now it transpires that Lord and Lady Ormiston are travelling to Ireland. We are palmed off with some paltry children's party." Sally Featherton pouted in distress, and missed Lazenby's own astonishment.

"Ireland? Whatever takes them there?"

"Oh, business, business—when is it ever anything but business? They go to inspect estates and speak with tenants and make improvements that no one wants instead of staying put and doing their duty by us dull dogs!"

Lazenby could hardly have put it better himself. How he was expected to find a rich bride while the Ormistons waltzed about Ireland he could not imagine. Still less could he use the interval between introducing himself to his rich paragon by flirting (and more) with the delicious viscountess. It was tiresome. It was inconsiderate, and really, thought the earl as he puffed on his cigar and sipped on his port in a most abstracted fashion, it was his public duty to prevent this rash excursion. He excused himself early from the Selbys' dinner and continued to ponder the question as his coach returned him homeward.

Lady Cecilia was in the garden when he called. After a short delay, he was walking across Hatherley's lawn and up a rise of land to where the viscountess stood, examining her latest project, the construction of a simple stone summerhouse with an unobstructed view of the house itself. The building appeared to be well advanced, with the windows nearly in place.

"Good day, Lazenby. Look how our building is coming along! It even has fireplaces so we may use it in the winter." Cecilia was pleasant as always, her enthusiasm for the project lending vivacity to her even features. "Dacre huffed and puffed so when I first suggested it, but he is quite taken with the project now, and badgers Ormiston to start painting his great portrait of the house without delay."

"But I hear there must be some delay, for you are going away?"

"How did you hear that? We have scarcely decided for ourselves!"

"At Jane Selby's table, one always hears the latest doings of all one's neighbors. It is better than the *Thunderer*."

"Or the *Stamford Gazette*. Yes, there must be some delay, but we are planning to return before Christmas. Do you get much snow here?"

"Sometimes in January and February. Rarely before then. Where are you going?"

"To Waterford County in Ireland. Dacre has not visited his estates there for years, I believe, so we are sent as inspectors or emissaries. The truth is that Ormiston is restless. He claims he has not spent an uninterrupted five-month at Hatherley since he was a child."

"Why can he not go on his own?"

"He could, but I am eager, too. If we sort well together on this journey, who knows but that I may persuade him to visit Italy. I so long to see Italy. My father went there on his Grand Tour, and we have such lovely things as a result. Intaglio cabinets, exquisite ceramics, and, of course, some wonderful paintings. Like Ormiston's Guardi." Cecilia's diversionary tactics did not succeed. Lazenby swung the conversation back to Ireland.

"How do you reach these estates in Waterford? Do you sail from Liverpool or Bristol?"

"I know none of the details. You will have to inquire of Ormiston. He is in charge of our arrangements."

"Do you know when you depart?"

"As soon as can be contrived. Next week, ten days, no more than a fortnight, I believe. But here is Will now—you may ask him direct."

Ormiston clambered up the rise and came forward to shake Lazenby by the hand before bestowing a kiss on his wife's brow.

"Good day to you, Lazenby. By the time we get back from Ireland, we shall be able to meet here for hot toddies and sledging."

"So I gather. A belated wedding trip?"

"I am not sure that Ireland in the autumn is the most salubrious spot for a wedding trip. Southern France or Tuscany, perhaps, but I have heard that Ireland is prone to damp and chills at this time of year. But Dacre tells me we have pressing business there, and one can hardly deny one's father. Ceci is good enough to keep me company, though I fear I have earned Reggie and Amelia's disgust for spiriting away their sister."

"It will be my pleasure to entertain them in your absence." The undertaking had escaped Lazenby's lips before he had quite understood that he would make it, though why he should suddenly take such an interest in nursery brats was incomprehensible to him.

"How kind of you, Lazenby! But well beyond the bounds of friendship," exclaimed Ceci. "The children have more than enough to occupy them, what with lessons, the Harvest party, and all manner of diversions."

"I shall be popping around to see Dacre while you are gone, so I will be able to spare a moment or two for your brother and sister. But tell me, Ormiston, what route are you taking?"

"Liverpool seems most convenient, although Ceci assures me that a longer sea crossing would not trouble her. Have you travelled to Ireland yourself?"

"Five or six years ago, for the hunting. You will find good sport there, and fine horseflesh, which I am sure will interest Lady Cecilia."

All three began strolling back to the big house, chatting most amicably about Ireland and Lazenby's experiences there. The earl did not notice the glances that the couple exchanged, but he did note that Ormiston's arm firmly encircled his wife's waist, and they walked together smoothly, as though quite accustomed to each other's pace.

The afternoon passed quite comfortably, or so it would have seemed to an observer. Yet, once Lazenby had made his bows and departed, Ormiston and Ceci found themselves sighing in simultaneous relief. They grinned at one another.

"How wearing it is to be watching one's tongue so carefully!" said Ceci.

"Does that mean you do not guard your tongue when we are alone?"

"Almost always."

"There is no need for flippancy. There should be no need for flippancy." Ormiston could not mask the hurt in his eyes. Cecilia's smile faded. She reached out toward him, but his hands did not rise to meet hers. She dropped them once again by her side and took a step away from him.

"I did not mean to speak with unbecoming levity."

"Everything you do becomes you. I wish . . ." He could not complete his sentence, the rawness of his longing stilling his tongue altogether.

"What do you wish, Will?" Cecilia spoke with urgency. "Tell me. Perhaps it is the same thing I wish."

But Ormiston had turned away and the moment was gone. He was careful to forestall the chance of any such moment developing again before their departure for Ireland. He wanted nothing to prevent their journey, for he felt that if he could only get Cecilia away from Hatherley, he would have a chance to woo her as she deserved, an opportunity to persuade her of his true and tireless devotion without interruptions or misinterpretations.

The morning of their departure, some days later, was cool and brisk, with a bustling breeze sending waves chopping across the ornamental lake and clouds scudding across a cerulean sky where the moon still hung like a stray guest lurking at the tail end of a ball. Buchan endeavored to occupy a rather glum Reggie and Amelia while Lavauden and Dorcas supervised the loading of the last of the viscountess's bags, the bulk having been sent on ahead.

Dacre had insisted that his son and daughter-in-law use his most comfortable coach, a huge, black monster which needed six horses to haul it. Ormiston settled Cecilia in the coach and sat opposite her. They waved farewell, the post-boy blew a flourish on his horn, and the horses hauled the great coach around and down the drive.

The marquis kept his roads well, going so far as to experiment with a new method, suggested by a Scotsman, of mixing chipped stones with tar, although the black track made by the drive winding through the landscape seemed to Cecilia an ugly scar. The coach made good progress to the toll road, but it was noisy and confined, despite the luxury of the red leather seats and padding. But Ormiston pulled out from some secret compartment in the coach a board which served as a table for his backgammon set. He introduced her to the game and the time seemed to slip past as swiftly as the countryside. Cecilia grasped the rules of the game swiftly, and they enjoyed themselves with inventing ever more ridiculous stakes for their games, most of which ended in stalemate as the coach lurched over potholes and verges, scattering all the pieces across the board haphazardly. Cecilia found herself gazing on Ormiston as he pondered his next move, longing to reach out and trace the line of his brow with a finger, to cup his cheek with her hand, kiss him casually as she had seen Aunt Letty bestow kisses on the admiral, or simply hold his hand. But still she stifled these impulses, afraid they would be unwelcome, afraid that such behavior would reveal too much.

Cook had prepared a picnic in the Hatherley kitchens so that no halts need be made until it was time for a change of horses at Nottingham. They were to break their journey at Stoke-on-Trent before continuing through Nantwich and into Liverpool the following day.

At Nottingham, Ormiston escorted Cecilia into a parlor at the inn and ordered some tea. A spread of ham, Stilton and cheddar cheeses, celery, radishes and tomatoes, scones and cakes was laid out for the grand visitors.

"I cannot do justice to this spread. Riding in a coach hardly promotes appetite and our veal-and-ham pie seems quite sufficient," commented Cecilia.

"They will not be unduly offended, I am sure. I am hungry enough for two, at any rate." Ormiston tucked into the meal with a will. "The journey so far has been easier than I expected. The weather has been dry enough so that the roads are fast, I suppose."

Cecilia sat and watched her husband. Soon enough they would be called back to the coach for the next stage of their journey, there could be no other interruptions for the next few days of travel. They were without distractions from each other for days now. There were no knotty relations between father and son, no call to cheer up or arbitrate between the two children. Even after they arrived at the house in Ireland, there could not be so many calls on their time. The concerns of her everyday life seemed to evaporate, leaving only the great conundrum of her feelings for Ormiston and his feelings for her to be solved at last.

Cecilia's reverie was interrupted by a pounding at their parlor door. It was the coachman summoning Ormiston. The viscount rolled his eyes at being dragged away from his meal but obliged the man, who looked anxious. On returning minutes later, Ormiston appeared a little exasperated.

"The old fellow is anxious that we move on. There is word of some band of highwaymen, and apparently the tiger is convinced that we are being followed. Would it inconvenience you if we returned to the road now?"

"Of course not. I am quite ready for our next stage, provided our horses aren't blown."

The coachman's fears appeared unfounded, and they made good time to Stoke-on-Trent. The inn there was comfortable enough and Cecilia found it easy to manage without Dorcas, who had been sent ahead with the greater part of Cecilia's wardrobe, an assistant, and an escort of two footmen. She retired early, leaving Ormiston to sample an excellent port before following her upstairs. He knocked on her door, but there was no answer.

The following morning was dank and lowering, with a sudden chill in the air presaging the coming winter. The coachman was once again eager to make a prompt start, although he was well aware that when the Dacres travelled, all manner of delays might be placed in his path, particularly if there was decent port to be had. He was agreeably surprised when the viscount and his wife appeared promptly, fully dressed, their fast broken, by half past eight. He did not fancy making for Nantwich in the heavy downpours which, according to local lore, were likely to fall before nuncheon.

This morning, both Ormiston and Cecilia occupied themselves with books. He read a novel while she leafed through a detailed guide-book to Ireland and its folklore, which seemed to her charmingly colorful. Conversation was impossible with the rattle of the wheels, the pounding of the horses' hooves, and the jingle of their harness. Both readers glanced up as the coach seemed to decelerate, and were surprised to see not the town they expected, but rather, dense woodland which seemed to have been savaged by high winds. Trees were down in every direction, brambles, bushes, and ivy rampant, and great tree stumps marked huge craters in the soil. The coach came to a gradual halt. Ormiston poked his head out, then opened the door and climbed down to inspect the damage.

"Stay in the coach, my dear. There is a tree down. I shall try to help move it. I daresay if we can harness the horses to the tree, we will be able to shift it, but it will take some time, and then we will have to rest the cattle before setting off once more."

"Is it all right if I stretch my legs a little?"

"Of course."

Cecilia emerged to inspect the tree which blocked their way. It was an elm—not thick, but substantial. It had fallen in such a way as to impose an insurmountable barrier, for on one side was a sharp incline and on the other, dense bush. Cecilia called her husband.

"Look, Will, it's been cut down!"

The viscount came over to inspect the base of the tree. It did indeed bear fresh axe marks. His eyes met Cecilia's. She did not look apprehensive.

"Could you manage one of the horses, Cecilia?"

"I believe so," replied Ceci steadily.

"Even without a saddle? Or proper reins?" Ormiston laughed shortly. "Of course you could. Would you ride ahead and summon help?"

"You want me out of the way."

Ormiston shook his head and took her in his arms. "There is no one I would rather trust to extract us from this mess."

"And if you are attacked by highwaymen?" She looked up at him, steel in her voice and flint in her eyes. She did not want to be sent off on some fool's errand.

"Please, Cecilia, if this is some form of ambush, I would feel far easier if you were riding away from it. In the meantime, we are four sturdy fellows and five horses—we should be able to shift this obstacle."

"Then there is no real need to send me away. This is not some track in the wilderness—other coaches are bound to come."

"We could wait, but we will be much quicker if you can summon help in Balterley, which I believe is the next village," reasoned Ormiston. "I cannot force you to go, of course, but I think it might save us a good deal of time."

"Very well."

"Brave girl, I know I can rely on you." He kissed her and before she could prevent herself, she twined her arms around his neck and returned his kiss. She was full of foreboding although there seemed no ostensible reason for it. But in the face of unexpected danger, she revealed more passion than she ever had before. Ormiston cradled her face in his hands, and sighed as he pulled away. "A swift return, sweetheart. Do you have money?" He handed her a pouch of coins, readied the lightest of the great horses for her, and helped her onto the beast's back. Then he reached into the pocket of his greatcoat. "Take this. It's one you've practiced firing." He handed over a small pistol with a mother-of-pearl handle.

"Will, is this really necessary? You yourself said it is more of a toy than a weapon."

"It will make me easier if you have something about you."

"I will be back. Never doubt it," vowed Cecilia fiercely.

"I never shall." Will smiled as she wheeled the horse about and took it over the hurdle presented by the tree trunk. She did not turn back, but cantered away, her back straight.

The ride was straightforward enough, for the road was in reasonable condition, although from time to time, Cecilia was certain she could hear the sound of more hoofbeats behind her. It took no more than twenty minutes to reach Balterley, which was a mean-looking place. She went immediately to the tavern, ringing the bell in the yard furiously. She dismounted and went in search of a blanket for the horse, which was more used to a steady canter than the pell-mell gallop she had forced it into. The tack room was a filthy jumble, but she found a serviceable enough cover just as a dishevelled ostler emerged from one of the stalls.

"Here, look after this animal, if you please." She threw the makeshift reins the coachman had fashioned from the harness at the man and strode into the public house. A slatternly woman appeared.

"I need some men and horses, or oxen if you have them in this place. I have money. There is a tree down in the woods and it impedes my coach."

The woman looked incomprehensibly at Cecilia, then shrugged.

"I've a private parlor if you wishes to wait there. There's a gentleman there, waiting for some friends of his, but he won't mind."

"I don't want a private parlor—I want men, and quickly, too."

"It'll take some time. It's harvest—everyone's out in the fields, especially with rain coming. Make yourself comfortable and I'll call you when the men are come."

Cecilia saw the sense in what the woman said, and certainly did not wish to wait in the taproom in her current state of dishevelment. She followed the woman up some stairs and into a low-ceilinged room where a fire burnt. There were two wing chairs. As Cecilia approached, the occupant of one of the chairs rose.

"Well met, Lady Ormiston. I might have guessed that you would be riding to the rescue. How convenient for us both."

Lazenby smiled serenely, and Cecilia saw the pieces of the jigsaw fall into place.

Eighteen

The arrival of the viscountess was not exactly as the earl had planned. He had intended that she should be abducted and brought to him here, where he might pose as the unexpected savior of her fortunes. Certainly, there was no calling off the attack on the Dacre coach. He could still appear in a favorable light by ensuring that assistance reached the viscount. But he had given away his position in his welcome. He must salvage the situation and then decide what to do with Lady Ormiston. Remaining at this tavern, with its brutish innkeeper and slatternly wife, was out of the question.

The lady was very still. She stood in the doorway of the parlor until Lazenby went over to her and drew her to the fireside. She untied her bonnet and unbuttoned her travelling cloak, which Lazenby eased from her shoulders and draped over a chair. He was about to help unbutton her gloves when she snatched her hands back and did the task herself. She went to the fire and warmed her hands.

"How surprising that you should be on the Liverpool road, too, Earl Lazenby. Perhaps your men can assist my husband. Our coach has been halted by a fallen tree. The greatest nuisance."

Lazenby weighed up the viscountess carefully. He turned to the fire and prodded it with a poker.

"I only have a boy with me, my dear. I'm in my curricle, with a tiger to keep an eye on the bays. Allow me to escort you to Nantwich and the boy can go to your lord's assistance. We might round up some villagers to assist him in his labors."

The earl did not look at Cecilia as he spoke. She understood the unspoken threat quite clearly. If she did not comply, the earl would ensure that no help reached Ormiston at all. Even if she waved the bag of gold in the villagers' faces, they would take a little money and a promise of more from an earl over a finite sum and a woman's word. The earl's game seemed unfathomable, but if she played along, Will might genuinely be assisted out of his predicament. Additionally, if she appeared to acquiesce in the earl's plans, he might drop his guard. But this would be the last time this Lazenby interfered with her family, she vowed.

"I would welcome your assistance and your escort as far as Nantwich, where we have bespoken a private parlor at the Crown Hotel for lunch. Perhaps they will be able to provide us with rooms for the night. I don't believe we will reach Liverpool today."

Lazenby nodded and summoned his tiger and the landlord of the tavern to give them their instructions. Cecilia insisted that she see the men and the few beasts that could be spared for the shifting of the tree trunk before paying out any of her money. That at least would cut the start that Lazenby would have on the viscount.

Half a dozen villagers were brought forward with a single team of wiry oxen, along with the carriage horse that Cecilia had ridden to Balterley. Cecilia found the landlord and deposited with him money for the hire of the men and oxen, to be paid once all had returned to Balterley with the viscount and his coach. She could think of no alternative. She watched the men heading along the Stoke road until Lazenby tugged at her elbow to escort her into his curricle. She knew the landlord and his wife were watching, were almost certainly wondering why she chose to accompany another gentleman rather than wait for her husband, despite her tale of having to reach Nantwich to secure rooms for the following day.

That, of course, would have been done by their out-runner earlier in the week.

She gazed at the curricle, reluctance freezing her steps. Lazenby's reliability was another issue. She would not put it past him to drive straight through Nantwich, or bypass it altogether. Still, she was equipped with Will's pocket pistol. She checked its position in the spacious pocket of her cloak. She also felt a pencil there, one that Amelia had left on the lawn at Hatherley. At least she should leave a proper message with the landlord.

"Wait!" She dashed back inside and chivvied the landlord into giving her paper, ink, and a pen. She scribbled a brief note, making it as innocuous as possible given that she had no time to seal it. She turned and left the inn, her back straight, her demeanor as calm as she could summon.

Although strained, Lazenby's smile was still charming. Cecilia's swift visit within had wasted another ten minutes or so, but it would take hours to clear the road. In the meantime, Lady Cecilia would provide entertainment enough, one way or another. They would not be going to Nantwich, certainly. Crewe was equally handy and would delay matters a little further.

Lazenby had no real notion of what he wanted to achieve by removing Cecilia from Balterley. But it was as though he had climbed into a boat and set it adrift on a rising river and inexorably, he must flow where the current took him. As he set the curricle in motion, he almost convinced himself that he simply wished to provide assistance to Lady Ormiston, who clearly could not remain unaccompanied in so low a dive as the Laughing Crow of Balterley. He had done nothing irrevocable yet; he still could simply escort her to Nantwich. She was desirable, but he had spent time with desirable women before without wishing to seduce them. More specifically, he had spent time with this desirable woman without wishing to seduce her.

The trustworthiness of the earl did concern Cecilia. She

watched him carefully as he cracked his whip and guided his team of chestnut geldings out of the inn yard. He seemed a reasonable enough driver, but he also appeared preoccupied, as if faced with an absorbing dilemma. His gaze in the inn had reminded Cecilia of visiting a menagerie in Paris at feeding time. There had been a crocodile that appeared to be fast asleep. The keeper gingerly threw the carcass of a goat into the animal's enclosure. An eye had seemed to open and then as swiftly close again. A long minute passed and then the great lizard had lunged at the dead goat as swift as lightning.

Ceci tried to gauge how long it had been since their departure from the Laughing Crow, how long it would be until the men reached the Dacre coach, how long it would take to reach Nantwich. The calculations passed some time, and all the while, she was alert to Lazenby's every move. They came to a junction where their road widened as it joined with the route from Newcastle-under-Lyme. They were fast approaching the fork in the road which would determine her next action. The map in the taproom had been quite clear. If Lazenby kept to the left, he was also keeping his promise to take her to Nantwich; if he turned to the right, he was heading for Crewe and some less reputable course of action.

By now, the tree might have been shifted sufficiently to get the coach past it. The ride to Balterley had been no more than twenty minutes, but she had been pressing the horse. The coach would take longer. Then it would stop in Balterley and Will would be puzzled to find her gone to Nantwich. Would the landlord remember to hand the note to him?

The milestones marked the approach of the turning to Crewe and Cecilia reached into her pocket, taking hold of the small gun and cradling the pearl handle. If he turned the wrong way, she would fire the gun into the air. It would startle the horses, keep Lazenby thoroughly occupied, perhaps give her a chance to get out of the curricle and onto the road. It was another five miles to Nantwich from the crossroads, but she could walk that easily enough. And Will would be behind her. If Lazenby took the wrong turning, it would take him time to turn his team around and catch her up, and even if he did catch her up, he wouldn't be able to get her back into his curricle without a struggle.

Lazenby himself did not know which turning he would take until he reached the signpost which marked the road to Shavington and Nantwich. But the horses were going at a considerable pace, the road curved naturally around to Crewe, and he found himself guiding the curricle past first one and then the second chance to take Cecilia to Nantwich.

He kept his gaze steadily forward, but was distracted by a flash of the brilliant silk lining of her cloak. She was holding a gun, fiddling with the safety catch. His hands full with the reins, he jerked the horses back suddenly just as she fired into the hedgerow. The horses reared and plunged, whinnying and braying as the lightly sprung carriage swayed and swooped like a dinghy in high seas. Cecilia found herself half thrown, half jumping clear from the curricle just before there was a sickening crack and Lazenby disappeared as the axle disintegrated.

The terrified horses tried to gallop away from the source of their fright, but could not shake off their traces. Cecilia approached them gingerly, grabbed onto the harness, and gentled the animals with soft murmurings and strokings. When it was clear they were calm, she turned back to the mangled wreckage of the curricle. The carriage had caved in, and Lazenby appeared to be trapped within, one leg caught in splintered wood, his right arm tangled in the reins and awkwardly angled, his forehead grazed. He was unconscious.

Cecilia yanked back the leather hood so she could at least reach the unfortunate driver, but the tangle of reins and spokes seemed to be clamping the carriage together. She turned her attention to unwinding the mass of leather and buckles, queasy as she noted the blood beginning to ooze through the fine wool of the earl's trouser leg. She steeled herself to concentrate on the task at hand. Eventually, she managed to free the horses from the wreckage, easing them from the shafts of the curricle and leading them to the sign-post a hundred yards down the road, where she tethered them.

Then she returned to the carriage. Lazenby was still unconscious. She pulled at one side of the carriage and then the other, easing them gradually apart until she was able to squeeze in and start unlacing the reins from his right arm. Then she tried to free his leg, but this caused him to moan and she squeezed out again. She felt at a loss; she hadn't anticipated so dramatic and grim a turn of events. The earl clearly needed medical attention immediately. His horses were still in a nervous state, which meant that riding either back to Balterley or on to Nantwich to rendezvous with Ormiston would be impossible.

The most sensible plan seemed to be to wait at the cross-roads to hail the first passing vehicle and get some help in transporting Lazenby away from the scene of the accident. Cecilia walked back down the road and stood, feeling guilty, helpless, and increasingly cross as time wore on. In fact, she had only to wait a quarter of an hour before she heard the sound of a cart approaching from Nantwich. She flagged it down anxiously. It was fully laden, driven by a clean-shaven man in his forties.

"Sir, sir, please, can you help me? There's been an accident."

The carter drew his horse to a standstill and accompanied Cecilia down the road to where Lazenby still lay. The man shook his head and tutted, but managed to free the earl from the carriage immediately.

"Best take him back to Nantwich. Roundell can set bones. My cloth will wait till tomorrow. I'll bring the cart up and we can lie him on the tarpaulins. Let's hope the rain holds off."

So it was that over an hour later, Cecilia arrived in Nantwich at the Crown Hotel. The landlord, Bloxham, was a very different type to the man at Balterley and snorted when he heard of Cecilia's experiences at the Laughing Crow. She contrived to explain that her husband was imminently expected and had been fully conversant of her excursion with Lazenby. It took the carter and two ostlers to transfer the earl to the private parlor which had been reserved for the Ormistons, where he was laid out on a long oak table. Cecilia was shown up to a bedroom overlooking the High Street. She was offered refreshment and washing facilities.

In the privacy of her room, Cecilia removed her outdoor garments and looked at herself in the mirror. Her hair was slipping from its pins, one cheek was streaked with mud, and her eyes were glittering in her pale face. She did what she could to calm herself and set herself to rights, splashing water over her face and lathering her hands with the rose-scented soap left by Mrs. Bloxham, before taking down her hair and recoiling it into a simple chignon. Finally, she sat down on the bed and suddenly gave way to the fear that she had kept at bay since she first saw Lazenby at Balterley. What had happened to Will? How long could it take to shift a tree and come the eight miles to Nantwich? Would he think the worst and assume she wished to be with Lazenby? There had been no sign of him at the Crown—surely he would have stopped here as they had arranged? And now she had caused this hen's broth of an accident, and must take responsibility for Lazenby's care. His wounds certainly appeared serious. Cecilia rubbed her temples, breathed deeply, and set off downstairs to discover the doctor's verdict.

The examination took some time, but finally, Roundell emerged from the parlor into the hallway where Cecilia sat on a wooden settle, her hands knotted.

"Lady Ormiston, you were in the company of our injured friend?" The doctor's tone was neutral and calming.

"I was. He was escorting me here following an accident to my husband's coach."

"He is not your husband?" clarified Roundell.

"Oh no! Earl Lazenby is a friend of our family, a neighbor. When our journey was delayed by a fallen tree, he offered to escort me here to greater comfort. Then we had this accident." Cecilia did not feel equal to a fuller explanation, and hoped that she would not be called to account for the fudging she had done.

"On the Crewe road?" queried Roundell.

"Yes, we had taken the wrong turning and his lordship was trying to rectify matters. That is how we came to have the accident."

"Well, he has broken some ribs and his right arm and I cannot yet tell the damage to his leg. He will need considerable nursing for the next few weeks. You say he is an earl?"

"Yes. Does that make a difference?"

"We may get the local gentry offering him shelter and assistance. An inn, even so fine an inn as the Crown, is not a suitable place for a sick man. I think I will speak to Lady Tollemache and Miss Wilbraham."

"I expect my husband will be here shortly. I do not know how long it will take to move the tree and settle with the Balterley people."

"Settling with the folk in Balterley will take as much time as shifting the damned obstacle, I should think. In the meantime, I've made the poor fellow as comfortable as can be expected, but I shan't move him until I can find a permanent home for him. I shall be back as soon as that is done. He's had laudanum after I set his arm, so he won't wake just yet."

"Thank you, Doctor."

He bowed and left. Cecilia peeked into the darkened room where Lazenby lay, prone and frighteningly still. Then she closed the door and returned to her room where she paced and paced, watching the afternoon drag by, leaping to the window every time she heard the sound of harness and horses' hooves.

It was half past four when she caught a glimpse of the Dacre coach pulling round into the Crown mews. She ran downstairs, outside, and around into the stableyard. Ormiston was already out of the coach before it had fully stopped and before she knew it, Cecilia was in his arms, his mouth on hers, his hold on her tight. At last, he lifted his head and released his grip on her.

"Will, you're safe! Were you attacked? What has kept you so long?"

"Let us go in, and let me see Lazenby before I answer your questions. I assume this nonsense was his doing? He shall certainly pay for it."

Cecilia bit her lip. "I believe he is already paying for it most grievously." She led him into the inn and pointed out the parlor. "Lazenby is in there. The doctor here is looking for someone to take him in while he recovers from his injuries."

Ormiston popped his head around the door, then followed Cecilia upstairs, where he demanded an explanation and heard Cecilia's story with mounting ire at the earl's folly in trying to stray away from Nantwich, and a mixture of amusement and horror as he heard about the accident which Cecilia had caused.

"You are a brave girl, but very foolish. You could be in Lazenby's position yourself, if you had not been so fleet and nimble." Ormiston stood and went over to Cecilia. He knelt by her chair, took her hands in his. "If you had had another accident! It does not bear thinking about."

"I did not think of that. I will be more careful, I promise you. I did not mean to cause you any distress."

"My dearest girl, it is Lazenby I hold responsible for this business." Ormiston stood and pulled Cecilia gently out of her seat. He took her place and tugged her onto his lap. "You did what you thought was best and must have experienced agonies in the last few hours."

Cecilia looked in wonder at her husband. It seemed extraordinary to her that he should find nothing to blame or question in her behavior. "So you are not angry that I did not wait in Balterley?"

"No. Your note was quite clear, Ceci. You did not say it in so many words, but it was obvious that Lazenby intended to throw every obstacle in our way unless you accompanied him. To answer your earlier question, we were attacked, but luckily the Balterley men arrived and frightened off the villains. I assume that it was Lazenby behind that plan."

"Yes. He was astonished to find me in Balterley and gave himself away. I believe he meant the men to abduct me and then to claim the credit for rescuing me singlehanded. How this would profit him I cannot imagine."

"He is a man in a terrible muddle, in which state I can sympathize." replied Ormiston ruefully. He cradled his wife more closely. "However, he must cease this interference in our affairs. I cannot question his taste in women, but I will not have him harassing you any further."

"What should we do?" asked Cecilia. "I do not feel we can abandon him while he is so terribly injured. Besides, I have given the doctor the impression that we were travelling together. I thought it might cause a scandal otherwise."

"That was well judged. I think we might be plagued with some awkward questions otherwise. But if this Roundell can find the earl a safe haven, we may safely continue on our journey. Unless you wish to turn back after these events?"

"Is that what you wish, Will?" Cecilia stood and moved to the window. It had not occurred to her that they might return to Hatherley with matters between them still unresolved. She found she wished more than anything to continue travelling with Will. But if he found her too much trouble, despaired of the time he spent with her, then she might as well be back at Hatherley where at least she could find occupation to fill the chasm left by his lack of interest in her.

A weak and watery sun was beginning to cut through the clouds. A shaft gleamed on the diamond panes of the window, so that Will could no longer see Cecilia's face clearly. But it was as though the light had severed the last thread of self-control by which he bound himself.

"No!" he shouted. "No, there is nothing I want more than to be with you, alone, without distraction, without interruption, without interference or complication. Dear Lord, Ceci, why must everything between us be fraught with confusion?"

The force of her husband's words propelled Ceci backward until she was sitting, dazed in the windowseat, her hands clasped tight to stop herself from reaching out toward him, for she was still afraid that if she did, he might turn her away.

Will waited for her to answer. But she was frozen, trapped by some panic he could not understand. He stood, the seconds drawing out. She could not speak. Here was the choice, the fork in the road. He had either to turn away or to open his heart to her. After all the years and months and weeks of knowing her, now loving her, it was not enough to tell her when she was feverish that she was essential to his very soul; it was not enough to watch over her as she slept; it was not enough to take her away with him. He must speak, for if he did not, nothing could ever be right between them, and it would be better for them to part. And then his life would be nothing but cold ashes in an empty fireplace.

"Cecilia, I beg your forgiveness. I did not mean to shout. But if all I can do is make you unhappy, then we are better apart. All I want is your happiness. Tell me what will make you happy and I will ensure you have it, even if it means you never wish to set eyes on me again."

"Will, don't you understand? All I want is you. You make me happy. When you want me and hold me as if you'll never let me go, when you make plans for Hatherley and our future together, when you sit and draw with that fierce scowl as if there is nothing else in the world but the image you are drawing—all that, that makes me happy."

"Then why do we seem so distant from one another?"

"Because you do not love me. You never have. I thought I had love enough for both of us, but it is so hard, Will."

Ormiston closed his eyes in pain. "What a fool I have been, Cecilia. Can you forgive me? I've loved you to distraction for so many months now."

"Why have you never said so?" asked Cecilia, suspicious, wary, uncertain.

"Because you did not love me. You despised me and mocked me in Paris, and you were distant and cool at Sawards. At every turn, I pressed you, I bound you, because I thought if I did not, you would leave me. You wanted revenge for my coldness when we were first married, justly so. I was callous and cruel."

"No, Will, no. I told you, that's what I wanted at first. But then that night at Hatherley, you said you did not believe in love. You said you knew nothing about it. You wanted honesty and respect, and I have tried to give you that."

"You have tried, but we have failed each other. If we had been truly honest, we would not have reached this pass. Can you believe me now when I say that I love you?"

Silence fell between them. Cecilia looked up. Then she stood, slender, straight, trembling slightly. She stepped over to her husband and laid her hands gently on his shoulders. She looked into his eyes.

"Will," she whispered, "I vow I love you. I will always love you. I promise you this." She stretched a little and sealed her words with a gentle kiss, then pulled back. "I believe you love me and I believe that we have been fools." She smiled up at him. "Your turn."

"I love you, Cecilia, and I always shall. I swear this. I believe you love me, and I believe that we have been fools. But we shall go on better."

His arms tightened about her, and he picked her up and whirled her round until they were both dizzy with delight and laughter, the sun glinting through the window to warm their glowing faces.

Epilogue

There was great excitement at Hatherley: Viscount Ormiston and Lady Cecilia were returning home after a full three months in Ireland, and were expected by midday at the latest. Mademoiselle Lavauden had great difficulty in containing my lady's exuberant brother and sister. The marquis himself kept harassing his unfortunate servants with alterations to his plans to welcome the travellers, first in the music room, where Buchan had arranged the hanging of numerous watercolors from the viscount's Italian travels, then in the Great Hall, before finally settling on the stone summerhouse the viscountess had left half-constructed, but was now complete and pleasant in the unseasonably warm weather.

The autumn had passed quietly enough, with frequent letters exchanged between the estates in Waterford and Hatherley, but epistolary exchanges hardly matched the reality of presence. Dacre in particular had found life flat, for his great friend Earl Lazenby had left the neighborhood around the same time as Ormiston, and had vanished without trace.

But all thoughts and fidgets were dispelled when the sound of the tiger's horn came echoing along the drive, along with the jangle of the harness and the pounding of the horses' hooves as they hauled the Dacre coach down the drive at a spanking trot. Reggie and Amelia were hopping about on the stone steps above like merry monkeys, each held back by Lavauden's firm hand on their shoulders. Finally, the carriage came to a halt, the boy leapt down, opened the door, and lowered the steps. Ormiston emerged first, escorting his lady out, stepping back as she held out her arms to her sister and brother.

The marquis waited for his son. He looked into the young man's face and smiled. Will came forward and for the first time that either of them could remember, reached out toward his father. They embraced.

Later, as they watched Cecilia playing catch-as-catch-can with her brother, sister, and their governess, Will turned to his father.

"I have not thanked you."

"For what, my dear boy?"

"For providing me with the best wife a man could have." Will smiled. "Your wager was wiser than you knew, and you have made me the happiest of men."

"Ah, my dear Will, I have regretted that folly more times than I can count, but if, through my error, you have found contentment, I am paid better than I deserve."

"More than contentment. And Cecilia and I hope to pay you further. God willing, we shall have a child come April."

There was a pause in the game as Cecilia looked up the slope at her husband and his father. Both men were beaming. She waved up at them, until she realized that Amelia was racing toward her, head down, intent on buffeting her. Ceci sidestepped the small whirlwind and skipped away. Ormiston joined his wife and children on the lawn. Skillfully, he cut Ceci out of the pack and made off with her, descending like a wolf on the fold to spirit his love away, make her rest, and keep her safe.

ABOUT THE AUTHOR

Madeleine Conway lives with her family in England. Her next Zebra Regency romance will be published in August 2004. For more information check her website, www.madeleineconway.com